Shadeborn

Jason Craft   Amanda White

Supremacy PRESS

Acknowledgements

Jason

Thank you to all the Shadeskin fans out there, especially you, Joel. You guys are the real heroes of these stories!

Amanda

I owe many thanks to my supportive hubby, Lance, who ensures I have a working computer on which to document this far and away tale and for supplying a shoulder to cry on during the dark moments. It's been a tough year (or two) and your support has meant the world to me. Thank you to God for making this wonderful world on which we live and for supplying us silly humans with the capability for imagination, helping us to enjoy it ever more.

Table of Contents

Taking Flight

by
Amanda White

1

Darrus took a long drag of smoke from his cigar and exhaled it into Trent's face.

"Uncle Darrus, I'm sorry things turned out this way," Trent said.

Darrus walked to the side of the room and slid a bronze statue of a Doberman to the side, revealing a small hand-shaped compartment. Darrus pressed his hand to the palm print and a small safe opened. He removed a velvet bag, untied the bag's drawstring, and emptied its contents onto the Persian rug in front of Trent's chair.

Trent made a startled noise and struggled to shuffle his chair backward. Darrus clamped his hand on Trent's enormous shoulder. "What? Does this little trinket make you uncomfortable?"

Darrus retrieved the skull-imprinted amulet and held it within inches of Trent's face, dangling it by a green ribbon. "You don't want to take a closer look?"

"No," Trent said. His face and forehead flushed red. "I'm good, thanks."

"Wanna try it on? It will bring out the color in your eyes, I think." Darrus moved to place the green ribbon over

Trent's head.

"No! Don't put it on me!" Trent struggled against the plastic binding that held his wrists together.

"Oh." Darrus took a step back and let the amulet sway between them. "I didn't realize you had an aversion to fine jewelry." Darrus bit down on his cigar and thrust his face within inches of Trent's. "Or is it this particular piece?"

Trent glanced up to meet Darrus's eyes, then looked away to the floor and remained silent.

"I'm not sure what sickens me more," Darrus said as he grabbed Trent's face and forced him to meet his eyes. "That you two went behind my back or that you allowed that boy to suffer out there in the woods. You both need serious help."

"Uncle Darrus, there was nothing we could have done for him," Trent said.

"Nothing?" Darrus replaced the amulet in the safe and slammed it shut. "An Illumin's skill might have eased his suffering."

Trent shrugged and said, "I assure you, Uncle Darrus, he was completely out of it the whole time."

Darrus slapped Trent's baseball hat from his head and grasped a handful of his hair. "If you two hadn't put so much energy into superseding me, you may have realized that you were in way over your heads. Do you have any idea of the magnitude of what is behind the dam you cracked open?"

Trent whined against the pain and said, "Can't Katy's Illumin boyfriend smooth things over?"

Darrus kicked Trent in the center of his chest and he fell backward against the carpeted floor. He cried out in pain, and Darrus forced his fists into his pockets in an effort to restrain his hands. He thought of his two children as acid rose in his throat. The Raven family was unraveling.

Darrus looked down at his burly nephew and tried to remember the younger version he had once loved. "You do not speak to Katy anymore. Not after what you did to her. You are lucky she vouched that you weren't yourself that night at the pool." Darrus paused a moment then said, "So, what were you asking about her?"

"Nothing," Trent gasped. "I just meant…can't the Illumin smooth it out?"

"No, boy." Darrus opened the door to the underground room and motioned for his nephew Christopher to come in and upright his cousin. Trent's hair stuck straight up and sweat formed under his white t-shirt.

Darrus waved Christopher out of the room. "The Illumin are now dealing with an all-out war with the Shades because of the brilliance of you and my son. And as far as helping us, well, they haven't decided how honorable the Ravens are at this point."

Trent shifted in his chair so that he could sit up straight. He said, "I'm sorry, Uncle Darrus. Hunter promised me his plan would help the family. He said in the end you'd be pleased."

"Don't talk to me like I'm stupid. My son has been over-ambitious since the moment he learned he could make weapons. You've got 30 seconds to tell me his entire plan and who it involves, or I'm going to have Andy come in here with his jyo. Do you comprehend your situation?"

Trent's face reddened and he said, "You are going to have my cousin beat me up? That's rich. And you wonder why Hunter questions your ability to lead!"

Darrus backhanded Trent across the cheek. He stepped away for a moment, then turned to meet Trent's stare, whose bloodshot eyes met his in challenge. Only a tiny vibration across Trent's cheeks belied his nervousness.

"You know I don't want to unleash the hell that is Andy's skills all over your face, but I will, *nephew*. You think that after all that has transpired the last 14 days you can go back to life as usual?"

His nephew replied, "You are fine. Sure, being out cold was inconvenient, but we didn't hurt you."

Darrus leaned over and spoke within inches of Trent's face, "Do you see the purple dots around my eyes?"

Trent nodded once.

"Those are broken blood vessels from vomiting all night. This room spins every few minutes, and I keep thinking I hear someone call my name."

Trent attempted to hide a smirk. Darrus said, "I can see you think that's funny. I'm glad I can be here to amuse you. Please, let me provide you with more entertainment."

He opened the door and motioned for his nephew to come in. Darrus had hoped to avoid bloodshed, but clearly Trent saw him as an old fool.

Andy entered holding a long, wooden weapon he used in his Jyodo studio. He raised the jyo and only the sound of the air signaled that he had struck. Blood poured out of Trent's nose. "Are you serious, Andy? When I get out of this chair, I'm going to tear you up!"

Andy pressed his stick beneath Trent's chin and said, "That will never happen."

"You are a puppet, man. Just like the rest," Trent said. "What would your students think if they saw you striking an unarmed man?"

Andy glanced away for a moment then struck Trent across the face again.

Darrus pulled Andy back and said, "You have no reason to hold back information and lots of reasons to tell us everything. This is the least you can do to clean up the tragic mess you made."

Trent glared at the two men for a moment. "Hunter planned to use the amulet against the Illumin. He knew that Matt's dreams were coming true, so he involved the Shades to help him manipulate what the boy dreamed. But, it was too late. Matt was too far gone, and they couldn't make it happen."

"Go on," Darrus said. He felt the warm room begin to spin and held onto the arm of the chair for support.

"Hunter made a deal with Astrous to sell him weapons in return for his help with the amulet. He saw it as a win-win because he could make more money and get back at the Illumin."

"Get back at the Illumin for what?" Darrus asked.

"He believes they are at fault. For, you know… why Aunt Lilly disappeared."

Darrus felt a cold chill run down his spine and the back of his eyelids burned. He rubbed his forehead with his fingertips. "I just can't believe the two of you knocked me out for two weeks and proceeded to fan the flames of a supernatural war."

Trent shrugged and glared at Andy.

"Look at me when I speak to you," Darrus said as he brought his heel down onto his nephew's foot.

Trent cried out, "Look, I'm sorry. What else can I say?"

Darrus raised a shaking finger, "Your life is in my hands now. Do you understand?"

Trent's eyes widened. "Not really."

"I'm going to tell your parents that I'm giving you a pass. The reality is you are mine. You will do everything I tell you. If you slip up on a morning, you will have forgotten who you are by the next sunrise. Do you understand me now?"

"Yes, sir," Trent said.

"Not only did you betray this family, but you put my daughter in harm's way. You have years' worth of debt to repay."

Andy pulled Trent to his feet and moved to escort him from the room. Darrus said, "Once he's off the property, bring the next one in."

Darrus seated himself in a chair and rubbed the tight muscles in his neck. After a few minutes, he heard the hidden room's slot door open and footsteps descend the creaky stairs. Just the sight of Cooper's thin, freckled face caused Darrus's anger to resurface. Without a word, he crossed the room and punched him in the jaw.

Darrus entered the formal living room where his family was waiting. He removed his suit coat and gazed out of one of the plate glass windows that overlooked the wide lawn of his estate. He saw the small pond in the distance reflecting the noon sun. The conversation receded as the grandfather clock's second hand chimed in to mark the passage of time.

Darrus glanced at the reflection of the room on the window's glass and estimated that 30 family members were present. Cooper's mother, Cynthia, sat in a straight-backed chair and held a tissue over her mouth. His chest tightened when he saw his daughter, Katy. She sat in a remote corner of the room with her eyes directed to the floor.

Darrus faced the family and cleared his throat. "Thank you all for coming. I want to apologize for the difficulty of the last few weeks. Your support and discretion has not gone unnoticed or unappreciated."

Cynthia started to talk, but Benjamin squeezed her shoulder. Darrus continued, "I know you have many questions, and I will answer them as best I can. Let me summarize what has transpired and share with you our plans for action. Everyone will have a chance to speak when I am finished."

Darrus turned back to the window for a moment when

the room began to spin. He hardened his eyes at his own reflection and straightened his suit jacket. His dark hair and eyes magnified the pallor of his appearance. A few people whispered and shifted in their seats.

"Silence," his voice cut into the room. "Yes, to answer the questions burning on your faces, it is true. My son caused my coma. Hunter was the mastermind, but Cooper and Trent volunteered their services. They wanted me out of the way so they could create an alliance with the Shades. Hunter discovered an ancient relic that originally belonged to our family, and, through a series of poor decisions, chose to involve the Shades in hopes of making a lucrative deal."

Stephanie, Katy and Hunter's same-age cousin stood and handed her toddler over to her mother. She walked to where Katy was seated, shoved a finger in her face and said, "What about her? There's no way she didn't know what her twin was up to."

"Yeah!" Violet, Cooper's sister, closed her tablet's cover and slammed it on the room's wet bar. "My brother loses his job and gets roughed up, but what about her?"

"We all know Katy's the favorite. Pretty Katy can do no wrong," Sarah mimicked.

Darrus spoke just above a whisper, "Get your finger out of her face and take a seat." Katy squared her shoulders and remained silent, her face blank.

"Katy had no idea what her brother was planning. If you'd spent more time with her during this crisis, you'd know that."

Stephanie started to speak, but changed her mind and returned to her seat.

"I thank God Katy is sitting here with us unharmed. She made some wrong choices, but she did what she thought was best at the time," Darrus said. "Does anyone else have any accusations they need to get out? Otherwise, I'll hear no more of it."

Cynthia moved away from her husband when he tried to silence her and stood beside her son. Cooper was seated behind his family, bruising evident on his face. "I'll not tolerate you mistreating my Cooper. We all know he followed your manipulative son around like a lap dog. Stephanie's right, when will your children be held responsible for their actions?"

Darrus walked over to Cynthia and moved to take her hand. She snatched it away; the rejection elicited a stir of murmurs around the room. He took a step backward then told her, "I think if you examine the evidence you will see that Cooper has been treated fairly."

"And just how is that?" she asked. Violet came to stand by her mother's side. She pushed her glasses up and clasped her hands behind her back.

"Exhibit A," Darrus said and gestured to Trent, his bulking 32-year-old nephew who was seated on a bar stool. Trent's face flushed red, and he inspected the bottom of his boot as if it held the mysteries of the world.

"The facts are that Trent helped Hunter in this little coup. He even assaulted Katy in my pool, yet here he is in all his glory, still in one piece." Darrus clapped his hand on Trent's shoulder with too much force.

"Here we go with 'poor' Katy," muttered Sarah. The teen let her blue bangs fall across her face and hid behind her father's back when Darrus shot her a look.

Darrus's cousin, Jerry, wrapped his arm around his daughter and said, "She's just upset. We all are."

Turning back to Cynthia, Darrus said, "Don't underestimate my fury with Hunter. When we find him… and we will, he will regret his actions. The choices he made have changed what could've been his future."

He moved to the front of the room and said, "Our situation is no longer as comfortable as it once was, and I have little solace to offer you all." Darrus held out a hand to silence the outbursts of moans and objections. "I am going to challenge you to step up and be willing to engage in our affairs with the Illumin as you never have before. Hunter, Cooper, and Trent executed a most grievous error in judgment. They have kicked us from the supernatural sidelines and forced us to play ball. We must now choose our side."

The family matriarch, Aunt Tebe, spoke up from the back and said, "We need to thank our stars the Illumin haven't shut us down. We have to prove we are still loyal."

Benjamin, Darrus's brother, stated, "I agree, Aunt Tebe. Our family has a responsibility to the Illumin and now we need their protection more than ever." Benjamin turned to address the room, "My nephews and my son have incited a war between the supernaturals. Katy has also played a part by participating in a battle between the two species, making herself and potentially us a Shade target."

Katy moved to the front of the room to stand by her father. Darrus patted her on the back. He imagined what they must look like to the family, just two where there used to be four.

Amos and Andy, Darrus's twin nephews, stood and walked to the center of the room. Andy spoke first, "Uncle Darrus, Uncle Ben, Amos and I stand behind you and have advice, if you will allow." Darrus nodded. Andy continued, "Let us renew our relationships with the Illumin. Become friends with them again, not just business partners. We must reconnect those old ties."

Darrus looked to the ceiling a moment and said, "I know I have not encouraged any of you to have friendships with the Illumin. If this hadn't occurred, I would still advise the same and in my heart, I wish we could remain business-like. But, Andy is right. We need them in a different way now." Darrus put a hand on each of his nephews' shoulders and said, "I want everyone to take a look around the room. I know things seem shaky among us. And maybe they are. But we are all we've got. If any of you get suspicious about an Illumin- no matter how paranoid you may think you are being-come talk to me. The only people we can rely on are in this room."

Amos said, "Let us be responsible for Cooper and Trent."

"Why would you want that?" Darrus asked.

"We need every Raven available. We need Trent for security," Amos said.

Darrus eyed his two nephews. They were his top security experts and he knew they were right. Trent was fearless and an excellent fighter. He looked at Trent, who seemed to be embarrassed and relieved all at once. "We'll see," Darrus said.

"I think you are right about the Illumin," Benjamin

nodded, and then said with a smile. "Let's take a survey. Who is in favor of us getting chummy with the supernaturals again?"

A majority of hands appeared in the air, and Darrus and Benjamin nodded to each other. "Then that's settled. We will arrange a party—like old times, right here at the mansion. Cynthia, you know how fond they are of your cobblers." Benjamin smiled at his wife. Some of the sourness lifted from her face.

"Uncle Darrus," Amos asked. "Where is the amulet now?"

"It is here," Darrus asked.

"It must be destroyed!" Aunt Tebe's cracked voice cut through the chatter.

"Yes, destroy it!" multiple voices rang out.

"I assure you, it is under lock and key for the moment," Darrus said.

"This is ludicrous," Jerry shouted. "This only entices the Shades further. Now that you can't trust Cooper's security system, how do you know they won't break in? Who knows what secrets Hunter divulged to them?"

Darrus stabilized himself on the side of a chair and said, "Yes, it is risky, but I promise it is well hidden. We plan to consult with the Illumin force to determine the best course of action."

"We aren't even sure of how to destroy it if it comes to that," Benjamin stated. "Jerry, do you have any suggestions on how to destroy it?"

Jerry shook his head and put his arm around Sarah. "They could come after any one of us."

"Yes," Darrus said, "they could. That is why we must demonstrate a united front." He walked to stand beside his daughter and glanced at Katy in time to see her wipe a tear from her face.

The family was quiet and tension filled the room. "I won't pretend we are all happy with each other right now. This situation has us all feeling uneasy. As you can imagine, I'm having trust issues myself," Darrus stated. "But, the way I see it, we only have one viable choice. We must stand together as a family."

3

The moonlight glinted on Katy's sword, the point just inches away from D'Nas's neck.

"Okay, fair enough," he said. "I relent. In the *Battle of Mountains* trilogy, Gillian's powers would give her an advantage over Milton's character, but you are missing my point." In a swift move, D'Nas deflected her sword and lifted Katy into the air with one hand, knocking her weapon across the field with the other.

"Which is…?" Katy struggled to say. She kicked him in the chest with her boot and he released his hold. She landed with a thump on the ground and rolled away to grab her sword and struggle to her feet.

D'Nas smirked and said, "Gillian would never use her powers over him because of her central weakness."

Katy snorted and raised one eyebrow. She readied her sword.

"Gillian," D'Nas said, "believes that every time she kills someone, it brings her closer to the likelihood of never being able to return home. Remember, at the end of the last book, the soothsayer told her overuse of her powers could prevent her from crossing back over the White Mountain range. It's what she fears most: Being stuck in the wrong world."

D'Nas rushed forward and tugged Katy's ear to alert her of her failure to dodge. She jerked her head and her pony tail whipped at her eyes.

"Unbelievable," Katy said, as she rushed backward to put distance between them. "This is the basis for your argument? That Gillian wouldn't win a hypothetical fight with Milton because she is afraid to use her powers?"

Katy dropped her sword and removed a small, silver object from her pocket. She ran to D'Nas' left and threw it in his direction.

D'Nas' mouth dropped open, and he flew into the air to dodge the silver object. It scraped his ear and blue liquid poured down his face.

Katy watched him struggle and felt a smug satisfaction when the weapon returned to her, its blades now retracted, "Milton's character is a hot-headed misogynist, and Gillian wouldn't turn away from someone with such a need for a beating."

"As long as Gillian lets her fear of being kept from home rule her, she will never be the warrior she was meant to be," D'Nas said. He flew 15 feet into the air and looked down on Katy.

He disappeared to her eyes, but a faint breeze on her right warned her to dodge. Throwing herself flat on the ground, she kicked upwards and caught him in the side as he flew past. "She's already a great warrior," Katy strained to say. She stood and held her sword out, circling as she smelled the air, tuning in to any shifts that would help her guess his next attack.

"What holds humans back more than anything?" D'Nas asked and paused between flapping wings to hover over her. She shrugged and he said, "Your fears. The imagined scenarios that keep you up at night."

"What if the soothsayer was right?" Katy said, lowering her sword, but not taking her eyes off the floating Illumin. "All Gillian wants is to be home again, comfortable and safe among her people. She'll be lost forever if she can't cross the range."

"No one can know the future. It is just imaginations that twist themselves into delusions over time. If you focus on what you fear the most, it becomes a self-fulfilling prophecy. It leads you to the very scenario you wanted to avoid."

Katy watched D'Nas as he floated to the ground in front of her. "What do you fear?" Katy asked. "Or are you Illumin impervious to everything?"

D'Nas's eyes glowed. Their faint blue light cut through the dimly lit field. "I used to fear being stuck here. For years, if I wasn't chasing or fighting Shades, I was like Gillian, with thoughts of home consuming me."

"And now?" Katy asked, meeting his gaze.

"Useless distractions could get us both killed." D'Nas dropped his sword and gave her hand a quick squeeze.

Katy watched as D'Nas began to gather up their weapons from the football field. "What do you think my fear is?" she asked.

"You don't need me to tell you," he replied. "It wraps you like a cocoon and stifles your every breath."

Katy's eyes filled with tears, so she busied herself with putting away her weapons. "My fear is no delusion. It's not a storyline from a fantasy novel." She held out the small silver sphere. "If I had been born into another family, I could live a normal life. I wouldn't have to spend my time making things like this."

D'Nas walked to her, a hint of a smile on his lips. "Exactly," he said, taking the weapon from her hand.

He threw it high into the air and her human eyes lost sight of the silver weapon. Katy heard the ball squeal on its way down, causing the hair on the back of her neck to rise. D'Nas stepped out of the way an instant before the weapon would have shredded the side of his face and it sank into the ground.

"Uh-oh," he said. He glanced at Katy and put his hand over his mouth, hiding a grin. "It didn't bounce back to me. And I think it's pretty deep down."

Katy shrugged and walked to his side. "Well, I only tested it in the air and on flat, nonporous surfaces. Big-brain move on your part, man." The little ball had driven itself into the dirt and a small puff of steam rose from the hole. "That was the only prototype, you know."

"I'm not leaving it. This weapon was a stroke of genius, my lady," D'Nas said.

Katy met his bright eyes for a moment and felt a jolt of

emotion take flight in her stomach. D'Nas's eyes were the typical mark of an Illumin, the supernatural beings tasked with keeping the humans in her city safe from Shades. As a member of the Raven family, unlike the general populace, she knew the truth about his kind and could see his features with accuracy. She took a deep breath and felt her muscles relax in response to his scent.

D'Nas stooped to the ground to inspect the damage. "I don't suppose you have a shovel in your car?"

"Of course. A shovel is as essential as one's purse," she said. When he did not respond, she stated, "Sarcasm," and placed her hands on her hips. "You Illumin really need to learn how to recognize the sardonic tone."

D'Nas smiled and picked up his weapons bag. "Come on, you are exhausted. I'll take you home, then run back to get it. I think I have something at the office I can use to pull this out of the ground without tearing up the field."

"Okay, but that will keep you out late," Katy said. There were only a few remaining hours before sunrise. They had decided to use the football field for their weapons practice since it was abandoned on summer nights. They figured that factor and D'Nas's keen sense of awareness would buy them some time before having to trek off into the woods for these meetings.

"I don't want to lose it. I've never had a Raven—or anyone for that matter—make a weapon especially for me." D'Nas tugged at her ponytail.

"I'm glad you like it. I guess you did find a glitch though. Bring it to me for our session Sunday and I'll start working on it again," she said.

D'Nas glanced at her sideways and picked up his pace, putting some distance between them as they returned to his car. "Sunday? So, you have other plans on Saturday night?"

"Yes," Katy said. She paused at the irritation in his voice. "I'm going with Miranda to watch that Russian film. I told you about it. It's based on one of my favorite books, remember?"

D'Nas turned to her with a smile across his face. "Yes! I had forgotten about that. Let me know if you want any company. You know, Dwight has expressed some interest in her."

"Oh, no!" Katy held up her hand. "Miranda is still trying to get her head wrapped around the information I blasted her with about your kind and the Shades. She does not need any distractions."

"Do you really think your father won't find out about your disclosure to her?" he asked.

"No," Katy said and sighed as she slid onto the leather of his front car seat. "But I'd like to put that off as much as I can. He's going to be super mad."

"You know," D'Nas said, "You were under duress at that moment. Your cousin had just tried to kill you in your own swimming pool. Somehow, I think he will be more understanding than you predict."

"I hope you're right," she said. "Now that she has the antidote to my family's water potion, she will be seeing more and more of the differences between humans and the supernaturals. I've tried to prepare her as much as possible, but I worry."

D'Nas started the car and pressed the gas, causing the

high performance motor to crescendo. Katy looked out the window as he exited the parking lot and passed her old school. The tennis courts brought images from long ago to her mind. She thought of a girl who had once tried out for the team. Katy shivered as she remembered the power from that girl. Her outward appearance was human, but there had been something completely unnatural about her.

"I mean, what if Miranda is flirting with a Shade, which by the way is something she has done before without knowing it. She is drawn to the clichéd bad boys." Katy smoothed her hair down and continued, "Anyway, let's say she catches this guy on a bad day and he becomes angry. She gets nauseous, her head hurts, and even worse, she see his eyes darken and his face morph into its creepy natural form. If she runs away screaming, what will people think? He'll just look like a normal guy to them."

"I think you should keep throwing scenarios at her. Get her mind prepared," D'Nas said. "You could let her come to one of our practice sessions."

"No," Katy shook her head.

"Your skills are really improving. She may enjoy seeing what you can do," D'Nas countered.

"You have to understand. She's been my best friend since we were little girls." Katy changed songs on D'Nas's mp3 player and then gazed out of the car's windshield. The street lights illuminated the empty highway, magnifying a feeling of loneliness. "I've told her about my family's role in keeping people in the dark and making weapons for the Illumin, but I don't want her to see me fighting yet. It may be the last bit of information that convinces her she never really knew me at all."

"Why don't you bring her around me a little more? I'll take flight for her one day. It will put the focus back on my kind, and, like you said, she needs as much information as she can get."

Katy smiled and said, "You know, Miranda would love that, actually. She's been begging me to let her spend more time with you. She thinks I'm purposefully keeping her working at The Spicy Perk, but in reality, Dad is insisting that I spend time filling Hunter's shoes."

"Do you miss working at the coffee shop?" D'Nas asked as they turned onto her street. Her cat, Megan, darted across the road and ran into her yard at the sight of his now-familiar car.

"I do. I miss my employees and some of the regular customers. And the smells of the coffee and lemon scones. It is a peaceful place," Katy said.

"I guess you miss the 'peaceful' part most of all," D'Nas said.

"Yes." Katy marveled at how much D'Nas knew about her despite their recent acquaintance. "I have no choice now that Hunter has abandoned his post."

D'Nas put the car in park and got out to help her with her bag. Katy unlocked her front door and her little dachshund, Oscar, ran out to greet D'Nas. He brushed against D'Nas's leg and excitedly wagged his tail. "Jeez, he doesn't even notice me when you are around," Katy said.

"I assure you, I am not stealing your dog's affection on purpose," D'Nas replied.

"There is just something magnetic about you guys,"

Katy said.

D'Nas patted Oscar's head and without looking at her said, "Good job tonight, Katy. Don't worry, I'll get my 'Sliver Lilly' back." He shot her a grimaced look as he descended the stairs.

Katy picked up Oscar and with a smirk said, "Sorry, I just couldn't resist. Every weapon must have a name."

"Right," he said and ran his hand over his damp, spiked hair.

Katy marveled–not for the first time–over his large size and build. She put her hand on her hip and said, "Oh, and D'Nas, despite her fears, Gillian would totally whip Milton."

"I guess since these stories are a part of your world, you know best," he said and made an exaggerated bow.

Katy watched him drive away, and Oscar whined as his car lights faded. "I know, my little stretched buddy, I know."

Darrus stared out of his bedroom window and rolled a burning cigar between two fingers. Lightning streaked across the sky. A loud clap of thunder returned his thoughts to the present. Through the sheets of rain flowing down the glass, he watched his daughter's red convertible approach the house gates. He released a deep breath that clouded the window and seemed to mimic his melancholic thoughts.

As the car made its way up the drive, Darrus pondered the

involvement between his daughter and the Illumin detective. During the weeks he was unconscious, his daughter had formed a bond with him. "Well, she had to turn to someone," he whispered into the empty room.

"That beige tie makes you look paler. Wear the blue one," Nila said from the bedroom entrance.

He started at her sudden appearance. "Good grief, Nila! What if I'd been in my underwear?"

She frowned and said, "You need to stay home and get your rest. The last place you should be going is the museum."

Darrus knotted the blue tie and said, "Katy will be with me. You know she can take care of this old man. Besides, you should take the night off. Go see those grandbabies."

When she did not move, he chuckled and said, "If you are so concerned about my health, maybe you should stop sneaking up on me."

"You don't look well, Mr. Raven," she stated.

"I wish you'd stop calling me that, Nila. We are the same age, and, as many years as you've worked here, I think we are past formalities," Darrus said. He peeked behind the curtain to gaze at the heavy rain and wind. "If this tropical storm doesn't abate soon, that big pine might fall over and squash the gazebo."

"I hope not," Nila said and joined him at the window. "She was so happy when you surprised her with it."

Darrus watched as tears welled up in Nila's eyes. In the few years that she had known his wife, the two had formed a bond not typical of the maid and lady of the house. He cleared his throat and let the curtain drop. "You know," he said, "I'm surprised you are this worried. Considering my feelings regarding certain museum staff members, you know I'll be in bed counting sheep before the ten o'clock news."

Katy appeared at the bedroom door wearing a blue evening gown. Darrus felt his dark mood begin to lift. He gave Katy a quick hug and said, "You just keep getting prettier and prettier, young lady." The three of them descended the stairs, and then Katy and Darrus slipped out into the stormy evening.

Darrus slid into the backseat of the limo and gestured a nod to the driver. He leaned back in his seat and took a deep breath. He hated attending events at the museum, but Shreveport's most stuffy segment of society was well-aware of his family's extensive collection of Aztec exhibits and expected his presence at any opening involving this type of collection.

The rain pelted the windshield and Darrus wondered at the driver's visibility. He patted his face dry with a handkerchief and felt a pang in his stomach when he saw the monogrammed image of a raven. He grunted in frustration and muttered aloud, "I've told Nila not to put these out." He sighed and rubbed his stomach. The familiar knots of grief were tightening as they always did when something reminded him of his wife. He recalled the Christmas his wife had presented him with the array of handkerchiefs, monogrammed by her own hand. It was the last gift he received from her.

Katy glanced in his direction and then busied herself by examining her face in a small mirror. "So much for dropping all that money to get my hair put up. Within the hour, this Louisiana weather will undo my 'do."

Darrus laughed and said, "Honey, every woman there will have to walk through this mess. You will still be the best looking one by far."

"Thanks," Katy said. She smoothed her dress and placed her small matching purse on the seat beside her.

"I'm glad you are coming with me. I hate these things," Darrus said.

Katy straightened her posture and looked forward. "You hate going to the museum, you mean."

Darrus's stomach constricted further as the driver turned down the road leading to Shreveport's most prominent museum. He moved his thumb across the raven on the handkerchief and frowned at the sting in his eyes.

"We are here, sir," the driver stated.

Darrus grabbed his umbrella. "I tell ya, Bruce, I could think of better ways to spend an evening."

Bruce ran around the car and opened the door for them. He held an umbrella over Katy and asked when he should return. Darrus said, "Give me two hours…if I leave earlier than that I'll be forced to fabricate an excuse. I don't think they'd take to kindly to 'this is as long as I can tolerate you folks.'"

Bruce laughed and straightened his driving cap. "No, Mr. Raven, you might not want to say that."

As they walked to the front entrance, a gust of wind blew the rain sideways, making their umbrella useless.

An aged woman dressed in formal attire complained to her husband as they moved to walk beside Darrus and Katy. "Oh, my dress! I'm going to be soaked and freeze from that air conditioning."

"Good evening, Dr. Willow, Mrs. Willow," Darrus said and slowed their pace to match that of the older couple. They were one of Shreveport's most elite pairs.

A younger couple jogged past them. The woman slid when her high-heeled shoes struck a shallow puddle on the concrete, but she managed to catch herself.

"Finally!" Mrs. Willow stated as they reached the museum's front entrance. "I'll never understand why they don't put a covered walk." She lowered her voice and pulled on her jeweled necklace. "Mr. Raven, you are friends with the curator. Perhaps you could mention something?"

Darrus nodded as if in agreement then busied himself with handing his coat and umbrella to the doorman. Katy shot him a frustrated look when two men raced to greet her, each attempting to speak over the other.

Darrus headed to the open bar and requested tonic water. The sharpness of the bubbles would help to clear his head. He surveyed the crowd. A couple hundred well-to-do people milled about. Darrus heard a familiar too-loud laugh from a young lawyer always eager to impress. He jumped when a hand touched his arm. He turned slightly and encountered two women standing with drinks in their hands and plastic smiles on their faces.

"Good evening, Mrs. Hawkins," Darrus said and contrived a fit of coughing that enabled him to step a few paces away.

Mrs. Hawkins let her hand drop from his arm and swayed a little. "Oh, are you still not feeling well?"

At least that is what Darrus thought she said; the words came out pretty close together.

"I'm fine, just a bit tired. How are you ladies?" he asked.

"I am well. You remember my cousin Rebecca, don't you?" Mrs. Hawkins smiled at the other woman, who cocked her head to the side and flashed a mouth of stark white, perfectly aligned teeth.

"Hello, Rebecca, nice to see you again," Darrus said and moved as if to step away.

He was stopped by another grab on the arm. "I was just telling Rebecca about what a nice man you are and such a community activist. You work so diligently for those less fortunate. I mean, just think of all the people who will never get to attend an event like this."

Darrus looked down at her and said, "I imagine the 'less fortunate' have much regret about not getting to wear formal attire and spend time with folks such as yourselves." Mrs. Hawkins nodded her head in earnest, but Rebecca frowned in his direction. Darrus smiled at her and enjoyed that despite the heavy makeup and drink, at least she could recognize satire.

An hour later, Darrus was able to break free from the group. He had made his usual speech about the importance of supporting the local museum and reminded everyone of his family's interest in Aztec history. Despite his lack of enthusiasm, judging by the elbow rubbing he had endured, the museum's finances would soon be much improved.

"Good talk," Katy said. She blew a stray piece of hair from her eyes and took a sip of champagne.

Darrus noticed the museum's curator edging through the crowd. He took Katy's elbow and guided her in the opposite direction to the permanent exhibits. Katy's heels clicked against the floor as they walked in silence for a few moments.

"Let's go down here." Darrus gestured in the direction of his favorite wing.

"I figured this is where we were going," Katy said. She pulled him to a stop and said, "Dad, have you even talked to him yet?"

"No," Darrus said. "I'm sure it's unavoidable, but why not delay that for a bit?" He chuckled to himself and squeezed her arm.

"Don't you miss Sams?" Katy asked. She pointed to a room of pastel paintings, so he followed her there.

"No," Darrus said. "And yes."

"Any thoughts about rekindling the friendship?"

"It was a long time ago, Katy," Darrus said. "You remember what I've told you through the years?"

"To pay my bills on time and say no to drugs?" Katy beamed and made a smoking gesture.

"When it comes to relationships, always trust your instincts. If something feels wrong, it probably is. If you think someone is lying, they probably are."

Katy looked away from a tall painting of a grassy meadow and faced him. "What if our instincts about the Illumin were wrong?"

Darrus placed his hands on his hip and shook his head, "Katy…"

"Just hear me out," Katy interrupted. "Maybe we were wrong. Maybe our 'instincts' that they were involved with Mom's disappearance was just our emotional upset talking. It's possible that our perceptions were off."

"She did not just run off Katy. We both know the Illumin resources. Something didn't sit well with me then and it still doesn't now. They should have found her."

"I trust D'Nas," Katy said.

"That scares me, Katy. To my core."

"I wish you would give him a chance," Katy said. "Dad, it's been over 20 years now. We may never know what happened to Mom, but we have to go on living. And we can't fully live inside the walls we built around our family. Especially now. Like it or not, we have to patch our relationship with the Illumin."

"I hate every bit of that," Darrus said. A spell of dizziness came over him and he leaned on the wall for support.

"You know, I was looking at the picture on your desk. The one of your last fishing trip with Sams before Mom's disappearance. You both looked so relaxed and happy." Katy pulled on the edge of his sleeve. "Won't you at least talk to him? Just give him a fresh read now that time has passed."

Darrus gestured for Katy to follow him and he led her past a room of antique war rifles and into an area that contained his favorite painting. They crossed the room and stopped in front of a piece he had desired for years. It was the portrait of a two-story white house with a wide porch and blue shutters with vine-laden trellises. The gothic architecture was an interesting juxtaposition of the otherwise feminine features.

Darrus turned to face Katy. "How do you know you can trust D'Nas?"

She met his eyes and said, "His behavior has been consistent. He isn't afraid to tell me hard truths. But, mostly I just feel it in my gut."

"He looks like a hothead to me," Darrus said. He adjusted his tie in an effort to help himself breathe better.

"I have an idea," Katy said with a gleam in her eye.

"I can't wait," Darrus said.

"Why don't you ask Sams what he thinks about D'Nas?"

"That makes a heap of sense. I should ask someone of questionable integrity about the integrity of another."

"You were friends for years," Katy said. "You saw something in him then. Won't you at least consider it?"

"All right, Katy." Darrus found himself feeling somewhat lighter. He returned his attention to the painting and began laughing to himself.

"What's funny?"

"You are taking quite the risk, you know?" Darrus said without taking his eyes from the art. "Sams was always very protective of you. He won't mince words about D'Nas. If he provides an ill report, how will you feel about him if I forbid you to date that detective?"

"Well, then at least we will know for certain," Katy said and threw her hands in the air.

"Know what for certain?" Darrus said.

"That Sams does indeed have questionable integrity."

Darrus laughed and gave his daughter a squeeze. "Quite the comedienne. You should sell the Perk and go on the road."

Katy watched Miranda pick the radishes out of her salad. "I'll take those if you don't want them," she said.

"Gross. They just taste like watered down black pepper." Miranda tossed some slices onto Katy's plate. "I love that you are back at the Perk today. I also love that we are taking an actual lunch break."

"It is nice to have dependable employees," Katy said. She took a bite of her salad and cherished the taste of the lemon vinaigrette.

Miranda took a bite from a huge hamburger. "Mmm... this is good," she mumbled through her food.

A loud clap of thunder sounded and the chandeliers flickered. "Guess that storm is early," Miranda said.

Katy was about to take another bite of food when she felt a familiar dip in her stomach. She put her fork down and resisted turning around to watch the Shades walk into the restaurant. The ancient beings walked past their table and Katy laid her hand across the bottom half of her face to block the inevitable smell.

"What is it?" Miranda asked.

Katy darted her eyes in their direction.

Miranda watched wide-eyed as the two males seated themselves. One man was wearing a navy blue pinstriped suit, and his black hair was slicked back. Katy mused that he looked like he had just taken a time portal from the 1920s. The other man was dressed more casually, but he sat with his back to her.

"Katy," Miranda whispered. "The guy in cargos is Hunter's friend, Thomas. The one he brought to the store that day. The Shade."

"Is it?" she replied. Anger appeared in an instant and deleted her rational thoughts. "Maybe he can tell me where my brother is."

Katy shook off Miranda's hand when she tried to stop her and walked across the patio to their table. She stopped next to Thomas and did her best to keep her emotions in check.

"Well, just when I thought the beauty of this day could not be surpassed," Thomas said, winking.

"It's funny isn't it?" Katy asked and cocked her head to one side.

"What's that, little human?" Thomas replied with a smile and winked at his partner.

"How you choose to make a quip about my presence enlightening your day when your entrance so darkened mine."

Thomas's russet eyes darkened to black, and Katy felt the vinaigrette turn in her stomach.

"Ms. Raven, I think it would be wise to return to your table," stated the suited man. "Thomas is not a fan of your family as of late."

"Well, Astrous, I can't imagine why. After all, Thomas and Hunter were such pals." Katy leaned close to Astrous and whispered, "It was so cute, the way they bonded over weapons. Can't you just imagine them sitting on the floor in little seersucker overalls, building things like little boys work on their blocks."

"Smart mouth for someone so defenseless," Thomas snapped.

"Where is my brother?" Katy straightened and returned his stare. Thomas's face had begun to shift. His cheekbones elevated into an unnatural shape.

"Who knows?" Thomas said. "Since he wasn't my brother, I figured it was someone else's responsibility to make sure he got off the battlefield alive."

Katy grimaced as the guilty feelings resurfaced. She had been forced to leave her brother wounded after he had turned against her and their family.

"Cat got your tongue?" Astrous smiled and took a sip of his tea. He laughed, displaying pointy teeth. The odor of his breath, even across the table, threatened to send her reeling.

"Thomas, do you not know where my brother is? I know he is alive." Katy said.

"No," Thomas said. "It's too bad, really. He and I were just getting to know each other, and like you pointed out, now I don't have anyone to play with."

Katy looked at Thomas's plate as the waitress placed it down; she considered throwing it in his face. Miranda appeared at her side and in a breathless voice said, "Katy, we better be getting back."

She took Katy by the shoulder and said, "You guys have a nice day." Her smile wavered as Astrous grinned widely at her. Unbeknownst to either Shade, Miranda was no longer blind to their true appearance.

Miranda steered Katy out of the restaurant and toward their car. Katy stopped suddenly when she thought about the bill.

"I already paid it," Miranda said. "Just get in, I'll drive."

Miranda drove in the opposite direction from the coffee shop.

"Where are you going?" Katy asked.

"We need to de-stress before we head back," Miranda stated and turned onto one of Katy's favorite streets. Tall oak trees lined each side. The pair rode slowly through the rain while listening to meditative music.

"I've always loved that house," Miranda said and gestured to an old yellow house with a wide porch. She pulled over to the side of the street and parked. "Do Shades always smell so bad?"

"Yes," Katy said. It was refreshing to be able to talk to her friend about a world that she had been forced to hide from her for so many years. "It's a weird odor, isn't it? Sort of like hot moth balls."

"For a minute there I thought you were about to vomit," Miranda said.

"So did I. It was my fault. I don't think he would have cooperated with me either way, but I made Thomas angry. The physical effects are always so much worse when they are angry."

Katy shifted in her seat and looked out her window, not focused on anything in particular. "I wonder how he is doing…"

"Katy, I'm sure Hunter will turn up soon," Miranda said.

"I know. I just can't believe it's come to this. I knew Hunter and I had our differences, but to have no relationship at all?" Katy said.

"Who do you think he could be with?" Miranda asked.

"I don't know. I'm sure he had bank accounts my father didn't know of, so he was able to get money. He could be anywhere by now."

"Well, if he did leave, let's face it, he'll be back. No offense, but your brother is quite the little climber. His whole life is about money and prestige. He can't be the 'big dog' if he's separated from your dad's money."

Katy laughed and drew a smiley face on the foggy car window. "I've thought the same thing myself." She paused then said, "You know, while Cooper is feeling guilty for helping Hunter, I'm thinking of coercing him into to going with me to Hunter's apartment. See if I can find a clue."

"Why would you need Cooper? You and I can go right now."

"No, Dad has cameras on the place. Cooper will be able to locate them and buy us some time."

"Why wouldn't your Dad want you in there?" Miranda asked.

"He says he doesn't want me associated with my brother in any way. He's afraid I'm already in too much danger with the Shades. He has my cousins watch me all the time."

"Really?" Miranda said. "What about now?"

"See that motorcycle, the blue one parked on the corner?" Katy said.

"Yes," Miranda said. "Wait! That's Christopher's bike!"

"Right," Katy said. "When it's not Christopher, it's

Andy, or Amos, or one of their friends."

"Their friends?"

"Andy has a lot of friends who are well-trained in martial arts, just like he is. They all know Hunter is missing. I'm sure my Dad pays them handsomely to watch out for me and not ask questions," Katy said.

"This well just keeps getting deeper," Miranda said.

The two women entered Katy's coffee shop and were greeted by the sound of music and laughter. The shop's feline resident wound herself around Katy's leg in greeting. Familiar customers welcomed her back and inquired about her well-being. Katy was finishing a conversation with an elderly family friend when Miranda passed by her and said, "Big man is here."

Katy felt a lift of excitement to see D'Nas, but was disappointed to see that Gabriella was with him. He was always so much more business-like when she was around.

"Hi," Katy said with a forced smile. "Can I get either of you something?"

"No, we are fine," D'Nas answered.

Katy rolled her eyes. "Gabriella, I'm sure you can answer for yourself. Is there anything I can get you?"

Gabriella seemed pleased at the direct communication since they typically ignored each other. "I'm going to get some tea, but I can order it from the front. D'Nas needs to talk to you." She looked back on her way to the counter. "Thanks."

Katy nodded to Gabriella and looked up at D'Nas. His eyes were emitting more light than usual, which indicated something was wrong. Katy sighed, "Yes, I know I shouldn't have approached them. Yes, I know I was asking for a scene, but I had to ask about Hunter."

D'Nas held a frown for a moment then said, "You pretty much just made my speech for me."

Katy laughed in relief of one less lecture and patted his shoulder. "Everything is fine. Besides, we were in a public place. Astrous may be a Shade, but we both know formality is important to him."

"Please be more careful. We will find your brother. After your appearance at the cabin battle, you are no doubt on the Shade target list. Don't give them an excuse to come after you." D'Nas said.

"Ping!" Katy said as she formed a small circle with her hands over her head.

Katy bit the inside of her lip and paced the length of her porch, her empty backpack slung across her shoulder. A cool breeze blew wispy strands of hair into her face. Behind her, Oscar jumped against the low-lying window, his little nails squeaking against the glass. "Get off the curtains, Stretchy," Katy said. He made no movement, but stared back at her with innocent brown eyes.

"Ugh," she said aloud and went to sit on the steps next to Miranda. A few moments later, Cooper drove an unfamiliar black truck into her driveway. He wore a baseball cap pulled down low over his face. He motioned for them to get in.

Katy used the handle to pull herself up to the truck's immense height. "Whose truck is this?"

"I borrowed it from the impound yard," Cooper said.

"How did you manage that?" Miranda asked. She looked around the dirty cab and drew her feet up onto the seat.

"The guard thinks I'm cute," Cooper said and backed out of the driveway.

"Really?" Miranda asked with raised eyebrows.

"Hey, everyone looks good to someone. Even guys like me." Cooper removed his hat and ran his hand across his curly hair, making it look somewhat electrified. The women laughed and the tension among them lessened.

"I don't think the family is watching Hunter's apartment at night. Dad pretty much expects Hunter to just lick his wounds and later brazenly show up at the mansion. It's more his style," Katy said.

"What are we looking for exactly?" Miranda asked.

"Anything that might lead me to Hunter. Surely he had a Plan B," Katy replied, trying to sound more confident than she felt. "Right, Cooper?"

Cooper glanced back at her and sighed, "Katy, like I said earlier, he told me only what he had to." He dropped his voice. "I'm not sure why he involved me to begin with."

The truck turned into a parking lot near Hunter's luxury apartment complex. Miranda and Katy stayed in the vehicle while Cooper crossed the space and disappeared around the dark side of a building.

"I hope you are right in trusting him, Katy." Miranda poked Katy in the side.

"He's our only hope. No one else could stop the cameras. I'm a little surprised they got them running without Cooper's help."

After what seemed like an agonizing amount of time, Cooper reappeared and signaled for them to join him. He gestured upwards when they neared. Katy saw the red glow from a cigarette where someone relaxed on a balcony.

Miranda started to giggle and held her hand over her face to stifle sounds. "Miranda, get a grip," Katy whispered.

Cooper rocked his body from side to side and squeezed his cap in his fist. "Let's go. Standing in a huddle by the bushes in the middle of the night may prove suspicious."

They ascended the staircase. The soles of their shoes created a soft tinkling on the metal stairs. Katy held the key at the tip of the lock and looked back at Cooper, "Are you sure we are clear?"

He gestured to Katy and back at himself, "Who will get in trouble here?"

The three entered the apartment. Katy's chest tightened at the familiar scent of her brother's home. She illuminated a small glow stick and handed two more sticks to the others. "I'll take his bedroom; you guys start in here."

Katy entered Hunter's bedroom. It was meticulous, just like his personality. The faint smell of his cologne hung in the air. She combed through the room and found nothing out of the ordinary. Her father had confiscated his computer. The space seemed barren.

Cooper lay across the couch. When he spotted Katy enter the room he said, "Katy, this is fruitless. You know how Christopher is. He's thorough on a good day, and

Christopher was super mad at your brother when he searched this apartment."

Katy shrugged, tossed her glow stick onto the leather couch, and walked out onto Hunter's balcony. The balcony opened to a secluded area adjacent to woods so that little streetlight permeated the area. Moonlight provided just enough light for Katy to see the furniture and other items in the small space.

Katy walked to the railing and looked outward. She breathed in the scents from the pines and the autumn night. Katy turned to face the balcony and noticed that the left half was empty. This asymmetrical look was not Hunter's style. Her eyes drifted across the space and stopped on an intricate spider web, the strands of which shone silver in the moonlight. Hunter hated spiders. Katy was overcome by a sudden impulse to tear down this symbol of her brother's absence.

She thrust her finger into the middle of the web. To her amazement, the web made a clicking sound and vanished. Katy stumbled backward in response to a gush of wind that came from the corner of the balcony. She stared dumbfounded at the black metal cabinet that had appeared out of nowhere.

"What is it?" Cooper rushed onto the balcony, followed by Miranda.

Katy shook her head and turned the handle. The door opened with ease, and she jumped in place several times from excitement.

"What is it?" Miranda asked.

"See for yourself." Katy stepped back and watched Miranda's expression change from curiosity to understanding.

"Hunter's stash o' weapons," Cooper said.

"My stash now," Katy said and placed the weapons in a black bag stored in the bottom of the cabinet. She was forced to leave a bow and arrow, as it was nearly as tall as she was. "Let's go," she said and closed the cabinet, leaving it unhidden.

Cooper opened Hunter's apartment door and stepped behind it so the women could exit. Miranda took a step across the threshold, then screamed and knocked Katy flat in her clamber backward. Cooper leapt in front of them and gasped. A large figure stood in the darkness of the door, wings outspread and eyes glowing red. "I didn't even have to knock," he said and grabbed Cooper by the neck, tossing him like a banana peel into the air; he landed with a crash into the glass coffee table.

Katy pushed Miranda deeper into the living room and tossed the bag down. She grappled for the zipper, but the figure grabbed her pony tail with his hand and pulled backwards. "Hello, my lady," he stated. His proximity caused her to tremble, and her ears felt like they were on fire.

"Shade," she said through a clenched jaw.

"Quick study." Another voice entered the room. Katy sensed the presence stand behind them. It spoke in its own language and pushed her captor to his side, forcing him to let go of her hair. Katy moved for the bag of weapons, but a boot landed on her hand. Katy winced, but the pressure from the cleats was mild. "I'll take that. Thanks for solving this little problem for me. I knew he had this stashed somewhere."

"Thomas." Katy dug her claws into the Shade's leg.

Thomas grabbed her by the arm, pressed his face to

hers, and whispered something into her ear. His tone seemed to suggest he was trying to comfort her, but she could not understand his language, and her stomach heaved in response.

Miranda shouted for her several times. Her voice wavered through sobs from another area in the apartment.

"Let her go!" Cooper said. In the darkness Katy could hear glass tinkling as he struggled to disentangle himself from the coffee table frame.

Red eyes cut through the darkness and with incredible speed crossed the room in Cooper's direction. The Shade screeched and its red eyes were thrown in the opposite direction. Its body smashed through the balcony glass, and wings thudded against the railing.

Thomas rushed to defend himself and threw Katy to the ground. The lights in the apartment flicked on as masked men raced into the living room, striking at the Shades with short staffs. Katy's stomach twisted in fear as she watched her cousins attack the powerful beings with human weapons.

Katy felt her brother's weapon bag lift from her side as Thomas retrieved it. He glanced down at her. His black eyes contrasted against his pale skin. He used the bag to knock one of the men out of the apartment and then jumped outside to the balcony. He muttered in his dark language to his partner, who growled in response but followed Thomas when he jumped into the air, leaving the humans alone in the apartment.

Christopher pulled off his mask and slammed the broken balcony door shut. The apartment was in shambles. Cooper had managed to pull himself out of the coffee table and was lying in glass between it and the couch. Christopher threw his jyo to the floor and spat at Cooper. "Serves you right!" He kicked Cooper in the side with a resulting sickening thud.

"I'm sorry, man. She asked for my help!"

Christopher helped Katy get to her feet. Blood from his left arm was beginning to soak his gi. "Are you okay?"

"I think so," she managed. When she met his sympathetic eyes, the trauma of the event settled on her. She choked back a sob and she said, "I'm so sorry."

He glanced away for a moment and then looked back at her, "Save that for Uncle Darrus, Katy. We are so lucky they left."

A noise came from the kitchen and Christopher started. Katy said, "It's just Miranda."

Katy found her friend sitting on the floor. She hugged Miranda while she cried and Katy apologized over and over. Christopher stared at them with a scowl on his face and held his injured arm.

Amos stumbled into the apartment. His face was splattered with blood. D'Nas and Gabriella raced in after him. Their wings were outstretched and weapons in hand. The pair muttered something to each other in their language, and Gabriella rushed to the balcony. D'Nas covered the length of the apartment in three steps and met Katy's eyes. As usual, his emotions were impossible to discern.

Miranda whimpered at the sight of D'Nas in his supernatural state. Katy put her arm around her shoulders and whispered, "Welcome to my life."

7

Darrus caught a glance of his shadow and chuckled at the vision of his duck-like walk as he lugged his ice chest, tackle box, and fishing poles. Once he reached the small flat-bottomed boat, he tossed the items inside. A refreshing autumn breeze blew across the lake, and he tightened the strings under his chin to make sure his hat stayed secure.

Darrus leaned against a pole and surveyed the lake. The morning sun peeked through grey cloud cover. A flock of ducks landed in the water near the dock. The ducks' chatter reminded Darrus of the days he and the children came to the lake to feed them. Hunter never took much interest in the animals, but Katy insisted on feeding them until the entire bread package was extinguished.

Footsteps at the beginning of the dock pulled Darrus back to the present. He walked in his old friend's direction. "Good morning."

"We couldn't have asked for better weather," Sams said. He adjusted his fishing bag and shook Darrus's hand. Sams placed his equipment in the boat, and Darrus started the small engine and drove them across the pond to his favorite spot.

Neither man spoke for the first half hour. The silence blanketed the two men and seemed to roll itself across the water.

"Any chance that painting is for sale?" Darrus asked.

"No, I'm afraid the museum intends to retain it." Sams met Darrus's eyes with a somber expression. "For any price." He tossed his line into the water. "There are several paintings we just obtained from a California museum that you might find of interest."

Darrus grunted his lack of desire. He would get that painting one day, even if it meant increasing his donation. Something about that house called to him. "Since you are unable to help me through your day job, maybe you can help me in another way."

"Certainly."

"Tell me what you know about a detective on the Illumin force. Named D'Nas," Darrus said.

Sams straightened and was silent for a moment. He reeled in his line inch by inch and kept his gaze on the water. He brought his hook into the boat, checked his line, and cast it back out into the water. "D'Nas is good at his job, but manages to stay in trouble with his superiors. He tends to disregard the rules of both Shades and humans."

"How is that?"

"He does not hesitate to fight if he thinks a Shade is out of line. Most of the Illumin Force consult their superiors to develop plans of action, but not D'Nas."

"Well," Darrus said and felt his mouth curl into a smile. "I owe most of my success to my youthful 'unorthodox' behavior. What I want to know is this. Is he dangerous?"

"To Shades, yes. To his Illumin partners, probably, due to his impulsive aggression."

"What about to humans?" Darrus asked.

Sams frowned and adjusted his long, silver ponytail. He lay his pole on the side of the boat and placed his sunglasses on top of his head. "The rumor among my people is that D'Nas has entered a relationship with your daughter."

Darrus recast his line. "Is this something I need to put a stop to?"

"What's surprising to me is that D'Nas has whined for years about wanting to serve elsewhere. He resents this world and…until now, the inhabitants herein." Sams replaced his sunglasses over his eyes and leaned back in the elevated chair, placing his boots on the side of the boat for support. "What is even more surprising is that you haven't put a stop to it already. Instead, you and I are fishing like two decades haven't passed since our last real conversation, and you are asking my advice."

"I know we haven't been on the best of terms."

"Not since Lilly's disappearance," Sams said.

A shiver ran down Darrus's spine. He paused for a moment then said, "It has been a long time. Look, I know you cared for Katy. Advise me on how to protect her." He held his hands in the air and shook his head. "I can't lose Katy too, Sams."

Sams turned his face and stared unmoving at the water.

Darrus said, "For goodness' sake Sams! A few weeks ago I woke up from a coma—induced by my son—and find my daughter has thrown herself into a supernatural battle."

Sams rubbed his hands across his chin. "What does Hunter have to say for himself?"

"We have no idea where he is." Darrus paused. "You

telling me you didn't know that?"

"I did. I was hoping maybe he had returned since I'd last heard news." Sams said.

"Katy is my primary concern. I've also got D'Nas running a few errands for me," Darrus said.

"You've run out of 'errand nephews and nieces'?" Sam asked and raised an eyebrow.

"Hmm…" Darrus dug around in his tackle box then slammed it shut. "I'd forgotten how hard it is to keep you on topic."

"Deviation drives an ordinary conversation to extraordinary places."

"To tell you the truth, with the mess Hunter's got us in, I need more than my nieces and nephews. I'm also trying to keep D'Nas close, and I don't think for a second that he's unaware of my motive."

"My advice is this." Sams removed his pocket watch from his shirt and glanced at the time. He snapped it closed and rubbed the engraving with his thumb. *"D'Nas is a little wild, but that tendency coupled with his distaste for the Shades makes him an effective protector."* He sighed and shrugged his shoulders. "With Katy, it's a double-edged sword. Excuse the cliché.*"*

"Explain the sword," Darrus said.

"For starters, D'Nas will ensure she is high on the Shield List," Sams said.

"I should hope so." Darrus said. "They had better keep their eyes on her. Tell me the bad news."

"D'Nas has been a Shade target for years. He has enemies among the top of their hierarchy. Without him, she's exposed. With him, she will have increased chances for being caught in a melee."

Darrus rubbed his chest from the stabbing heartburn pain. He took a long drink of water and nodded for Sams to continue.

"I'm not going to sugarcoat it. She's put herself in a dangerous position."

"Between her brother's antics and D'Nas's reckless choice to bring her to that battle, she's not the one to be blamed," Darrus said.

"Either way. It's not good, but most of the Shades have bigger things on their mind." Sams motioned with a wave of his hand in the air. "You know as well as I that that war has been brewing for years. I think the best action is the one you are taking. Keep D'Nas close to your family affairs. The more he's invested in her, the more she's protected."

Darrus felt a headache coming on. "Maybe." He shifted his weight in his chair and looked across the lake. "I sure do hate my daughter being in a romantic relationship with one of you."

"I'm sorry about Lilly, Darrus. The Illumin did everything we could. Hell, so did I." Sams placed his feet on the bottom of the boat and swiveled his chair to Darrus. "We are the protectors of your race, not the predators."

"Yeah, well, the jury is still out on that," Darrus said.

The men sat in silence for the remainder of an hour and watched the sun rise and wipe away the dampness in the air. Darrus reached into the water and drew in their lines. Two decently sized bass and about eight white perch gleamed in the day's light. "You ready to go in?" Darrus asked.

Sams nodded and they packed up. The low rumble of a muscle car drifted across the pond as they paddled toward the dock.

"Your errand Illumin?" Sams asked and nodded in the direction of the house.

"He's not due here for hours," Darrus said.

Darrus tied off the boat and Sams climbed up on the dock. D'Nas and Cooper walked down the dock in their direction as they unloaded the boat. Cooper's shirt was stained with blood, and his arms and forehead were bandaged. "Do I dare ask?" Darrus said and moved to inspect Cooper's face.

"I'm sorry, Uncle Darrus. I didn't expect something like this would happen," Cooper stated.

"Spill it, boy."

"Katy asked me to help her break into Hunter's apartment. She was hoping we could find something that would tell us where he is. Shades must have been watching the apartment."

"Get inside the house, now." Sams put a hand on Darrus's shoulder, which he shrugged off. Darrus fumed on the inside. He was losing control of the whole family.

Turning to D'Nas, Darrus demanded, "Where is Katy?"

"Katy is at your house. She's not harmed," D'Nas said. "If you hadn't had me monitor Cooper's phone, the situation may have been different. When I saw where he was, I sent Amos and Christopher to the apartment while my partner and I made the trip across the city."

Darrus stalked down the dock and motioned for them to follow him on the walk to the house. He paused at the bottom of the back door steps to rub his eyes with the palm of his hands. Sams was right about D'Nas. That Illumin was good in a pinch.

Nila opened the back door and walked out onto the top step. She shoved her hands in her apron and said, "Don't be too hard on Katy. She's had a long couple of months."

Darrus nodded. "She's had a long couple of years." Nila narrowed her eyes at Sams and D'Nas, and after a tense moment stepped aside so they could pass.

When Darrus entered the kitchen, his stomach sank at Christopher's condition. He was holding his side and blood stained his clothes. "Have you called Benjamin to have yourself looked at?"

"Yes, sir, he's on his way." Christopher turned around and motioned behind him saying, "Come on, ladies. It won't be that bad."

Darrus watched in horror as Katy entered the room accompanied by Miranda. He stomped his boots in anger and flung a nearby ceramic vase onto the floor. It shattered, sending flowers and water across the kitchen.

Katy knelt next to the broken pieces and began to cry. "That was Mama's." She picked up a few fragments, the blue roses now dismantled.

Darrus's thoughts swirled, and he tried to think of a course of action. He turned away from the group and dug his fingers onto the countertop and looked out of the window. Lilly's white gazebo was bright in the morning's sunlight. He felt the burn of regret cross his chest. That vase had been one of Lilly's favorites.

Miranda moved to stand between Katy and Darrus. Christopher and D'Nas left the room. Sams appeared holding a trash bag, patted Katy on the back, and began picking up the shards.

"I'm sorry, Katy. That was unnecessary," Darrus said. Katy avoided his eyes, but Miranda stared at him. She must think him such a cruel father. He saw Nila at the kitchen's entrance wiping her eyes.

"Mr. Raven," Miranda spoke with ice in her voice. "Katy only told me because she had no one. Your family is isolating. Why should she be alone? She just wants a normal life!"

Darrus rubbed his face and stared at the ceiling, "Miranda, I've imposed strict punishments on any Raven who betrays our involvement with the supernaturals."

"They won't know if you don't tell them," Miranda said.

"That ship has sailed, young lady," Darrus said and gestured to the edge of the kitchen where Christopher and D'Nas lingered.

Nila placed a soft hand on his shoulder. "Darrus, those boys love Katy as if she were their own sister. Besides, Miranda is practically family. You can't tell me she didn't already suspect something was a little, how do you say it, 'bizarre' about this family?" Her face softened into a smile and Miranda nodded a response.

"I won't tell anyone, Mr. Raven." Miranda stood and crossed her arms. "I don't keep the secret for you, but for Katy and Mrs. Lilly."

Darrus nodded. He looked at Christopher. "How long until Benjamin gets here?"

"Any minute." Christopher's face was pale from his injuries.

"Did you hear our conversation?" Darrus asked.

"Yes, sir," Christopher replied. "Amos and I won't tell that Katy blabbed to Miranda. Besides, Nila's right, Miranda is practically family."

Darrus looked at Cooper, who was seated in a chair in the corner of the living room. "You are in no position to tell anyone anything. Understood?"

Cooper nodded. "I promise I won't say a thing."

"Katy, I want you and Miranda to go upstairs with Nila and stay in her rooms. The last thing we need is to have to explain this to Benjamin. At least yet anyway."

"But what about Oscar?" Katy asked.

"I'll go get him when I leave here," Christopher said.

As soon as the women were upstairs, Darrus glared at Cooper. "You are lucky you're all banged up. I'm so sick of you I could spit. Fortunate for all of us I had D'Nas tracking you." He leaned down, within inches of Cooper's face, and pinched his jaws firmly between his fingers.

"For a second time, you've put my daughter in danger." Darrus stared at him and wondered how soon he could get Cooper on a plane. The worst possible places he could send him swirled in his mind.

Sams moved beside the two men. "Darrus, why don't I take Cooper home? I'm sure you and D'Nas have business to discuss."

Darrus stepped away from Cooper and withdrew some tea from the refrigerator. He took his time draining the glass and gazed out of the window. The trees' shadows swayed in the light breeze.

Sams snapped his pocket watch closed, and Darrus

turned around to face the group. The usual stoic look on Sams' face had disappeared. His forehead seemed to crease from worry; the skin above his jaws worked beneath his taught pale skin.

Darrus glanced at D'Nas. The tall, blonde Illumin watched Sams with a questioning look on his face. "What's gotten into you Sams?" Darrus asked.

"Oh. I just need to get to the museum. On second thought, Darrus, I think I'll have to abandon the boy to his fate with you. Let's go fishing again real soon." Sams waved and bolted out of the kitchen.

Katy woke to a prod on her shoulder. "Your Dad wants to speak with you." Nila stood over her where she had fallen asleep on the couch. Katy looked across the room and saw that Miranda was fast asleep on a makeshift bed.

"Now?" Katy asked. She pushed herself to a seated position. The clock on Nila's wall showed midnight.

"Yes, now," Nila said. "Be quiet when you come back in. There is no reason for everyone to lose sleep." The old housekeeper clucked her tongue against the roof of her mouth and walked to her bedroom.

Katy wriggled out of the blue nightgown Nila had loaned her and dressed in her clothes from earlier that day. The clothes still held the faint scent of Hunter's apartment.

When she was ready, she closed the door behind her and descended the twisting staircase. She padded the length of the hallway and stopped at the door of her father's office. D'Nas was alone in the room. He sat in a chair across from her father's desk and stared at the floor.

"What are you doing here?" Katy asked.

D'Nas looked up in her direction and raised an eyebrow. Katy ran her hands across her wrinkled t-shirt and walked across the room. She tripped on the rug and landed with a thud on the couch next to the fireplace.

"You must be a morning person," D'Nas said and laughed. He shifted in his seat and popped his knuckles.

"I would say that you don't appear well-rested either, but that would be rude," she snapped. "Where is my father?"

"He went to get the amulet."

"Why?" Katy said.

"I guess he has questions he wants answered," D'Nas said.

"I don't see why this can't wait," Katy said.

"No, it can't wait." Darrus entered the room still dressed in his fishing clothes. A velvet bag swung from his hands. "Let's talk about this now before there's another disaster."

Katy moved to stand next to D'Nas. Her father untied the strings of the bag and allowed the amulet to slip onto the leather desk pad. "It's hard to believe that ugly little thing caused so much heartbreak and strife," she said.

Darrus sat in his cushioned leather desk chair with too much force. He met their eyes and said, "We can't leave this thing here. I'm thinking of shipping it out of town. By way of ground transport, of course. Maybe stash it in one of my safes on our hunting property in Colorado."

"Can't we just destroy it?" Katy asked. She sat halfway on the side of the desk and rested her chin in her hand.

"No," Darrus said. "It's made of supernatural material. Doesn't melt or shatter. We tried."

"I don't think sending it to Colorado will keep this amulet out of Shade hands. They know you have it, and they will use whatever methods they can to track it down. It's likely your hunting cabins are known to those outside the Raven family," D'Nas said.

"What do you suggest? That I turn it over to the Illumin?" Darrus said.

"I think that's the best choice," D'Nas said.

"Of course you do," Darrus said.

"Maybe we should just give it to them, Dad. It gives us one less thing to worry about."

"Over my dead body," Darrus said. He picked up the string of the amulet and let it hover in the air. To Katy he said, "This may be a burden, but it is our burden." Darrus gestured in D'Nas's direction. "We both know putting it in the hands of these folks is no guarantee of anything."

Katy tightened her lips and widened her eyes at her father in hopes he would tamper his rudeness.

"You have made your concerns about us clear, Mr. Raven. I for one have concerns about you," D'Nas said.

"Do share," Darrus said. He let the amulet drop with a thud on the desk.

"You want me to train with your daughter. 'Keep an eye on her,' you said. Why do that if I can't be trusted?"

"I don't know that you can be trusted, and it's a risk

I resent having to take. The last time I allowed an Illumin into this family's hearts my wife disappeared. I can't prove anything against Sams, but something didn't sit well with me then, and it still doesn't now," Darrus said.

"Why do you blame the Illumin for Lilly's disappearance?"

Darrus sighed and peered through narrowed eyes at D'Nas. "You people can find anything or anybody. You have the strength of superheroes. Yet, my wife was never found."

Darrus's forehead reddened, and he leaned closer to D'Nas. "Despite my misgivings, Katy is in this mess because of you, which makes her safety your responsibility. But don't misunderstand. I debate every day whether or not I should build a wall between you two."

"That's a little ridiculous, Dad," Katy said. She pressed her hand to his shoulder and tried to lighten the mood. "Let's face it. I'm starting to roll down the hill toward 30. It's time I pick my own boyfriends."

"You can pick your own *human* boyfriends," Darrus said. He leaned back in his chair and lit a cigar. "It becomes my business when you intertwine yourself with a supernatural. That's a relationship that could affect this whole family."

Katy glanced at D'Nas. He sat motionless with a passive face. "So, what are we going to do with this old thing?" She picked up the amulet and swung it in the air. In her exhaustion she underestimated her force, and the relic swung toward her face. Like a flash of lightening, D'Nas was out of his chair and snatching the amulet just before it struck her.

Katy jumped off the desk and shouted, "Drop it, D'Nas!"

D'Nas let the amulet lay flat against his palm. "It's not

burning my hand this time."

"And why not?" Darrus demanded.

D'Nas glared at Darrus. His eyes flared, and his skin began to emit a blue light. "You tell me, Mr. Raven."

"It hasn't been out of that safe, boy, and it can only be unlocked by my hand," Darrus said.

The two men glared at each other. Katy touched D'Nas's arm and shook her head. His eyes dimmed and he returned the amulet to the desk and inspected it. He picked it back up and tossed it into the air and caught it. "It feels barren." D'Nas sighed and returned to his chair. "This Shade relic is a vessel no longer."

"You mean the Shade is gone?" Darrus asked.

"If he's gone, then where is he?" Katy asked. She touched D'Nas's arm and he handed her the amulet. She rubbed her thumb against the skull engraving. "He would have no choice but to transfer to another vessel, right?"

The reality crept into her mind. Katy told them, "I know where he is." D'Nas and Darrus stared at her with wide eyes. "He's in that kid, Matt."

Darrus leaned back in his chair and covered his face with his hands. D'Nas stomped across the room and leaned against the wall. He rubbed his neck and said, "That's why his body disappeared after I ripped off the amulet. A human's body could never have withstood such power on its own."

"So, his body wasn't taken by the Shades. He walked out of that battle," Katy said.

"D'Nas, this means a pure Shade is loose in the city?" Darrus asked.

D'Nas paced the floor. "I was sure the Shades had

removed the body. That kid was dead when I was in the room. No breathing." His shoulders sagged and he met Darrus's eyes. "I didn't think to check the amulet again after I gave it to Katy. I still have the burns. I was sure the vessel was active." D'Nas held out his hand to show that his fingertips had not healed.

"Wow," Katy said. "You should have been healed almost right away, right?"

"I don't think my hands will ever heal. Not after touching such a powerful Original."

"D'Nas," Darrus said. "We have to keep this information under lock and key."

D'Nas shook his head. "We have to tell my Captain, and he will tell the Force. This Shade will threaten all we fight for. If he joins forces with the rest of the Shades he could be unstoppable."

Darrus said, "I agree we can't just keep the secret between us. I just worry about the security among your people. What if there is a leak?"

"There is no one disloyal to us. Illumin are even loyal to you humans," D'Nas said.

Katy felt a stab in her heart. "What wrong with us humans?" She glanced at her father, who gave her a knowing look.

D'Nas said, "That's not what I meant."

"Katy," Darrus said. "There will always be an 'us and them.' You need to accept that."

The three were silent for a moment. "Look," D'Nas said. "I will make sure we keep this information as secure as possible. Only the fighters need to know right away. We must begin an immediate search."

Darrus stood and stretched. He yawned and turned down one of the lights. "D'Nas, do you think the Shades know an Original is about?"

"I don't know. That may explain why they haven't searched harder for the amulet." D'Nas said.

Darrus replaced the amulet in the velvet bag. "Not sure what to do with this now. It certainly doesn't require a trip to Colorado."

"Let me have it," Katy said.

"No," D'Nas and Darrus said together.

"And why not?"

"The Shades could still be looking for it," D'Nas said.

"I'm with him on this one," Darrus said. "That's entirely too dangerous."

Katy picked up the velvet bag and walked across the office to one of Darrus's Dobermans lying on the rug. She dangled the bag in front of the animal, which sniffed a moment then resumed its doze.

"Ok, so the Shade's residue is gone," Darrus said. "You still aren't keeping it."

"Here's the deal. You both want me to be more involved in this life, so let me be involved. The Shades are more likely to look in all kinds of hidden places rather than out in the open," Katy said.

"What do you mean 'out in the open'?" Darrus asked and exchanged a glance with D'Nas.

"Hand it to me," Katy said. She took the amulet out of the bag and placed it around her neck. Both men gasped and she laughed. "I'm fine, calm yourselves. Too bad it's so big or I could put it on Oscar's collar."

"This is not a joking matter, young lady," Darrus said.

"That's the problem. That's the problem with this whole stinking life. Nothing ever is funny. Or humorous. Or lighthearted. Or normal," Katy said. Her father looked to D'Nas, who shrugged. Katy thought she detected a hint of a grin on his face.

"You both just need to trust me."

"Katy, you can't wear it around your neck. That's too easily seen," D'Nas said.

"I know," Katy agreed. "I was thinking of framing it inside one of my Halloween decorations. It would match perfectly and no one would suspect a thing."

"What will you do after that?" Darrus asked.

"Something creative," Katy smiled and kissed each man on the cheek. "This has been enlivening, but I'm off to bed now." She left the room with the feeling she would be called right back. All she heard was the sound of her feet striking the staircase.

9

Katy slipped out of Nila's bedroom, tiptoeing on bare feet as she crept down the wooden stairs. She smiled to herself when she was able to dodge the creaky areas. Her memories of sneaking up and down those stairs when she was a child filled her with a sense of familiarity.

She wanted to walk around the lake in the coolness of the early fall morning. When she reached the second floor, she breathed a sigh of relief that her father's door was still closed.

The chilly air refreshed her as she walked down to the small pond. She used the paddleboat to cross the water to an old spot where she and Hunter used to play. The sound of the paddles hitting the water relaxed her. A small fish jumped, and a turtle poked its head out of the water.

Katy pulled the boat to shore and stood on the bank, relishing the feel of the sun on her face. It warmed her body, and pretty soon she needed to push up her thin, long-sleeved shirt. The sky was a bright blue and cloudless. She gazed at her father's home. It was a familiar sight standing proud among the pine trees. She looked at her bedroom window across the distance and thought about how many times as a girl she would gaze at the very place she was now standing and wish she could play at their fort.

Katy turned and followed the overgrown trail to enter the small patch of woods that had once been Hunter and Katy's special place of adventure. They often brought their friends across the lake to play with them. The boys hung ropes for swinging and would push the girls across a small creek. Katy stooped to pick up a worn rope covered in shredded pine straw. She sat at the base of a tree and pulled the straw from the rope piece by piece.

A twig snapped and she whirled around in time to see a fat squirrel dash from one tree to another above the metal fence that bordered her family's property. She sighed and leaned back on the tree, marveling at the beauty of the sun-dappled woods. A slight breeze blew her hair and she closed her eyes.

"It still feels like another world here, doesn't it?"

Katy snapped her eyes open and, with her heart racing, withdrew her knife from her pocket. "Where are you?" she asked as she whirled around in circles looking for the assailant.

"Katy, it's just me." Hunter jumped from the top of the fence.

"Jeez! Hunter?" Katy said. She backed away and held her knife where he could see it.

He inched toward her with his empty hands in the air. "I'm sorry I startled you, but there was no way around it." He laughed and said, "I've been here all night trying to figure out how to catch your eye. I thought I was going to have to sneak in the house."

Katy let her knife fall to her side. She glanced away and tried to blink back tears. "So, you are okay?"

"Yes, I'm fully recovered," Hunter said. He smiled at her and walked near, leaving a few feet between them.

Katy thought about the sleepless nights spent wondering if he was okay or if he needed help. She felt the urge to hug him, but decided against it. "How did you get around the alarms?" She looked back at the house. There was no movement.

"Easy. Cooper weakened this section of the fence for me last year." Hunter said.

"Why are you here? The whole family and the Illumin are looking for you," Katy said. "I searched too. I'm still mad at you, but I've been worried." She pushed her hair back when wind blew strands into her eyes. "Are you coming home?"

"No, not yet Katy," he said. He leaned against a tree, "I came to find you. We need to talk about Sams," Hunter said.

"What?" Katy shook her head in disbelief.

"Keep your guard up around him. He has always had a strong attachment to you."

"Big deal. So he and Dad are talking again." Katy shrugged. "He was actually comforting during a super un-fun situation yesterday. Just like he always was when drama was going down."

"That's exactly what I am worried about, him sneaking his way back in. Just because you are all cozy with D'Nas, Katy, don't forget our suspicions about the Illumin. They are supposed to be so powerful, but were no good when Mom disappeared. Remember how attached Sams was to her? Yet when she disappeared, he didn't stay upset long."

"No, we don't know what happened. We have no idea and neither do they. I doubt even the Shades do." Katy paused and felt her heart harden in anger. "I'm beginning to think she just left. Maybe she couldn't take all this supernatural crap. I can understand that now more than ever."

"She would have taken us with her, Katy," Hunter said in a soft voice.

Katy studied his face. He looked tired, but physically well considering that he had been stabbed by Cooper less than a month ago.

"Look," Hunter said, "I didn't come to argue with you. I just want to tell you that Cooper was wrong; I wasn't going to hurt you. We were mad at each other, you especially, but I would never hurt you."

"I know," Katy said. "I'm sorry Cooper stabbed you and we left you. I just wasn't sure who you were anymore. I'm still not."

"I'll always be your brother. No matter what happens, just remember that," Hunter said and started to back away. "And Katy, watch Sams. Tell Dad I'm sorry too, and that I'll make it up to him."

Hunter hopped back on the fence. Katy pleaded, "Hunter, just come home. You'll be in trouble, but Dad hasn't killed Cooper or Trent yet, so I'm guessing that means he'll spare you. I think he's getting soft in his old age." She paused then said, "And, you should know, Thomas has your weapons. The ones from the apartment."

"Great," he said. "Oh, well, they aren't anything all that special." He hopped over the fence and said, "If there was ever a good time for you to leave town, now's the time. I think it's going to get pretty rough in Shreveport. Very soon."

"Why? Where will you be?" Katy asked, but the sound of his retreating footfalls told her there would be no answer.

Katy dropped Oscar on the floor, and he ran through the house straight to his food bowl. Christopher was not a dog person and was one human Oscar was happy to avoid. She flipped on the lights as she went through the house and when she reached the kitchen, began pulling dishes out of the cabinets. Amos would be staying the night with her and was bringing takeout. She was not happy about having a babysitter, but it was better than being stuck away from home at her father's house.

She put on a load of laundry and closed the blinds to

the nighttime darkness. Katy lit some incense to freshen the house and turned on the heater for the first time in months. She could smell the dust burning, a familiar smell that she found comforting. Oscar yelped several times; Katy's chest turned cold. She ran to the back of the house and tripped on the laundry basket in her rush to see what was wrong.

"Oscar!" Katy called out. Another series of cries confirmed his location. She switched on the light, but the room remained dark. "Oscar," she called, and fear washed over her when she spotted two red eyes glowing from the corner of the room.

She started to run, but the creature was on her in an instant, gripping her by the arm. "No reason to run," he whispered. "I'm just here to visit."

"What do you want, Thomas?" she asked. "Where is Oscar?"

"Oh, no worries, he's fine. I just tossed him out the window. He was biting at my ankles," Thomas said.

"Just when I think you couldn't be more of a jerk," she said. Her stomach began its familiar turn, her vanilla incense mingled in a sickening way with the Shade's bitter odor.

"I was underwhelmed by the weapons in that bag," Thomas said and twisted her arm. "I don't like disappointment, but my boss finds it intolerable."

She turned and looked into his face. He was illuminated by streetlight coming through the blinds. "I don't see how that's my fault."

Thomas loosened the grip on her arm, and his eyes returned to their natural russet color, which, much to Katy's relief, indicated he was calming down. "Maybe not, but," he hesitated. "My boss would like very much to see your stash."

"Your kind cannot use my weapons," she said, surprised by the change in his tone. His face had softened, and in the glow he seemed almost human. "Even Astrous can't wield them, Thomas."

"He wants them just the same," Thomas stated. "Let's go." He placed his hand on the indention of her waist and urged her toward the hallway.

"I don't have any here," she stated. "I store them at my father's house under lock and key, and for good reason, as is made obvious by my current predicament."

"Katy, don't talk to me like I'm some Illumin fool. I can feel them. I'm not sure why, but it's like your weapons are calling to me. It's like they are tied to me in some way."

Trying to buy time, she smiled at him and widened her eyes. "Maybe that power you feel is just me."

"Well, you do have a potent effect," Thomas said. He wrapped his arm around her and drew her to him.

Katy's fear accelerated, and Thomas seemed to misinterpret it for excitement. He turned her to face him, his expression almost boyish. "You are so beautiful for a human," he said. "I'm sorry if I hurt you the other night. I just wanted to get to you before my counterpart did. You don't mean anything to him."

"I mean something to you?" Katy asked. Her mind was racing.

"You've had me enchanted since Hunter brought me to your coffee shop. I loved how you were unafraid, even though you know what I am," he said and stroked her hair. He pulled her to him and kissed her forehead. "Most human women don't recognize the real me; they are just drawn to the power. You would be making an informed choice."

Katy shivered and almost cried aloud when she realized that in her panic she had led him to the pocket door that protected her weapons storage. Realization dawned on Thomas, and he placed his hand on the door, removed it, and touched the tips of his fingers together, as if they tingled. "I don't want to force you. Please, just let me take Astrous your weapons. Then you will be safe from him." He paused. "For a while, at least."

Katy paused, buying time to think. Her most precious weapon, the knife she made for her mother, was in her weapons closet. It also contained her newest weapons for D'Nas, including one that she was quite proud of and he had not even seen yet.

She put on a pout and said, "I don't think I have much choice, really."

"Sadly, no," he said.

"Then can I ask one favor?" she asked. She placed her hands on his chest and felt his muscles tighten in response.

"Anything," he whispered and tightened his grasp on her waist.

"Let me keep the small blue knife," she said. "It was the first weapon I made, and my mother held it the last day I saw her."

Thomas's jaw tightened, and he stared over her head in the direction of the door. He intertwined his fingers in hers and placed his lips to hers. Katy's heart raced, and she choked back a sob. D'Nas had not even held her like this. She felt awash with guilt and ice cold terror. She forced herself not to pull away, hoping that her careful behavior would win her the knife.

He pulled away and said, "Okay. You keep the small knife."

Katy gestured for him to move the small bureau blocking the door. In his distraction, she stepped inside. She grabbed the knife and held it out with a little grin on her face. She tossed it onto the bed behind him, and he nodded his satisfaction. She moved to the side and waved her left arm across the weapons as a child would during Show and Tell in school.

As she predicted, Thomas was forced backward by the repellent built into the weapons, giving her time to grab a small sword and push him away from the closet. "These are mine, you can't have them, Astrous can't have them. Now, get out of my house."

Thomas looked stricken for a moment, then his eyes darkened to blackness and Katy realized the fault in her plan. Her ears began to whine and pain radiated through her body as Thomas's anger charged the atmosphere. She struggled to hold the sword in the air until her stomach heaved and she bent forward. He grabbed her by the hair, slapped her face, and then threw her across the room. She hit the wall and covered her head with her arms, waiting for the inevitable assault.

The window above Katy broke and glass shattered around her like rain. D'Nas flew into Thomas and knocked him through the drywall and into the next room. She heard loud bangs and the sound of flesh hitting flesh. Katy saw a flash of red, and then heard the sound of someone hitting the metal refrigerator. She grabbed her sword and ran into the kitchen, her anger beginning to drown out her fear. This was her house and her almost-boyfriend. No Shade was going to destroy what belonged to her.

Katy raced into the kitchen and saw Thomas punch D'Nas. Black tendrils began wrapping D'Nas's sword arm. Katy jumped behind Thomas and slashed on the bias of the webbing, just as D'Nas had taught her. Thomas cried out and reached for her. She met eyes with D'Nas for the first time and he saw the mark Thomas had left on her face.

D'Nas's glow illuminated the entire room, and Katy jumped from Thomas's reach. She ran into the hallway and bounced into the wall as a result of the blinding glare. D'Nas clotheslined Thomas and wrapped him with his razor-tipped wings, shredding his thick skin. Thomas was forced to the floor, and D'Nas straddled him, punching him in the face over and over. Katy flinched at the savagery. D'Nas's eyes were a bright blue. Between punches, D'Nas yelled at Thomas in his strange language. Gabriella raced in and touched D'Nas's shoulder. Thomas lay still, covered in his thick, black blood.

"It's finished, D'Nas," Gabriella said. She touched D'Nas's arm and continued to speak to him in their Illumin language.

D'Nas made an effort to slow his breathing and resume his human form. He stood and crossed the room. "Tie him up. He goes to the holding cell tonight."

"I'll call ahead," Gabriella said and began wrapping Thomas's hands with a silver wire.

Katy used the wall for support as she struggled to stand.

Thomas opened the less swollen eye, now back to its natural russet shade. He coughed and blood trickled onto the floor. He mouthed something, but Katy could not understand him.

D'Nas crossed the kitchen and placed his boot on Thomas's neck. "You don't speak to her." He pulled what looked like a syringe and stabbed Thomas with it. His eyes closed.

Gabriella said, "Move, let me drag him."

D'Nas stepped back and watched Gabriella take Thomas's body to the door. He then turned to look at Katy standing in the doorway. She heard herself laughing aloud in response to the swift change of his facial expression. He ran to her and lifted her to him. She wrapped her arms around his neck and through her laughter said, "My hero."

"I'm not sure why you are making jokes," D'Nas said.

"I'm not sure either." She looked into his blue eyes and breathed in his sweet scent. It was such a drastic improvement from Thomas's invasive nearness. She stared into his face and said, "I'm so sorry."

"What for?" he asked.

"For doubting your kind." She placed her hands on his face. "For doubting you. My mother's disappearance wasn't your fault, or any other Illumin. I'm sorry for any cruel jab or discourtesy I've thrown at you or any of your people." Katy's knees felt weak, and she held onto him for stability.

"There are no hard feelings between us, you know that," D'Nas said. "Right now, I'm so proud of you," D'Nas said and smiled as he bent down to kiss her neck.

"Why are you proud of me? You saved the day, not me. I was stuck under the window, helpless... again... when you arrived." Katy squeezed his fingers.

"You rushed in here to fight by my side. You even remembered what I've taught you. You are better at this life than you think," D'Nas said.

"A-hem." Amos stood in the doorway, holding a trash covered Oscar in one hand and a bag of takeout in the other. "Mind telling me what I missed."

Katy ran to him and took Oscar from his hands. "My little stretch, are you okay?" He wagged his tail and started clambering for D'Nas. "Per usual," she said and put the dog down to see if he was walking okay. He trotted up to D'Nas, who said, "Whew, he stinks."

"I guess he got into the neighbor's trash. Maybe he's a stress eater." Katy laughed.

"I get the feeling I'm going to be in trouble for not being here," Amos said and slumped his shoulders. "Are you okay?"

"Yes, you have nothing to worry about, you were there last night. I never got a chance to thank you for that." Katy hugged her cousin and kissed his cheek. He smiled at her and touched her face. "You've got a mark."

"It's just a scratch. Everything heals with time," Katy said and snatched the food out of his hands. "Who wants to eat?" she said and stepped over the black substance on her kitchen floor.

by
Jason Craft

1

Chaos tore through the sterile, whitewashed room. Nurses dressed in crimson scrubs skittered about, attending to the woman lying with the blue curtain drawn around her body. Her screams were not only from the pain riveting her, but also of expectancy. The nurses encouraged her, commended her, and instructed her to push. What little strength she held back she put into her grip on her husband's hand.

Nathan stood at her side with all the concern of a helpless, soon-to-be father. His eyes darted across the faces concentrating on the mystery behind the blue curtain, the miracle of life hidden by such a thin barrier. Unsure of everything, he squeezed her hand, hoping it gave her some help beyond the blue veil. He knew enough about life to keep him from even wanting to know what lay behind that curtain. His sole job was to keep his wife pushing.

Agony trampled his wife through her hours of labor until the doctor held their screaming newborn. It was a baby girl, not that he was surprised; they had found out weeks ago. The doctor presented him with their hard-earned bundle of life. With his daughter in his arms, he stared into her beautiful face and wiped off the blood from her cheeks.

"What is her name?" the doctor asked.

"Clara," Nathan replied, tears blurring his vision.

"And what is her destiny?" The doctor's voice sounded distant in this joyous moment.

"What?"

Nathan looked up to see the room cleared out. The doctor stared at him with dark and familiar eyes, the rest of his face hidden behind a surgical mask.

"See for yourself," the doctor said, motioning to his daughter.

Clara's eyes opened and she smiled up at him. A soft glow shone from her face. He wiped a tear from his eye. Her tiny heart pulsed a faint beat.

The sterile light in the room flickered for a moment before settling into a darker state. Nathan watched his daughter's face go pale and heard her heart speed up.

"No!" he yelled, looking for the doctor, but he was alone.

He rushed for the door only to come against a solid grey wall. The entire room was enclosed. Clara reached up for him with her miniature fingers. The chaotic rhythm of her heart stopped and her eyes fell shut. More tears welled in his eyes. His first and only daughter went limp in his arms.

Her smooth skin cracked and turned black as if it were on fire. Flakes of ash peeled off her until she was no more than a sack of remnants. Nathan cried out, dropping her blanket so he could hold her closer. Ash spilled through his fingers and filled the air. His tears dropped into empty palms, creating an oily mess.

His lungs burned, throwing him into a violent cough. Around his feet a pair of black tendrils snaked up each leg, stinging him as they climbed. He held strong through the pain, remembering how much his wife endured all those years ago.

The walls grew darker and venous like cracked glass. In the opposite corner, the doctor watched Nathan. He reached around the back of his ear and took off his mask.

"She's mine now, Nathan. You gave her up."

Nathan glared at his old ally, an ancient rage pulsing from his heart. "I showed you how to control this place, and I will show you what a fool you are for bringing me here."

Zyne laughed and raised his hands. The tendrils crawled up and wrapped Nathan's arms. Pain burned through his chest–Zyne's reminder that Nathan had failed to save his daughter. She was lost.

Daniel scrutinized the ring, determined to find at least one more blemish to wipe away. Most of the lights were turned off in his shop except for the one above the counter. The closed sign had been posted for a couple of hours now, but his last customer had yet to arrive.

Headlights beamed through the glass doors before cutting off. He looked back at the ring, deciding it was as polished as he could get it. He put it back inside the glass display case. The doors swung open and a disheveled heap of a man walked through. His dark hair had grown into sets of tangles that flopped over his ears, and his clothes were covered in dirt. He was clearly not as kempt as most BMW owners.

Daniel knew the news wouldn't be good. The man waltzed right up to the counter and slapped his hands on the glass. He kept his head down.

"Sorry, Uncle. He got away," Hunter muttered.

Daniel contained himself. At least his nephew was alive. Darrus would be glad to hear it, if he still cared.

"I sent you out almost a week ago. What happened?" Daniel calmed down and put his hand on Hunter's shoulder. Hunter looked up at him, his eyes filled with a dark echo. "You tried to tap into the relic didn't you?"

"Not only that, I had worked a deal with Astrous."

Daniel shuddered at that thought.

"I gave you specific instructions to pick up Matt and keep him safe." Anger built inside him at the thought of Hunter abusing his trust. He tightened his grip on Hunter's shoulder.

Hunter looked at him like a dog in trouble, waiting for his master to yell. "I know, but like you I'm just tired of Dad only playing one side. I needed a deal to start my own business."

Daniel shook his head. "The safety of your family should be your primary business. Don't think I go off trying to disrupt the way your father does things just to feed my ego. I do what I do to keep us safe. Astrous never makes fair deals; he only feeds himself. I'm actually shocked you're standing here intact, more or less."

Hunter brushed Daniel's hand off his shoulder. "I can

handle myself."

"Obviously. I guess you haven't told your father yet?"

"Huh," Hunter said, looking away. "Can't imagine what he'd do to me now. I knew he wouldn't like me helping you, but now that seems like a petty crime compared to working with Astrous." A hint of a smile crept onto his face.

"Darrus is on the warpath, but he needs to know both his children are alive and safe."

"Well, at least I'm alive." Hunter looked at him with a nod.

A trickle of fear broke inside Daniel. He braced himself against the counter.

"Leave him out of this, Zyne," Daniel said.

Zyne materialized out of a thick cloud in the corner of the store. He walked up to the two of them. Hunter shrank away to give room for their small circle.

"This was his choice, Daniel," Zyne said. "I gave him the option, and he chose to join the winning team."

"Or is it punishment for trying to tap into the only power greater than your own?" Daniel challenged.

Zyne smirked at him. "I have little use for slaves. Hunter is free to go whenever he wants. Though, I will need a reference from his most recent employer. How would you say his job performance was?"

Zyne's pulsing fear tightened around Daniel's chest. Then he realized it was his own.

"That was a family affair, Zyne. You shouldn't have been involved. I had to wrap up my mistake before it grew out of hand."

"Who are your allies, Daniel? Your family has disowned

you, yet, you still have the gall to go behind my back and take what belongs to me. You can't stand against me alone."

Daniel regretted putting that ring back into the display case. "Stay out of our family business and let me handle it for you like I was trying to," he said, sliding his hand beneath the counter.

Zyne put his hand down hard on Daniel's shoulder and stared straight through him. "Keep your hands where I can see them. I know what relics you hide in this shop."

Daniel jerked his hand back onto the counter to steady his shaking body. Zyne looked at Hunter and snapped his head back toward the door. Hunter nodded and left the shop.

"I understand how you feel, now more than ever," Zyne said after the door chimed at Hunter's exit. "You are the closest friend I have left on this world, and I need you with me. Your family will always hate you for what you've done and keep you out, but your reserved place in my organization will always be there."

Anger boiled up inside Daniel at Zyne's patronizing. This being had no concept of what he was going through. All he knew was power and control.

He opened his mouth to speak but found himself tapping against his counter with both hands. The shaking moved up his arms and into the rest of him. He gritted his teeth and flashed a scowl at Zyne. His legs buckled, knocking his knees against the back of the counter.

Zyne lifted his hand from Daniel's shoulder as his knees gave way. The edge of the counter met his head on his way down to the floor. The room spun around a bit, and the fear returned to him more potent than before.

A blurry Zyne rushed around the counter and knelt down to help him up. Daniel waved him away.

"Get out of my shop!" he growled. A thundering headache stormed inside him. The door chimed again, leaving him in peace. He was going to need that ring later.

Zyne looked over his glass desk, happy to see nothing out of place. An organized desk allowed for a free and clear mind, or it would if he were actually as neurotic as the business persona he wore at the office in an attempt to be more human. The one thing out of place wasn't on his desk, but across from it.

Two brown eyes begged to help him. Sweet, auburn hair draped over a shoulder covered by a fine suit, tailored exactly to his specifications. Hands clasped in anticipation finished the ensemble. How could he ever refuse her?

"Astrous is just trying to turn you against me. I wouldn't put much stock in his words," Zyne said, hoping to dissuade her.

"It's not really what he says that I want to take stock in," Clara replied. "When he taunted me with the fate of my parents at your hands, I just wanted to rip into his face. He doesn't know the pain I still feel. I just..." She paused, wiping a tear from her eye. "I have to see what I did to them."

Zyne stood up to go and sit next to her. He reached for her hands, feeling her warmth trickle into him.

"It wasn't just you, it was me. I had that score to settle;

you were just caught in between your mother and me."

"And all I'm asking is to help you. Let me finish what we started," she said, squeezing his hands.

He smiled. "This must be why nepotism is frowned upon in business."

"Well, it isn't technically nepotism yet." She raised her left hand, tapping the inside of her naked ring finger with her thumb.

"Committed to the human experience. Now that is why I love you." He pushed in and stole a kiss from her. She moved her hands around his neck and took one back.

She playfully slapped his cheek. "If you hadn't come along, I'd still be method acting."

"Okay, you win this round. I'll take you down there, but you have to take it slow. Your father is pretty much intact, but your mother is completely under the Shifting Plains' power. I really have no idea where you will fall in that spectrum."

"I've heard you explain it no fewer than a thousand times, Arthur."

He loved hearing his human name vibrate off her lips. "Alright then. I trust you've gotten your work finished for the day?"

She stood up, pulling him with her. "It's me, remember? I went to college for this stuff."

Her smile was good enough for him. "Fair enough. With you down there, I'll be free to deal with other issues up here."

The calm darkness tortured Nathan more than the rest of Zyne's punishment. It was the slow anticipation of more pain that drove him to the brink of insanity. He refused to give Zyne what he wanted, and now Nathan had nothing left to lose after Clara was stripped from him.

A faint pulse teased his bare feet through the floor. Like a drum beating far away, he wasn't even sure he heard it or felt it. He moved his feet through the grimy floor and felt the pulse again.

He breathed in the stale air, reminding himself he didn't even need to breathe. In this place, keeping up human appearances did more harm than good. However, his breathing kept him in a steady rhythm to help resist the torture to come.

Trying to move, Nathan struggled against the tendrils wrapping around his torso as they kept him against the tall spire eating away at the flesh on his back. He tried pulling his arms down to him, but they didn't budge from the network of tendrils drawing them up to the point of the spire that curved out over him.

Sparks of light ignited throughout the room, filling him with more dread. One of them grew into an ember no bigger than a fleck of burnt paper. Its orange light spiraled down to the ground and erupted into a fire. The blaze spread out in erratic lines running all around the floor. One of them ran directly underneath Nathan. The trail of flame inched toward him while the rest quickly covered the room and ran up the blackened walls.

The yellow tongues rolled forward at an impossibly slow rate. He pulled his arms down toward him again as hard as he could. The spire seemed to bow a little. A cracking sound echoed through the chamber as the spire snapped in half. It slammed down into the ground, bending him over with it.

The fire shot along the broken spire and burst into a full flame. Thick heat blasted into him as its tongues now lapped his skin. His naked, human flesh burned with pain. The fire purged him of all thought of what lay beyond this chamber, or even why he was here.

"Nathan!" A whisper floated on the air, reminding him who he was.

He looked around with his limited view to see where it had come from. One of the walls had disappeared and, in the distance, a pair of ghosts floated toward him. Terror sank into him. He pushed out with his legs, trying to gain any leverage he could to escape his bindings.

The ghosts moved closer, becoming more solid with every step. They weren't ghosts at all, but a dark haired girl leading a woman wearing an orange dress with a brown sun pattern dotting it. The woman's angelic face pored over him, staying his fear and melting his heart. He knew her, but only with faint memory. The pain searing his mind cooled long enough for him to notice her eyes. Eyes that used to be the truest blue were dulled to gray.

"Jailyn!" he screamed, his senses rushing back to him. "It's me, Nathan!"

She looked at him with fear and confusion, saying something to the child at her side. The little girl fished a tiny white ball out of her pocket and threw it at him. Several white creatures jumped out of the ball and spread wings. They barreled into him, biting through his skin with their razor teeth.

"Jailyn!" he shouted even louder. "Pull these bindings off me and I can get us out of here!"

The winged creatures swarmed around him and flew up into the ceiling. Jailyn and the little girl were gone.

Nathan's hands shook with fury. He launched himself back upright, flinging back the broken portion of spire. The tendrils fell out from his hands, freeing him to grab the ones still holding his torso. He dug into the layers of rough, slimy texture and ripped them off with a scream.

He tore off running to where his love had disappeared. A smoky cloud reached out of the darkness and hit him in the chest, knocking him on his back. The cloud poured into the room, congealing into a human form.

"She isn't your prisoner, Zyne!" Nathan yelled.

Zyne smiled down at him and kicked at his face. Nathan caught Zyne's foot and held it, shaking in place.

"You look detestable," Zyne said. "Grasping for something that was never meant to last."

Nathan used his grip on Zyne's foot to twist him off balance. He swept his other leg, tripping Zyne onto his face. Crawling backward, he moved through a few waves of fire before standing up.

Zyne also got to his feet and brushed the black soot off his dark suit. "You've lost who you were, who you still are, Nathan. I'm here to put you back in order. And if you let me destroy her in the process, that will be a decision you'll have to reconcile. She matters nothing to me."

Fear returned to Nathan. Zyne's promised reconditioning was upon him.

Daniel spent most of his day locked away in his office with a cold press on his head. The previous night had taken away all his ability to handle customers. He didn't even look beyond his blinds, trusting that Ryan had things covered in the front.

Truth be told, he didn't even care. The whole store could be burning before he even wanted to move. His head throbbed something awful. The only reason he even came in today was to rig up a solution for his problem. Well, it was more of the city's problem, but they were one and the same now. He had tried to avoid situations like these his whole life.

He twisted a small blue ring-box in his hand. The trinket within might be just what he needed to stop the new evil rising up. Cracking open the box, light shimmered off the silver ring. A line of stones sat on a raised track running around its center. Each stone glowed with swirling colors that moved with the light. He held the ring between his left thumb and index finger. With a swipe from his other index finger, the stones chased each other around the ring on the spinning track.

It made a unique enough wedding band, but coupled with a charge from an Illumin or proximity to a Shade, it become something else altogether. It probably would have saved his ex-fiancée's life had he made her keep it. At the time, it was an impossible argument, an insane request from a crazy ex-lover.

Telling her exactly why she needed it wasn't an option. Since they didn't get married, Darrus had made it perfectly clear she could never know about family matters. They were all taking a calculated risk that Daniel had caused. He snapped the box shut on the memory and grabbed his phone. Daniel was an outcast in the wrong family at the wrong time.

Waking his phone, he navigated to a long unused contact. Starting the call, he hoped Darrus hadn't changed his number.

"Hello," Darrus answered.

"Darrus, we need to talk, can we sit down?"

"I suppose it is time we tried again. Swing by my place. I have come across some information you may want to know."

Daniel's heart sped up a bit. "See you then."

"And you know what I expect."

"Sure, bye."

Darrus hung up.

Daniel snatched up a stress ball and squeezed it a few times in his hand. No matter how hard he crushed it, it always stretched back out.

"Some things just can't be suppressed forever," he said

to himself, hoping he might listen.

The world twisted all around Zyne as he watched it from multiple angles. He flashed through the skyline, looking for the Illumin he needed to see. In a crimson patchwork of buildings, a single blue light shimmered against the background. He focused on the rooftop, and the world slowed down at his command.

Faint moonlight steadied his twisting vision and brought him back into the real world. A few feet away from him, Gabriella sat with her feet dangling off the edge of a school building.

"You're alone quite a lot these days. Where's your boyfriend?"

She didn't even turn around. "We're not prone to romantic involvement as your race is. Hey, isn't your lackey falling head over heels for you? Or is she just drawn to your overbearing personality?"

In reaction, he took a few quick steps toward her before calming his rage. "Touché," he replied. "Daniel is the one you should be watching, though."

In the far distance he saw D'Nas and Katy practicing swordplay at a high school football stadium.

"Is jealousy something else you Illumin are not prone to?" he asked.

She jumped to her feet and turned to face him. Blue sparked through her eyes.

"Easy now, even Jailyn couldn't overpower me, and my 'lackey' has put you down before. I came because we are in a transition period here and, like you, I am interested in transitioning to a better state. Astrous's gambit with Hunter didn't pan out, but that won't stop him from trying something else. Now I've got Hunter under control, but I am worried Daniel may step out soon."

Gabriella eased away from him. "I've never trusted him anyway. He's betrayed me before. But why is he the one you're watching?"

"I'm watching everyone at the moment, so if you have information I need, tell me."

Putting her hands on her hips she said, "I can feel the residuals from the Shifting Plains all over you. You better drag yourself away from there and pay attention to what is going on up here."

Something had changed; he felt it. Here he had come to her with a warning, and she instead fed one to him.

"What has Astrous gotten his hands on now?"

"Nothing," she replied. "This goes beyond him. This is about the rise of a new Shade."

"Matt's imprint in the Shifting Plains is minimal, so I'm not all that worried yet."

She shook her head. "Keep your eyes above ground, Zyne. Matt's moving all around this city, and I can't track him down. Meanwhile, D'Nas is flirting with Katy, Astrous is terrorizing citizens, and Darrus is shaking down his own family. Matt is going to overrun us while we're distracted with each other."

"Once I pull Nathan back to my side, we'll see what

happens with Matt."

Taking a few steps toward him, she said, "We can't wait for that. I need your help now if you still want the chance to rule this city."

"Like I said, I need Nathan. However, I can send Clara to help you once she finishes tying up a few things for me. But, you have to keep Daniel in line. Send him back to his family, even."

"I'll do what I can. I still have a few murder investigations to look into."

He cocked his head at her. "Amazing how trustworthy I become after all your friends desert you."

"You're just the best choice for our broken system."

He laughed, looking in the distance to see Katy take a few swings at D'Nas. "Now you understand the problem. We Shades are Earth's new settlers, held back only by your temporary protection. How long will you keep up with us?"

"As long as it takes."

The iron gate paused for what seemed like an eternity. Daniel wished it would remain shut, keeping him from begging the help of his elder brother. The gate shuddered and rolled away from him. He drove his car through this thinly guarded prison where the warden was also the sole inmate.

He parked beside Benjamin's car, relieved to not see any others. Maybe the three of them could remember their younger bonds and put their recent grievances to rest.

His shoes drummed against the thick wood of the porch as he approached the door. He wiped down his glasses one more time before hitting the doorbell. Nila answered it with a smile.

"Hello, Nila," he said.

"Welcome back, Daniel. Long time no see," she replied, courteous as ever. She stepped back, allowing him entrance. Looking up the stairs, she said, "They're waiting in the study. Good luck."

"Thanks."

He climbed every step with his heart beating faster and faster. It would be a wonder if he wasn't dripping with sweat by the time he made it to the study. The door was open, and his two brothers sat across from each other with Darrus's huge oak desk in between.

Without a word, he knocked on the door as if Darrus hadn't already seen him approach. Benjamin turned around, rising when he saw who it was. At least one of his brothers cared about him.

"Good to see you, Daniel," Benjamin said, wrapping an arm around his shoulders.

"You too, Ben." He turned to the other set of eyes upon him. "Well, I'm here."

"It is good to see you," Darrus said, breaking his solemn stare and walking around to give Daniel a handshake. "Please, sit down. Reunions aren't the reason you're here, though it should be; the next one is long overdue."

The three of them sat down. Daniel noticed a small velvet bag lying in the center of the desk.

"Is that it?" he asked. Darrus nodded.

Daniel loosened the string and paused for a moment before reaching in and fishing out the silver skull with cracked rubies encircling it. In all the years he guarded this dangerous relic, he had never felt the weight of it in his naked hand. Rotating it around, the skull seemed to sneer at him as the light flared off its teeth. He clutched his hand around it and dropped it back in its bag, pulling the string as tight as he could get it.

"The beast is out of its cage," Darrus said.

Daniel stared at him, feeling the throbbing grow inside his head. As with the other night, an outburst worked its way to his lips, but he pushed it back down with a breath.

"I can still fix this," Daniel said. "Just give me what I need."

"And what do you need that I can't already use myself?"

"I came to you for your help. You always wanted me back in with the family. Well, I'm back."

Darrus thrust his finger at him. "I want you to stand with the family because it's the right thing to do. You're only back because your own plans failed. I didn't see you around here when I woke up from Hunter's potion. In fact, I heard you sent him off in some crazy attempt to rescue Matt. By involving him in your scheme, you put the fate of your estranged son in the hands of a family traitor. Now both our sons are lost."

The words stung Daniel with latent regret. If he had only been there for Matt, he might have led a normal life.

However, Darrus had stopped that in its tracks.

"My son was lost the day you demanded me walk away from him. You stole the only joy that came out of my short-lived relationship with his mother. While you and Lilly enjoyed family dinners with Katy and Hunter, I ate alone wondering who you really care about. Anyone who puts a family name above a person doesn't understand the value of family."

Darrus's face grew red. "Don't try to switch that around on me. Anyone not bound to this family by blood or marital vows can't be allowed to linger. They will see too much, and all that we do for the city will crash around us. You knew the price, but you still hold on to that grudge. Matt had no choice but to stay with his mother after she left you."

Daniel's heart ached again. "I loved Matt from afar just as much as any father. Would you not hold the same grudge if it were Hunter?"

"The next time I see Hunter will be his reckoning. Do you know what he did to Matt after capturing him? He tied him up in a room down at the camp to show him off to Astrous like a prized fighting dog. Looks like you picked the wrong twin to trust."

Daniel hammered his fist into the desk with a loud thud. Benjamin laid a hand on his shoulder. Daniel pushed him away and stood up to look down at Darrus.

"Hunter carries the Raven name you worship. I should have been able to trust him, but you bred that air of superiority into him! You spent so much time building up your name in this city, you forgot to protect your own family. You lost him just like you lost Lilly."

Darrus came up swinging, catching Daniel on nearly the same spot he hit his head the night before. The renewed pain drove him into a rage. He jumped across the desk, tackling Darrus back into his chair. Daniel reared back to hit him, but Benjamin pulled him away.

Finding a table lamp within reach, Daniel snatched it up and tossed it. It flew until its cord went taut and it crashed into the ground. Darrus rushed to his feet and charged Daniel, ramming him into a shelf against the wall. Silver and gold trinkets rained down on the carpet.

Losing his balance, Daniel fumbled against the shelf for leverage, knocking more things down. Darrus punched him in the stomach and tipped him backward onto the ground. Sharp pain stabbed into Daniel's back. Crying out, he rolled over onto his side. The fire in Darrus's eyes simmered. He reached behind Daniel to pick up a broken picture.

Benjamin offered a hand to Daniel. He got back to his feet, watching Darrus shed a tear over the picture. The three brothers gathered around the broken photo in silence. It was an old vacation shot of Darrus, Lilly, and a very young set of twins outside the Coliseum in Rome.

"A brother's wounds inflict more pain because they cut with the poison of truth," Darrus whispered, looking into Daniel's eyes. "Leave before I cut into you."

An autumn breeze tumbled through the pine trees, rustling their branches into a soothing choir. Cicadas hummed along with them, adding a rhythmic vibe to the evening. Louisiana had too few days as perfect as this one.

The tree swing rose back up to Nathan, and he pushed it away yet again. Little Clara squealed with glee.

"Higher, Daddy, higher!"

"Hang on!" he said.

Her hands tightened around the ropes at her sides as she leaned backward. When she neared him again, he pushed down on her shoulders and ran a bit forward for a really big push. He couldn't see her face, but her laughter expressed her delight.

"Another big one?" he asked.

"Yes! Yes! Can I jump this time?"

"I don't know. Aren't you scared?" He only asked for his own sake.

"Not if you promise not to let me fall."

"Well, what happens after you jump?" He pushed her up with another big push.

"I fall!"

A rumble of thunder cut off her voice. She jumped out, stopping Nathan's heart in his chest. A crack of lightning struck down at the ground, blinding him. When he opened his eyes, the swing was up at its peak away from him. Clara, in full womanhood, stood on it, facing him. She swung back toward him with sadness in her eyes. He couldn't move.

Pine needles fell all around them in the growing winds. The sun hid behind clouds in the bleak skies. Clara crashed into him, shoving him back into a tree.

"Why did you let me fall?" she screamed at him.

The tree reached down and wrapped him up with its

branches. Now, he saw the place for the farce it was. Pine needles stabbed into his skin all over. His blood oozed out, masking their intoxicating scent.

"You jumped," he managed through the rush of pain. He looked up at her to see if she was real. Her brown eyes and auburn hair couldn't have been faked, not to this degree, despite all of Zyne's talents.

"Clara!" he exclaimed, trying to reach out to embrace her. Seeing her again eased all his turmoil and renewed the fight still left inside him. She just stood there, watching him through an inscrutable stare. He felt a twinge of longing from her, but Zyne's marks were stronger.

"Don't let him do this to you, honey," he said. "He's bringing you down the failed path I abandoned to be with your mother. Just like him, I thought I knew what I wanted, but your mother showed me otherwise. And when you were born, I discovered another world I never knew existed. Through all of that, I found what I needed."

A tear crawled down her cheek. She wiped it away and shook her head. "Dad, I've come into my own now. I...I wanted to see you again, to see you for who you really are. I need you to come back to me and show me who I'm supposed to be."

"Those are Zyne's words, not yours. He pushed you down here knowing I gave up everything for you." He turned up his head at the darkening skies. "Face me yourself Zyne! Don't pit my own daughter against me!"

"No!" She slammed her fist into the bark of the tree. Its branches ratcheted tighter around him. "I came for you. I know the dad who raised me hid everything he should have told me. Now, I have heard of the legend that is Nathan, and that is who I want for a father, not the deceiver who cowered under my mother."

"Zyne is the deceiver, honey. I was the one driven mad with power."

Her eyes sparked up at the mention of that. No doubt his true nature was vastly different from the father in her memories. She wrapped her arms around him and held tight. Their tormented souls connected once again.

"Show me who you are," she whispered. "I know you can control this place."

Being so close to her and smelling Zyne's power snaking all over her conjured up his desire to protect his family.

"Get back," he said.

The skies above them went pitch black. The roaring winds fell silent. He let fury build up within him and shot it back through the pine needles sticking him. The branches holding him decayed and grew black. He thrust his arms out in a cloud of ash.

He spun around to the tree that lay behind him and dug his fingers underneath its scaly bark. This place would be his again. He reached out with his senses and tore down the facade around them. The grass died and fell into a blackened, sticky floor. Walls of red rose up around them, sealing off the trees along the horizon. The tree he held onto morphed into a tall spire curling over his head. He was back in the room he had been in from the beginning.

Clara looked at him with so much awe that he almost mistook her for the little girl in the swing. Well, she was still a little girl in a swing, and he was the only one who could stop her from jumping this time.

Out of late-night habit, Daniel sat before the usual bone chess board. His normal opponent wouldn't show this time, giving him time to think over his fruitless meeting with his brothers. Even after going straight to him, Darrus refused his help, leaving him with few options. Zyne, Hunter, and Darrus had all failed and betrayed him at this critical point.

Raven blood was as cursed as any royalty throughout history. Everyone expected so much of you, yet never saw the slavery you had been born into. Matt bore the worst curse ever to face the Ravens. Somewhere in the city, he carried a beast within so great it threatened them all. He wouldn't carry it alone.

Walking to his jewelry cabinet, he took out the ring. With a proper catalyst, it could draw out the Shade and free Matt. Like venom, the Shade coursed through Matt's blood, and some of it would have to be spilled to get the venom out. The longer he delayed, the more the Shade grew inside his son.

He slipped the ring into his pocket and went back into his office. He rummaged through his disorganized bookshelves filled with almost everything except books. A handful of papers hid the tin cylinder he was after. Grabbing it, he sat at his chair and put the ring on his desk. He popped off the top of the cylinder and peered inside.

White strands of Illumin hair softly lit the inside. His

eyes darted around the room for the other pieces he needed for his contraption. Soon, his desk was littered with a strange collection of parts surrounding a hollow cane. The rest of his intended design formed inside his mind and he set to work, uncaring about the time. Raven blood may have been cursed, but it also fueled his inspiration.

He would save his son.

Nathan raised himself to his full height. He would show his daughter just what it meant to serve her chosen master.

"You want to see who I really am? Then take my hand." He reached out for her. She looked puzzled at his proffered hand. "Go on."

She moved to touch him, but a thick black cloud rose between them. He moved around it to grab Clara, but a hand shot out and caught him in the chest. The rest of Zyne's body materialized outward from his arm.

"Glad to have you back, my friend," Zyne said with a smirk. He turned to Clara. "You are weakening faster than you know down here. Go back and check on Hunter for me. He should be due back any minute."

Nathan pushed Zyne away and darted for Clara. Tendrils grew out of the floor around his legs and held him in place. Her eyes betrayed her confusion.

"I'm here for you, Clara," he pleaded. She took a few

steps back.

"No, you aren't who I know," she said, backing into the wall.

"Stay put," Zyne told him and moved to Clara's side. "It's okay, let's get you out of here."

She nodded at him. He picked her up into his arms and disappeared.

Nathan tore through the bonds on his feet, but more and more tendrils grew up to replace those he stripped away. In frustration, he drove his fist into the ground and let out a howl. The tendrils stopped coming after him, replaced by approaching feet.

"You shouldn't let her wander around down here, Zyne." He kept his eyes on the ground.

"I didn't know how she would end up. She lasted longer than her mother."

Nathan roared and launched up from the floor, landing a foot squarely in Zyne's chest. Zyne flew back into the wall.

"I own both your precious women!" Zyne yelled.

Nathan ran at him, aiming to smash that amusement straight off his face. He grabbed his throat and they fell back onto the floor. The walls disappeared in a rush of air, disorienting Nathan enough for Zyne to shove him away.

"You own a crumbling empire, Zyne. I'll see to that!"

Zyne swept his hands outward. "This is our empire. The one we built before you left it all for that–"

"I left it for an experience you may never know."

Zyne roared, "Look around you!"

Black skies soared overhead with cracks of lightning breaking up the otherwise monotonous scene. He walked to where the walls used to be. A sharp drop separated him from the barren landscape of reddish-brown soil below. One side opened up to a vast plain, while the other rose up into huge mountains on the back side of the tower. Specks of creatures roamed around, steering clear of the black pools dotting the ground.

They were up high atop the reflection of Mandrake tower here in the Shifting Plains. The tower's sides were glossy black in a grid pattern similar to the building in the material world. Four massive spires grew up from the corners and curved inward, high into the sky.

"This is our domain, Nathan. Help me reclaim it."

"Your empire has grown since I've been away. You don't need me."

"I will soon. A new Shades has birthed, and with him comes tremendous power. I tried to stop him before, but the Illumin, along with Astrous, blocked me."

"Is this why you destroyed my family?"

Zyne shook his head. "That was a score I settled with Jailyn, who is still our enemy! You must remember who you are and why we are here."

"I remember very clearly. I built this tower with little help from you. When we were sucked out into this realm, you clung to me for help. Now, you try to cling to me again."

Nathan felt his anger rise, and with it a spark of his old power. The ground around him heard his commands. A cord of tendrils shot out of the spire directly behind Zyne and wrapped around him. Nathan walked up to his smiling face and struck it as hard as he could.

Bits of flesh sprinkled the ground. Nathan drew back

his bloody hand. Black ooze trickled across his knuckles. With a slight gesture from him the tendrils tightened around Zyne, pulsing more waves of pain through him. Zyne's smile widened even more now that he was missing a portion of his face.

The pain coursed over Nathan's weary soul, quenching a deep-seated thirst. It reminded him of when he had trapped Jailyn, her blue eyes shining against his darkness. Snapping out of his memory, he ran back to the edge to locate his wife. She had to be out there, beyond the dark clouds protecting Zyne's tower.

"You can still be with her, if we can stop this new Shade, Nathan," Zyne said with a gurgle.

Nathan's hands twitched at his side, longing to exert more power.

Saturdays were always busy at the shop. Daniel roamed around, helping his customers with their questions. Ryan stayed pinned behind the counter ringing up and cashing out a steady stream of people. At some point Daniel was going to need to hire more employees. Of course, he was hesitant to do that because of his more eccentric clientele.

He answered a few questions from a couple about a child's bike with pink tassels dangling from the handles. Satisfied, they rolled their purchase to the counter just as a new group of customers entered the shop and took over the car audio section. They were just the customers he was hoping to see. He made his way to greet them.

"Martellus! What can I help you with today?" he asked.

Martellus turned around with a smile, showing off a row of golden teeth. "Aw, not much really. I thought maybe this time I might offer my services to you, seeing as how word is spreading of your boy."

Daniel quickly checked to see who all was in earshot. A few others had come in with Martellus, crowding out the car audio display. They all wore sagging, ripped jeans with gigantic t-shirts. Blue, tightly-rolled handkerchiefs on their necks gave them a signature look.

"Word gets out fast," Daniel said, walking over to a particular CD deck in the wall. He tapped through its menus until finding the setting he needed. A hum sounded out from it, letting him know it was working. "We can talk freely now, just don't get too loud."

"Always the man with the plan," Martellus jabbed, putting his hand on Daniel's shoulder. "What about now, though? I don't see you cuddling up to your brothers, and I know Zyne hasn't been to another chess match."

"You've been watching me?"

Jarvis, one of Martellus's friends spoke without taking his eyes off a subwoofer. "Only to protect what's ours. If the city goes crazy, ain't nobody going to like it. Hey, has this thing been used?"

"It's a pawn shop, what you think?" Martellus answered.

"You never know what kind of quality you gonna find in here."

"Gently used, but I have another in the back with a bit more kick," Daniel said.

"Ha! Nah, I just need a new sub today. Nothing more than that. We're still plenty equipped to roll over some Illumin."

"So," Martellus said, "You got a plan or what? I need to protect my best supplier. No strings attached."

"I don't believe that," Daniel replied, smiling. "I'm sure you want to earn yourselves at least a favor or two for what I need you to do."

The door chimed with a new group of people coming in, and a teenage boy headed toward them. Daniel went back to the cd deck and clicked the audio dampener off.

"Let me show you what I have in the back," he said to Martellus. They both walked past the counter. "Hold the front, Ryan," he said in passing.

They walked through the hallway, straight for the back door. Daniel stopped at his office to grab his contraption from the other night. He continued leading Martellus outside. Summer heat slapped them in the face like a hot, wet blanket.

"I am curious, Martellus. Why don't your kind like meeting new members of your family?"

Martellus's face crunched into a scowl. "Because they'll upset what we already have. Your boy will die, and my new brother of sorts will take whatever I have. We both lose."

"Well, here's what I have," Daniel said, holding his cane as if it were a sword. It was all black except for its silver handle shaped into the head of a hawk. "Now stand back."

Martellus took a few steps away. He looked in vain for any relief from the afternoon sun.

"I can bind the new Shade with this." Daniel flipped the unlock lever at the base of the handle and gave the shaft a quarter-turn. A small metal brand popped out of the bottom and grew red-hot. "It becomes a conduit. Aside from the heat, tell me what you feel."

He thrust it in Martellus's direction, seeing his eyes light up. Martellus took a few steps back, giving off a black vapor from his skin.

"That would burn right through me."

"Correct. I've connected this brand to the handle with Illumin hair. The burn will disrupt your mortal shell and then suck the life right out of you. Now, to complete the ensemble..." Daniel pulled out the ring from his pocket and put it on his forefinger. "This ring, under my control, would bind you inside. And once I bind that Shade from my son, we both win."

"Wait, is that a raven symbol?"

Daniel pulled the hot cane tip back to take a look at the simple, metallic raven. "Yep."

Martellus laughed.

"Hey," Daniel said. "It was the only thing small enough I had lying around. Plus, if I have to leave a mark on my son, it may as well be the family symbol."

"I like the personal touch. Now, if you want my help, you are going to have to prove your cane-thing works."

Daniel put the ring back in his pocket and re-hid the brand. "Guess you already have something in mind then?"

Martellus smiled with criminal delight.

Nathan walked through the living room, feeling the cold wood against his bare feet. Smells of gumbo wafted into his nose, guiding him to the kitchen. Jailyn's cooking was so good he was sure she could make it as a TV chef if she wanted. It was only a fantasy, though. They were stuck here in Shreveport.

His feet stepped from the cold wood onto the cold tile of the kitchen. The air was a glorious masterpiece of Cajun spice, okra, and chicken. A large pot simmered on the island stove. He removed the lid and breathed in a concentrated dose of home cooking. Gumbo was more of a southern Louisiana thing, but Jailyn's recipe could match the very best of theirs.

"I don't know if I can hold myself back, babe!" he called out, wondering where his wife was.

With no one to challenge him, he grabbed a spoon for a small taste before dinner. Scooping out as much as the spoon would hold, he held it in the air so it might cool off a bit. Blowing on it for added security, he dumped it in his mouth and savored the dancing flavors on his tongue.

"Mmhmm, that's some good stuff!" Still no response from Jailyn.

Footsteps pattered up to the laundry room door. A key scraped against the lock, and Clara burst into the house. She barreled through the kitchen before he even knew what happened. The only glimpse he caught of her face was of mascara trails falling from her eyes.

The door to her room slammed shut, prompting Nathan to approach it carefully. He gave it a few knocks.

"Hey, you okay?"

"I'm fine, Dad."

"Well, you want to sample your mother's gumbo while she isn't looking?"

"No."

"Can I at least see that you are fine?"

He heard her sigh loudly before opening up her door. Her room was a mess. Towers of books with clothes hanging over them filled up an entire corner while her bookshelves remained stuffed with even more books and trinkets only teenagers found worth in. Her computer desk was the only well-maintained and organized space.

"I'm fine, can I just be alone?" she asked. She had already changed out of her school uniform and put on a black skirt and blue t-shirt with white streaks. Surely even human teens didn't go through such crazy fashion phases.

"Hey, can I at least get a hug?" She curled around him for the minimal time he required. "Are they giving you a hard time again?"

"Who?" she asked. "The Raven twins or everyone else?"

"I'm sorry they pick on you, but they have to single someone out. Remember, they're just jealous."

"Jealous of what? I'm a nobody. They're the rich kids with all the friends."

"What did they say this time?" Tears welled in her eyes and her cheeks blushed. "It's okay, just tell me."

"I was reading *Ender's Game* and watching the band

practice. Waiting on my friends, you know. Then Hunter came out of the building by the practice field, and I could feel him heading straight for me. He's so tough when he has his cronies backing him up. Anyway, I was on the grass, and he comes up behind me and pretends to trip over my purse. All his friends laugh with all my stuff lying over the grass.

'Oh sorry, E-Claire,' he mocked and looked through my stuff. I just sat there, mortified, wishing he and his friends would take their hyena laughter somewhere else. Then Hunter got louder. 'Hey! Didn't take you for a burner; well, actually I did.' He reached down and grabbed one of my, um, tampons that spilled onto the ground beside me.

I jumped to my feet, trying to get it back. He pulled out his zippo lighter and clicked up a flame. All his friends just laughed as he stood there smoking my, um...you know. He said something else about the 'joint' tasting better than all the others he has tried and how he wanted to know the secret ingredient. I walked away crying.

The band director saw me and the burning thing in Hunter's mouth. He chewed Hunter out while a few of my friends came to check on me. After I was sure Hunter left, I picked up my things and came straight home."

Nathan pulled her close. "Oh, honey, I'm so sorry. Want me to talk to his parents?"

"No!" She pushed him away. "I want you and Mom to stop making me look so weird. I wouldn't be like this if I were just like everyone else at school!"

She slammed her door shut, but couldn't stop him from hearing her sobs. He didn't know what else to say to make up for the cruelty of teenagers.

Returning to the kitchen, his feet stepped onto a warm, prickly floor.

"No!" he exclaimed, coming to his senses.

Tendrils wrapped around his legs and continued up along his body. The house around him caught fire and burned away, revealing the black skies he abhorred. Zyne's laugh preceded his appearance in a cloud of darkness.

"I thought you were going to show me what a fool I was for bringing you here?" he asked.

Nathan stared daggers through him. He didn't have as much control as he thought.

Fifteen minutes left. The clock ticked away a slow approach to his last chance to save Matt. A nervous panic built inside Daniel, knowing that if his Shade-binder didn't work, not only would Martellus be furious, but he would also never get his son back.

An unfamiliar car parked outside the shop, prompting Daniel to head back to his counter. Hunter stepped out of it and burst inside. "Can I please talk?"

"You talked to your father since you've been back? Because I have," Daniel asked, his anger boiling up.

"Uncle Daniel, I need your help." He spoke in such a childish tone; all Daniel thought of was all those times in Hunter's teen years when he tried to see if Daniel could get him out of trouble with his father.

"Maybe you should have gone to him anyway, like I did.

He let me in on what you did to Matt right after I helped you save him." Hunter's eyes widened. "Yeah. Care to explain why you kept him locked up in a cabin instead of coming back to me?"

"It was Astrous, he had me–"

"That's your problem right there!" Daniel couldn't help but yell. "You went to Astrous instead of me. You took that dishonorable, slimy demon to my son and let him torture him to his heart's content. I know what Astrous is made of, and you are lucky Zyne pulled you away from him."

Hunter threw his hands up in protest. "I actually protected Matt from Astrous until he forced his way through me to your son," Hunter protested, trying to get back to the subject at hand. "Whatever you think I should do to make up for that I will. Just please, help me get away from Zyne. Every time he gets near me I feel like I'm changing into something else. He's got me doing all this stuff for him that will come back on all of us, I'm sure of it. He's even got–"

Daniel grabbed his shirt and breathed out through his teeth. "Our punishment for being family outcasts is we're forced to work with Zyne because he is the only Shade who works for us. I know the pain you're feeling. I live with it every day. This shop is my answer to it. Your Dad cares more about our name than who we are. The only way you're going to learn this is to get in deep with the wrong kind of people. Since Astrous didn't teach you, you're now in the hands of a master manipulator."

They looked at each other in silence before Daniel pushed him away.

"I don't care anymore," Daniel said. "Not that I ever

did. Now get out of my shop. I have my own demons to dance with."

Through the window he saw Martellus pull into the parking lot with his white SUV.

They started making their way to Downtown Shreveport. Daniel's head pounded not only from riding in an SUV with a group of Shades, but also from the terrible rap music blaring at them. He strained to hear Martellus over the guy saying something about how he "keeps his hoes at where he keeps his gat."

"Why do you guys listen to this?" he finally asked.

"What?" Jarvis replied from the driver's seat. "You just don't understand our culture."

"But it's not even *your* culture."

"It is now. Besides, shouldn't you be more curious of what we about tonight rather than our music?"

"I just find it hard to think when the music is some high school dropout trying to give me life advice," Daniel said.

"You don't think thugs can be poetic?" Jarvis asked.

Everyone except Daniel laughed.

"Anyway," Martellus began. "We got some straight imports on our turf, Chinese this time, so it'll get nasty. They've been meeting up at the veteran's park just outside downtown. They got whole crews of crotch rockets and rice burners up there to make themselves look bad enough to the locals."

"They have what up there?" Daniel asked, trying to figure out what they were talking about.

Martellus laughed. "Tiny motorcycles and cars, man. Keep up."

They exited off the interstate and cruised into downtown. Making a couple of turns, they got on the parkway that ran by the river. Veterans' Park was only a couple of miles away. Daniel held his cane close.

"So, who do we take down?" he asked.

"Ming-bling or something like that," Martellus answered. Daniel just looked at him. "What? Even I can't pronounce these weird import names. Point is, she is starting up some new foothold over here."

"This is another Shade, right?"

"Yes. You think I'd have trouble with a mortal gang? I don't want any real threat taking my turf."

"We get enough of that from Astrous and Zyne," Jarvis added.

They turned around a corner and Daniel saw the lines of bikes and cars he had been promised. Looked like at least 50 crowded the small parking lot. An uneasy feeling settled inside him.

"Wait. Are we just going to go right up to her and grab her?"

"Yeah," Jarvis said. "Where you been? They can't handle no blue-collared surprise!"

"Plus, backup's on the way," Martellus said, giving little assurance to Daniel.

They pulled into the parking lot, drawing strange looks from everyone. Their white SUV dwarfed every other vehicle. Jarvis parked beside the rows of double stacked bikes. A few people who were milling in the parking lot gravitated in their direction.

Martellus turned back to him. "Look Daniel, let me show you how to take control of a situation."

Martellus swung his door open right into the bike next to it. Like dominoes, the entire row cascaded onto their sides, stirring up the rest of the crowds. The rest of the guys got out of the SUV, leaving Daniel to crawl out from the back seat. As soon as he stepped foot on the ground, everyone seemed to be staring at him.

"Hope they still give out insurance on imports!" Martellus called out into the air. The owners came up screaming at him. He grabbed the closest one. "Hey, ching-chong, shut up and take me to your leader! I can break more than your toy bike."

Before Martellus could release him, the biker twisted around and kicked Martellus backward. The air rustled with hidden energies as a horde of Asian bikers surrounded them.

Daniel slipped his ring on and made ready for his move. He noticed each of the gang members carried a sub-machine gun hanging at his side. They didn't buy those from him. He hoped Jarvis was right about that backup.

A cloud of darkness spun in the air. Daniel watched it land ever so gracefully behind Martellus. A lithe, sexy form eased out of a crouch and stood up.

Martellus let go of the biker and faced the woman in the leather jacket and black pants. A sword hung down from behind her left shoulder and extended past the back of her knees. Her black hair was pulled into a tight pony tail. Fire seeped from her eyes.

"Tai Mei at your service," she said with excellent poise, bowing to him.

"That ain't how we start business around here," Martellus said, walking up to get in her face. He stood almost two heads taller than she. "I want you and your 'dynasty' out of here, or I'll introduce you to my friend...The Equalizer." He motioned over to Daniel. Daniel returned with what must have been an awkward look.

Jarvis slapped Daniel hard on the back, edging him forward. He walked up, spinning the inner ring on his finger to funnel his nervous energy. Martellus nodded to him, but Daniel just couldn't see how this could end well.

"My dynasty will live forever," she said to them with a liquid-cool voice. "I am only a messenger sent to prepare this area."

"Won't no imports be coming here!" Jarvis blurted out.

"Well then," she said, turning to Daniel. "I guess it's time we met."

A glint of silver flashed out from behind her back, and he threw up his cane in defense, holding on to both ends. Her sword bit through the shaft and stopped against the Illumin hair pulled taut inside. The blade hovered mere inches from Daniel's head, unable to cut through the white strands. Confused, Tai Mei pushed down, trying to cut through the rest of the cane's shaft.

Trails of light shot out from where the blade touched the Illumin hair. Her grip on the hilt loosened, and he twisted her sword onto the ground. He grabbed the part of his cane that was sliced and carefully turned the shaft, exposing the red-hot brand. Shoving it into her chest, he moved his ring to touch against the handle.

Tai Mei looked at him in horror. Fire poured out of her eyes and funneled through the cane and into the ring, just like he had planned.

Once exhausted , he pulled the brand off the lifeless body and hid it again. A blackened raven symbol showed on her sternum through the melted piece of her jacket. Daniel ducked to the ground as the other gang members drew out their guns and poured gunfire all around them.

"Aww, nah. We ain't havin' none of that!" Martellus yelled.

A group of bikers drew their swords and headed straight for him. Red sparks flew out of their eyes and ran over their bodies. With a howling scream, Martellus and Jarvis pounded the ground, black streams pouring out of their backs. The air twisted as if they were warping it around them.

"You ready for this?" Jarvis challenged with a deeper and more gravelly voice than before.

The red-eyes leapt in a whirlwind pattern, creating a line of spinning blades that Jarvis and Martellus tore into. Daniel kept low to the ground and tried to watch the fight playing out before him. Shimmering blades cut into the flesh of his comrades.

Martellus deflected a few blows with his sub-machine gun and emptied his clip into his attacker's head. With a kick, there was one less red-eye in the fight. Three more jumped on him, weighing him down.

Jarvis spun around like a furious tornado of black and red energy. Every quarter-turn or so, a shot rang out of his gun, catching one of the many red-eyes in the head. Daniel wished he had brought something more useful, but at least they were holding their own.

The melee chaos continued until Martellus and Jarvis stood with cuts slicing throughout them. At their feet lay the small army, barely squirming about.

"That's what I thought!" Jarvis screamed into the night.

The crowd around them holstered their weapons and backed away.

"Listen up everyone!" Martellus commanded. "Run along home and tell whomever you think cares that we run these streets. Ain't nobody going to take that from me!" He bent down and picked up one of the red-eyes by his hair. "This is your only warning. Shreveport belongs to the Blue-Collars!"

Daniel had never been so happy to see Black Raven Pawn again. His heartbeat had finally dropped down to a normal level just as they had gotten in the parking lot.

"We got you, Daniel," Martellus said. "That wasn't easy what you did tonight; I'm in your debt."

"I'll let you know when we should meet up again," Daniel answered, stepping out of the SUV. "Guess we didn't need that backup."

"Ah, I said that just 'cause. I knew you could handle up on it."

"Look it," Jarvis said, pointing. "Daniel is playing us."

"What?" Daniel asked, searching behind him. Gabriella leaned against a police cruiser in her usual parking spot.

Martellus jumped outside to join them. "Yo Gab! You ain't going to be trouble for my associate here are you?"

"Associate now?" She looked at Daniel. "No, I just want to know where he's putting his trust these days."

"He's picking the winning side—with me in the streets!" Martellus said.

Blue sparks shot out of her eyes. "Want to test that out right now?"

He laughed. "Nah, I'd never hit a woman."

"What is with this gang-banger act? Can't you just pick some more respectable form of human to imitate?"

He ran at her and rammed his fist into her cheek. She staggered backward.

"I will hit a ho, now," he said. "Culture is culture. You want to protect something you don't understand so you best back up."

She lunged at him for a punch, but dipped back at the last minute to wrap his feet up with her own. Twisting around, he fell on his face into the gravel. She continued her spin and landed a boot in the back of his head. He moved to get up, but she slammed her boot on the back of his neck and pinned him to the ground.

"You get up and we are going to have a *fo-real* fight. Am I speakin' yo' language now?" She looked back at Daniel. "Get a grip on your life, Daniel. You have no allies left, only these two-bit thugs who couldn't even hack it in the Old World. Go apologize to Darrus, or whatever you have to do. This city is shaking apart, and you need to be in cover when it all works loose."

She bent down and pulled Martellus to his feet. He tried pushing away, but she held him close enough that he could see her teeth.

"And you, Martellus the Gangster, you better keep your crew out of our way, or you'll be next on my list after I'm done with Astrous and Zyne."

She thrust him away to stumble back to the SUV. He yelled at the bystanders to get back in. They loaded up and drove off.

"I came here because I care, Daniel," Gabriella said. He felt the sincerity of her compassion. "The Ravens need to be together if we are going to survive this."

Brown waves of clay-laced water slapped against his stomach. Each tiny slap reminded him of the constant pressure from all sides. Ages had come and gone, but still he prevailed, thanks to support from his only believer, Zyne. Both of them were in it now.

He worked at his hands, trying to break through the simple handcuffs holding his arms behind his back. Something was different with them. Had they been pure metal, he could have snapped them with no problem. They burned his wrists and cut into him whenever he struggled against them.

Shreveport seemed like such an easy target with the economic downturn burning it to the ground faster than he was. With Reagan as a newly elected president, he had to work quickly to get his fingers around the pulse of the city. Even if he couldn't see the outcome of the current administration, economic upswings always follow such lows.

"We do things a bit differently around here, Nathan," a strong, female voice said from behind him. She splashed her way around to look him in the eye. "And you still haven't answered my question as to why you take such a human name."

Her eyes were blue flames tempered by the brown hair falling in frizzy waves across her shoulders. Even though she held no weapon, he wasn't foolish enough to think her defenseless. The Faith exuded from her. He was drawn in by her power.

"I have nowhere to go. I'm trapped here, in this mortal plane of existence." He nodded to the train bridge running over the river beside them. "You're still connected to your homeland by some bridge, right? Well that bridge has been burned out for me. Why shouldn't I live as a human?"

"That's cute how you make yourself to be the victim. My bridge, as you call it, is a toll bridge, and I'm still working off the cost. Part of which includes keeping you off the citizens."

"Well, speaking of human names, don't you go by one as well?"

"Yes, but not for why you think."

"Oh I think I know exactly why you go by one," he said smiling, "Because you see this world for the stage it truly is.

Neither of us really wants to be here. You do it to blend in, don't you? So that you can make more sense of why you're actually here."

"No, I keep it only so that no one gets confused. Besides, the human tongue can't even pronounce my true name, unlike yours."

"Sounds like you're the only one with confusion."

The words trickled out of his mouth like the water flowing by him. The bridge shook under the weight of a train rolling across it. The ground along the riverbank reverberated under the train's massive weight.

For a second, he saw a flash of black cover the skies, followed by a sense of déjà-vu. This Illumin that he could not name became oddly familiar. He stepped out to see through time.

Something like a sledgehammer pounded his chest, splashing him back into the water. The sky slowed its rotation above him as the Illumin withdrew her fist.

"I need your plans, not your tricks," she said with a hint of fear.

"Step with me and see."

Hesitating for a slight second, she threw another fist down at him. It broke his sternum, showering his nervous system with waves of pain. He laughed it off.

"Just tell me your name and let's end this!" He demanded.

The train continued its rumbling assault through the landscape, causing more flashing in the sky.

"Jailyn!" She answered.

All of this was wrong. It was devoid of the satisfying taste of danger he remembered. He felt nothing but a bland sense of boredom. A feeling that reminded him of what could be created in the Shifting Plains.

"I will unmake this vision, Zyne!" He yelled into the air.

Jailyn's fist came back at him, but he broke free of his bonds and grabbed her arm. He pulled her close, but felt nothing. Where was the original passion with which he won her?

The scene remained picture perfect, but it lacked the very element he and Zyne set out to conquer.

"I'm coming for you, my greatest love," he told the vision of Jailyn before him.

Closing his eyes, he pulled down the trickery that surrounded him. The river, the train, the bridge, they all burned away into the bleak horizon. He stood up back on Mandrake Tower. Jailyn remained in his arms before decaying into a skeleton that blew away as ash in the wind. The black skies above him renewed the power he had long forsaken. Breathing it in, he felt a new life rise in his heart.

"Welcome back, friend." Zyne said behind him.

A thick breath of coffee aroma topped off the satisfying pancake breakfast. Daniel took a sip and stared out of the window of the cafe. Drops of condensation trickled down at the top. He couldn't wait for fall to come and relieve them from this heat.

He moved his fingers around his head and found the trace of the bump. It still hurt when he touched it. Everything felt like a headache lately. The only comfort he had was the coffee in his hand.

The empty seat before him showed how many friends he had left. Martellus's partnership was born out of favors and would only last as long as Daniel's own usefulness. He imagined they would part ways before all of this was done.

"Can I get that plate out of your way?" The server caught him off guard with her perky smile.

"Yes, thank you," he said, fumbling around to hand her his plate.

"Need anything else today?"

"No, thanks. Just the check."

"Coming right up." She walked off.

He spread out his newspaper over the empty spot before him. Nothing ever happened in Shreveport. Looked like the latest front page news was typical fare. No unexplained murders, though, which was the best news he could have received. His greatest fear would be his son running around on a rampage.

A bitter wave of coffee splashed over his tongue and warmed him. All at once the room exploded with clapping that started out at the kitchen. A line of staff started singing some birthday-style song as they made their way to an unlucky target. Who even celebrated their birthday this early in the morning?

The celebration line moved past the only occupied table between him and the door. He looked around, but didn't see anyone near him. Sure enough, they surrounded him with a forced birthday song. His waitress sat a chocolate sundae with a single candle before him.

It wasn't even close to his birthday. He blew out the candle, hoping to end their song prematurely. After another round of clapping and patronizing smiles, his server handed him a sealed card in a pastel blue envelope.

"Someone cares about you," she said.

"I guess so," he replied, opening up his card.

The server walked off again, leaving him to his well-deserved peace and quiet. The card had a black and white picture of a father and son bent over a workbench hammering on a birdhouse. He opened it up and nearly dropped the card. Instead of a sentimental phrase printed inside, a handwritten note was scratched out in blue ink.

Happy Birthday, Dad! Come see me at my new club, Stonegate, at 7pm tonight for the surprise of your life! It's right next to the Arch. Don't forget! - Matt.

Every blood vessel in his skull worked to pump itching blood into the bump on his head. He rubbed it in a failed attempt to soothe the pain. How had Matt found him?

He looked around the cafe but couldn't see anything weird or the least bit supernatural. This place was clean. Looking back out of the window, he caught a glimpse of a young man walking around the corner of the building across the street.

The server appeared and laid the check on his table, which he handed right back to her along with his credit card. She took it and disappeared again. He dug his phone out of his pocket and called his last ally.

"Martellus, I've got our next move!" he said, hoping this move would be the right one.

Mandrake tower rose around the craggy landscape and cut into the sky with its four corner spires. Lightning constantly struck the spire tips, flashing down into the ground. It was hard to see from this distance, but Nathan could make out the smaller tendrils writhing all over the sides of the building like worms trying to burrow into impenetrable soil. They soaked up the energy from the lightning until Zyne pulled them into the world above for use as the disposable commodities they were.

Strange creatures lived among the Shades that dwelt here, outcasts too weak to survive outside this plain. They were the products of the Shades' effect on the Shifting Plains and tended to be enslaved to the Shades in whatever way the Shades commanded. The rarest of all creatures in this plane were the Illumin, as they were careful not to tread where Shades were strongest.

Nathan walked away from the tower to cross the ashen hills, following the pull of his aching heart. With Zyne away for the brief window, he conjured enough power to explore his old domain. It no longer felt like he remembered. Zyne's touch permeated the air and seeped deep into the ground. This place had forgotten Nathan's power, or Zyne had worked to cast it out.

The hills evened out, and the landscape transitioned into subtle greens and the occasional tree. Pools and streams of water dotted the ground, confusing Nathan. The air surrounding him replaced Zyne's taint with something he hadn't felt before. The trees grew thicker the more he walked, crowding out Zyne's touch completely.

Another familiar touch gently prodded him through the sprawling, quiet forest. He saw its edge just ahead and his heart beat faster. The prisoner he came to free drew ever closer. He broke out of the forest into a picturesque clearing covered in the greenest grass and surrounded by leafy trees and looming snow-capped mountains. A spark of light caught his eye in the middle of all the green. Jailyn knelt in the dirt, working at the tough soil to plant exotic flowers.

A charge of life jolted his heart. He ran after her.

She didn't even budge from her pattern of clawing the ground and planting flowers. Drawing her hands from the dirt, another spark of light flashed from her finger. A multicolored stone, cut like a diamond, sat on a band of gold. The ring looked as beautiful as the day he put it on her finger at their wedding.

He stopped to kneel in front of her, trying not to crush her flower. Staying her hands, she stared at him.

"Jailyn, I–" He couldn't say anything else before pulling her close to him. The stone's colors grew in intensity.

She locked her hands on his shoulders and pushed herself to her feet. "Get away from my garden!"

Fear played across her eyes. "Jailyn, no, I'm here to escape with you."

"This place is under watch. Better not have him see you here. He isn't fond of the dark ones."

"Who is watching? Zyne?" The effects of the Shifting Plains had already decayed her mind. He moved to grabbed her, but she backed away from him.

"Look at your ring!" he said.

Confused, she stared down into it. He reached out with his senses and connected with the stone.

"I cut out part of my heart to forever signify my love for you. Use it to remember who you are!" He stepped closer to her.

A small flash of recollection played across her face. "I...I..." She paused, lost in thought.

He pushed against the stone harder until it lit up her face. "Remember who you are, Jailyn!"

Her eyes softened. "Nathan?"

She ran into his arms. Their lips collided in a violent surge of love that ended all too quickly.

"Listen," he said, thinking ahead. "Stay close to me and I can protect your mind from this place's effects."

"Wait," she said looking down in thought. Her blue eyes rose back up to him in hesitation. "He's come back."

"Who?"

"I can't remember, but I know his face. He hides many secrets down here."

Just as they made it to the edge of the forest, a well-dressed figure stepped out from a tree, cutting them off. Nathan remembered the name behind the Illumin standing before them.

"Sams," Nathan uttered.

"Zyne hasn't burned all your memory yet, Nathan?" the figure said.

For once, Nathan felt back in his element. "What kind of Illumin would keep his own kind captive down here?"

"One who rejects core tenets of the Faith," Jailyn answered.

"So, blasphemer," Nathan challenged Sams. "Are you going to let me pass with my wife, or are you just going to stand there and goad me into tearing through you?"

Sams' face lit up as he swung his fist at Nathan.

A burning pain hammered into Nathan's side, and he bent over into the ground, losing his grip on Jailyn. With a turn, he retaliated with both his feet. Sams fell back from the double kick. Nathan threw his hands in front of him to summon tendrils. Only his fingers protruded forward. He stepped back and tried again.

"This is my own little alcove here, Nathan. I've removed your old encroachment and kept Zyne away in recent years." Sams dashed at him, stomping his boot straight into Nathan's chest. He fell onto his back, staring up at the emerald sky.

"I don't care about your turf war with Zyne. Let me walk away with Jailyn and you'll never deal with me again," Nathan pleaded.

"She's been corrupted by you long enough. I've been watching over her imprisonment until I can find a way to get her safely out of here. This isn't the world you left, Nathan."

Nathan pushed out with his senses to find anything he might use. The area felt distant from him, as if his own powers were being blocked. Nathan saw Jailyn cowering against a tree, confusion spreading back across her face.

Sams looked at her. "She's slipping from you every moment the two of you remain apart. In a few minutes, she won't even remember you coming to her in the garden. Even if she does, I'll rip that out of her mind."

Jailyn spoke only to Sams. "Take the dark one away from me!"

"Jailyn!" Nathan screamed, pushing out for the ring again. "You are an Illumin, a warrior sent to cleanse the earth! Remember the river where we discovered our bond?" Jailyn kept her blank stare. "Think of our daughter, Clara! The new life we created from our love!"

Nothing brought any real sense of meaning to her. She just stood there, waiting on Sams to remove the 'dark one' from her presence. His knees felt weak, and he fell over into the dirt. Crawling to Jailyn's feet, he lifted his hand to her, but she jerked away.

A heavy hand grabbed his shoulder and pulled him away. Another moved underneath his chin, putting him in a choke hold. He struggled to break Sams' hold, growing more desperate with every step as he was dragged away from his true love. Whatever strength he had found, he lost as Jailyn shrank in the distance.

A quick tumble sent Nathan into the dirt in Zyne's territory. He dug into the ground and pulled up a string of tendrils that wrapped around him for protection.

Sams just laughed at him. "How did you fall so far? You're a dim reflection of who you used to be. Even your name, Nathan, rings of a weakened being who is lost."

He thrust a whip of tendrils forward. Sams grabbed them with his hand and sliced them in half with the other. Moving in close, he wrapped them around Nathan's neck, pulling them tight.

"You're not even worth killing. You deserve much worse for dragging Jailyn into your apathy. She and I came so close to purging this area of your kind until you tainted her. I'll keep her exiled until she forgets all about you, then she will rejoin me and finish what we were sent here to do."

Sams kicked into Nathan's shin, dropping him facedown. Nathan gasped as the tendrils fell away from his neck.

"A part of you will always be with her," Sams continued. "I'm allowing her to keep the ring so you'll feel just how much of a curse immortality is. Every time I work to rid her mind of you, you'll feel me twisting that knife in her mind to cut you out. You'll feel her grow cold toward you until her resentment of Zyne bleeds over to you as well. You'll know the exact moment the love between you dies, and then when you try to reach out to her, you'll feel the same death you've brought to the Earth!"

Sams turned back around and walked away.

Nathan lay there in utter defeat, unsure of what meaning he had left. Lightning cracked in the distance, echoing the anger striking his heart. Footsteps crunched up behind him, preceded by the strongest presence he had ever felt in the Shifting Plains.

"You've taken everything from me. Even my ability to control this place."

"No," countered Zyne. "You sacrificed it all for a fleeting glimpse into a human life. That should have come after we finished what we started. Your own greed put you at mercy of a weakened Illumin."

Daniel tapped out a rhythm on his steering wheel to keep him from thinking about seeing Matt. They had both lived in the same area for Matt's entire life, yet they may as well have been across the country from each other. Of course, it was really Darrus's antiquated sense of propriety that had kept them apart. But, then again, Daniel never really bought into any of Darrus's other decrees, so it was his own fault for leaving Matt to his mother.

He pushed on his brakes and made the turn into the shopping center. A line of high scale boutiques ran along the side, ending at the Arch in the back corner. Pulling up to the door, he stepped out to let the valet take care of his car. Something definitely wasn't right about this whole setup. Not many former residents of Wheelbarrow Creek mingled inside one of Shreveport's premier restaurants.

Walking closer, Daniel wondered what Matt had done to the Arch. A long line of overly tan people in unbearably bright clothing ran down in front of the boutiques. Women in short dresses hung onto the arms of clean-cut men with messy hair. He followed the line with his eyes and saw it led to what must have been the Stonegate club Matt wanted to meet him at. He found it hard to believe Matt could have taken over a Shreveport cornerstone establishment so easily, yet the club looked to be in full force.

Stepping underneath the overhang on the adjacent side, a shadow moved for him. He reeled back just as a pair of hands landed on his shoulders. A pleading set of eyes gazed at him, followed by a mumbled sentence that got cut off when Jarvis appeared behind them and threw the shadow against the wall.

"Better get out of here, Hunter, if you know what's good for you," Jarvis told him.

Daniel shook his head and continued walking to the club, filled with an even greater sense of unease. He heard Jarvis and Hunter struggle some more, but didn't care. Hunter had gotten what he deserved. His nephew chose his fate and would have to live with it.

The cool metal handle of his cane reminded him why he came here. He had to force his way through a birthing Shade to rescue his estranged son, a son he barely knew, but Daniel wanted to recoup the lost time. All the missed birthdays and Christmases flashed through his mind, pushing him closer to the door.

"Daniel Raven?" a heavy voice asked him.

He looked up, startled to be standing before a hulking bouncer holding a clipboard.

"Yes," he answered.

"Right this way," the bouncer replied, ushering him through the glass doors.

The last time he had been to a club, a huge ball of tiny mirrors dominated the room and spun discs of light all over the walls to some of the worst music ever conceived. Worst until he heard the deafening noise of this place. The bright dance floor was filled with writhing bodies finding something to move to among the screeches and blips pumping out of the speakers. Everywhere else was dark and smoky with multicolored lasers tracing out lines through the room.

Between the lasers shining in his eyes and the music making his ears throb, Daniel had trouble spotting Matt. He sat on a plush couch that curved around a short table to the left of the dance floor. A blonde woman sipped from a tumbler and talked to Matt with animated gestures. Several empty shot glasses were stacked between the two of them.

Daniel leaned on his cane and forced himself toward his son. As he got close, Matt stood up and straightened his suit while easing around the other side of the table. He looked far too overdressed for this place. His hair lay slicked back across his head and gave a strange presence to his smile.

"Surprise!" Matt yelled at him to compete with the music. He threw his hands to either side as if expecting a hug.

Daniel couldn't stop himself from finishing the embrace. "I'm so sorry, son. Forgive me for all this time I spent away from you. I should have been there."

"It's okay," Matt said, patting his back. "We're together now."

The stench of death rushed into Daniel's nose and he pulled away. Matt's eyes filled with the purest black he had ever seen. They reflected none of the laser light streaming through the room. Dread sunk into Daniel's heart, weighing it down with hopelessness. He shook it off, realizing it for the effects of the Shade within Matt.

"I came here for my son. Don't step between me and him."

Matt laughed deeper than humanly possible. "Please, sit with me." He motioned to the table at their side.

Daniel followed Matt to the couch, laying the cane across his lap and ignoring the now silent woman at his side. "What happened to you?"

"Life."

"What?"

"Seems like yesterday I was staying up late playing video games and going nowhere. Then life happened. The life you left Mom and me to. Your amulet was the key to something greater than I could have ever made for myself."

"It wasn't supposed to be this way; we hid the amulet with you two because it was safest. She just didn't–"

"Let's not play the blame game. This is a reunion of father and son. We should be happy for my successes of late. I own a restaurant and have a father who now cares for me."

It all clicked into place for Daniel. "This is your base of operations? You've just awoken and already think yourself powerful enough for a physical foothold in the city? How much of Matt is left inside you?"

"Wow, one at a time. First off, I'm still me, just a little more cultured than how I was raised. Secondly, yes, this place is mine, and I intend to use it to punish anyone who stands against my will." He stood up and leaned onto the table. Flashes of red crossed his eyes and the lighting grew darker in the room.

Reaching into his pocket, Daniel slipped his ring on. He stood up to match Matt's gaze. Nausea dissolved throughout his body, but he forced himself through it. "I came here for you, Matt, not this thing that distorts you."

"I know, Dad. That's why I have to keep you from separating us."

Daniel flicked his ring into a spin and jumped back, twisting out the heated brand.

"It's too late for that. You can't stop this train," Matt said.

Shouts rang out from the club entrance. Daniel hurriedly backed away and watched Martellus and Jarvis burst inside, fully darkened into their Shade forms. Matt reciprocated by jumping onto the table. A dark cloud pulsed out from him. The drunken woman laughed and clapped her hands in applause.

"Who will make a stand today?" Matt proclaimed.

Daniel felt the heat from the brand through his shoes. It was ready. He led the charge against Matt with Martellus close behind. Matt stared them down.

Dark shadows flew overhead and landed in front of Matt, morphing into Jarvis and Martellus. When Daniel reached them, they jumped on him, tearing away his cane and pulling the ring off his finger. His cane flew to the side, clattering across the empty dance floor.

The club seemed to have emptied out except for the blonde woman who looked too infatuated with Matt to leave. Strong hands pinned Daniel's behind him.

"Don't move," Jarvis warned. "Your fight is over, but your life isn't. Unless you struggle."

"Sorry Daniel," Martellus said. "Powers are shifting, and your dinky shop can't match Matt's offers."

"Traitors!"

"What did you really expect?" Martellus asked. "I can't be seen with the weakest Raven."

Daniel's heart raced away with the Shades throwing his

senses off balance. Even knowing it was impossible, he tried wiggling out of Jarvis's hold. "No! I won't lose you before I've had any time to spend with you, Matt!"

"So sentimental, Dad." Matt jumped down and slapped his shoulder. "I'll make you proud regardless. Or," Matt said with a knowing smile. "We could rule this city as father and son."

"Strange how you haven't completely erased my son's existence."

"I've been trying to tell you that we have merged into a unique being. Now, let's try and talk one more time."

Jarvis pulled him to the side just enough for him to see a tiny silver speck fall through the air and land at Matt's feet. They all looked down at the spinning coin. Angel wings and fire came to a rest on the ground.

The coin exploded into the air in a burst of light. Jarvis shoved Daniel out of the way. Catching himself with the edge of a couch, Daniel saw a winged creature fly above them all to the point of light. He adjusted his glasses and Clara's form came into focus.

She steadied herself and reached out for the edge of light. The three Shades below her stood dumbfounded. Descending among them, she slashed out with the dagger forming in her hand. Martellus and Jarvis fell back with burning wounds in their chests.

Matt caught her wrist before she dealt him a blow. As Clara kicked up at him, he rammed her shin with his free hand. He tilted a bit, allowing Clara to use the leverage against him. The silver blade grazed his neck on his way to the floor. Sizzling flesh puckered and blackened where he had been slashed.

Daniel's eyes darted around the room and located his cane. While the Shades continued their fight, he ran for it. No one stopped him. Snatching it up, he reset the heater on the brand and prepared for another assault.

Three gunshots rang through the air. Daniel snapped around to see Gabriella lowering her sidearm as she came through the doors. She took position next to Clara amidst the fallen Shades.

"Stay down, boys," Gabriella commanded.

Matt rose to his feet again with a searing bullet hole through his front pocket. "This suit's not cheap."

"Unlike your crew's loyalty," Clara replied. "Now, Daniel, get over here and do whatever it is you were going to do."

"I think he needs this," Matt said pulling out the ring. "Think I'll just hold on to it until I can figure out how to use the Shade trapped within."

Gabriella leveled her gun at him, but before she could even take a shot, Matt lunged forward and laid her out with a punch. Clara brought her dagger down, but he pushed out into her stomach with his fist and sent her across the room.

"Get up!" Matt commanded. Martellus and Jarvis bolted to their feet and formed a shield around him. "Now, for those who wish us ill will, rethink your decision. I'm offering a chance to stand with the winning side in this crusade I have brought to this mortal plane."

Daniel watched the posturing by the five of them and knew it was hopeless. He closed up the brand and hunched onto the cane to support his hurting leg. He waved them all away on his short walk to the door. Matt had already gotten what he needed. It no longer mattered to Daniel what became of anyone else.

6

Nathan tumbled onto his back, the ground eating into his bare flesh. The sky was greyish-blue in this part of the Shifting Plains. Remembering what lay just a short distance away gave him too much anxiety to try and flee. A foot slammed down on his chest, pinning him to the ground.

Zyne leaned forward on his knee. His eyes were solid black and leaked out darkness. "Whatever freedom you thought you had was just as much an illusion as you reliving your memories. I had hoped you would come back to me through it, but now, here we are at our last resort."

Nathan pushed Zyne's foot off him and moved to throw him down. Tendrils snaked out of Zyne's arms and slithered around Nathan's chest, leaving trails of burning pain.

"You cannot hope to escape me!" Zyne yelled down at him.

The ground twisted away from him, and he soon found himself on his feet again face to face with his enemy.

"I control this place. I control Jailyn. And I will have your loyalty to our purpose!" Zyne roared like a ravenous animal.

"Don't leave Clara off your list," Nathan uttered

through clenched teeth. "She was precious to me, and you just emptied her out and filled her with yourself."

"No!" Zyne threw him outward and the tendrils let go.

A wall of cold stone flattened him out. Bones cracked along his spine. He stumbled before catching his footing. His entire body was at its breaking point.

"Why did you bring me back here, Zyne?"

"To show you what you sacrificed!"

Nathan turned around to stare up at the smooth wall behind him. It was several stories tall and formed out of the smoothest turquoise stone imaginable. He hadn't been here in a long time, but it still felt like coming home. Now that he knew where Zyne wanted him to go, he could walk freely. Resisting wasn't working anyway.

The two of them continued around to a break in the wall capped by towers on either side. They rounded the corner and peered into unfathomable depths. The rocky ground faded out from them into a black sea. Enormous stone pillars rose up in random patterns, sentinels between the shore and a round dais in the middle. The sky overhead bent down into a singular point at the center of the dais.

Just gazing into the point where the sky met the sea gave Nathan and Zyne dim reflections into their birth realm. The time spent on Earth had eroded much of Nathan's memories of where he came from, but he could still see the dark beauty coming through it even now.

"That is our true home, Nathan. Yet here we are, forever banished because of a now long-dead race of mortals who channeled the power in their blood. I've come here many times to see what I can never be again, to remember even the slightest fragment of what used to be my reality. I resent this world now for all its bleakness. We'll forever be restless."

Nathan walked past the wall to the edge of the sea, the farthest he could go. The stone pillars remained still, though his mind warped into believing they crawled toward him. A host of glowing red eyes sat on the edge of his vision, daring him to take one more step.

"Our destinies have only changed, my friend," Nathan said. "After we were torn from our realm and thrust into the world above, I knew our fates would never be what we wanted. That was why we set out to conquer the human spirit."

Zyne walked up behind him and pulled him away from the edge. "And we will, but I need you with me."

"I already have," he paused. "I found Jailyn, and with her experienced something beyond anything we had on the other side of that gateway."

"Your memory doesn't hold true then."

"It doesn't have to. I know why the human spirit is the way it is. Their life is finite, each step weighted down with meaning. They march with purpose toward an ultimate finale they only barely understand. You parade Jailyn and Clara in front of me to tempt me back into the eternal sadness we lived through when hurled from our world. After tasting what it is to be human, you hope in vain I will forfeit what I have learned."

Zyne's eyes went wide with a hint of weakness. "No. You will return."

"I'm forever tied to Jailyn. When we found each other in that dirty river, we forged an eternal bond that will never break, sealed with the piece of my heart that now adorns her finger."

Zyne grabbed him around the waist and dragged him back to the break in the wall. "You want Jailyn? You'll have to move the other way."

"I know you'll never let me have her again because I can't go back to what I was. Clara was born out of my love for Jailyn, and I gave up a part of myself to bring her into this world. My destiny is clear. This is how Jailyn and I will rise up against you!"

A surge rolled through Nathan, and he broke Zyne's grip to run back to the edge of the sea, stepping into it. His foot sank down until the sea touched the back of his knee. It felt like thick syrup that chilled his bones.

He struggled forward as fast as he could slog through the deceptively thick liquid. The pillars kept moving toward him, yet never seemed to change position. The air warped around to crush him with its invisible power. His eyes felt heavy and wanted to look down into the black sea. He refused them and waited to meet the pillars.

Razor-tipped wings unfolded from the pillars, revealing the texture-less forms underneath that transformed reality. Emblazoned red eyes filled the impossible forms with color unmatched by anything on Earth. Pure fear stormed inside them and leeched out to ensnare his heart. Ethereal snarling called out his doom. He was back among his own again.

Imagining Jailyn stood on the dais, he pushed as hard as he could. The gateway offered a sliver of hope that he knew was futile. The guardians were nearly awake and surrounded him with fear and dark fire.

"I did this for you my love!" he called out, watching the dais start to move farther away from him.

Everything was an illusion, except the love he had shared for his wife and daughter. That was real. The sky crushed down on him harder, reminding him he was no closer to the gate than when he started.

The guardians closed in on him, breathing dark flames that ignited within him and boiled his heart. Jailyn's eyes pulsed within his mind. Their bond stretched taut as he neared the edge of the gate.

Distortion and black flame barred his way, but he managed to struggle through, pulling his bond to its limit. The immaterial transformed into reality in this blend of everything. The sea rolled up around him. The guardians folded in on him with their formless maws.

The eternal love he shared with Jailyn kept him pushing until his last thought. He imagined what it would be like to see her again after she regained her true self. Her brilliant splendor enraptured his mind. Once the guardians destroyed him, his bond would surge back into her ring, freeing her from all the powers that controlled her.

His sacrifice meant life for both women who defined meaning in his life.

Daniel threw his car into park and flung open his car door. The moon's reflection peered down at him off the sides of Mandrake Tower like an eye of sadness. The streets were quiet in downtown. He looked around, still paranoid he was being followed.

Rushing up to the door, he fished through all the folds of his wallet to pull out the access card he had been storing for just such a dire situation. He tapped the card against the sensor; the door unlocked with a beep. He passed the two sets of glass doors into the empty lobby. He couldn't exactly remember where the elevators were. Stepping up to the help desk, he actually found them right across from where he came in.

The lone security guard gave him a curious glance as he waved at her and moved toward the elevators. The elevator responded to his call and he got on. None of the buttons worked for him. He tapped the top button several times. Then he saw another card sensor. In a huff of anger, he dug out the access card again and swiped it. Finally, he moved upward.

The door slid back to Zyne's personal lobby. All the lights were off.

"Zyne!" he called out. "I'm here!"

He flipped the light switch and worked his way to the side door. A faint light came from the hallway wrapping around the back of the lobby. He followed it and noticed it came from Zyne's office. He questioned what he intended to do, pausing just before the open door.

Little use that was, since Zyne could feel him anyway. He took a deep breath and prepared for the plunge. Turning to move inside, he knocked on the door in passing.

Surprisingly, Zyne wasn't at his desk. Instead he sat on a leather chair looking at a piece of bronze art on a square coffee table. The black orbs in his eyes rolled over to meet Daniel's stare. It was a rare moment to catch a Shade in a distraught mood. He motioned for Daniel to join him.

Daniel sat down in one of the two open chairs around the table. He looked at the statue that captivated Zyne. A thickly sculpted Atlas knelt down, supporting an empty globe of the world with the seas cut out to highlight the continents. What looked like fire spread around where Atlas touched the world. His hands and back were covered with it. Then Daniel saw the cracks running all throughout his body.

"I can't decide if I'm Atlas or the world," Zyne said after watching Daniel analyze the sculpture.

"I never understood art. The meaning of an object should be in how useful it is," Daniel answered.

"And how useful are you?"

"I must be of some importance with you sending Clara to watch my every move." A wave of fear pulsed through him.

"Not just her. I sent Gabriella too; well, I explained how you've been lately. She seemed to want you back on Darrus's payroll. Did you go crawling back to him?"

"I did," Daniel said, pulling his glasses off to get a blurry look at the sculpture. "That's why I'm here. If someone is going to keep me on a leash, it may as well be you."

"Those I like don't have leashes."

Daniel heard the sadness in his words. "Why are you here alone?"

"Because you are my last friend in this city. Nathan couldn't accept reality, so he broke himself against the Gate. The Guardians literally unmade him before my eyes. A being who was immortal just ceased existence, releasing all his power into the Gate."

"I'm sorry," Daniel replied in shock.

"Harrowing news I know. At least I can trust the rest of your family not to drag us to that place."

"I wish they would be so foolish."

"No," Zyne said. "Hold on to them as long as you can. They are our enemies, but they are still your family. Nathan and I were close enough to be brothers by your standards. A loss that great isn't something I wish upon you."

He couldn't believe Zyne's genuine empathy for his mortal existence. If Shades could cry, Zyne's eyes would have been faucets.

"Welcome to my inner dimension, Daniel. Now you can never leave our partnership again." In an instant, his entire face hardened into chiseled stone.

"I have nowhere to go."

"Good, because I have seen how to shut down that gate and lop off the head of the rising power in town." He gestured to the statue again. "We are Atlas, my old friend. And we won't let this world break us."

Resurfacing Memory

by
Amanda White

Mysti rolled the smooth, grey clay between her hands. The clouds changed direction, and a ray of afternoon sunshine appeared, warming her face. She shifted her legs beneath her on the cool floor and marveled at the view through the plate glass window that allowed her to see the tall mountains covered in multi-colored trees.

Mysti started at a sound behind her and leaned backward to peer into the front room. Maximillian, having nosed his way into the dilapidated cabin, stood next to the ancient woodstove. She smiled and held her hand out to him. The black spiky-haired beast trotted to her, his red eyes fixed on her hand. His hot breath and wet nose touched her fingers, and she reached up to stroke his coarse hair. Mysti laughed when he pressed his nose into her chest and knocked her off balance. "How do you always manage to find me here, Max?"

Max snorted and padded around on his enormous four paws through each of the shack's small rooms, sniffing the air. The floor creaked under his massive weight, and the red light emitting from his eyes bounced around the walls. Once satisfied, he re-entered the main room and sat beneath the plate glass window. Mysti watched Max for a moment, and he returned her gaze. His large torso rose and fell with his breathing.

Mysti scooted away from the window. "Move your feet, please." She pushed the animal's heavy legs to give her a bit more working room. Max shifted his weight, and Mysti felt the cabin's flooring move in response.

The clay began to dry, so Mysti dipped her fingers in the small bowl of creek water and moistened the clay so that it was malleable again. "This was the last of the clay," she said to Max. "I wonder if there is more in another part of the creek."

Mysti molded the clay in her fingers and, as always, was amazed when she could force her fingers to create something from nothing. She shaped the body parts and glanced at the animal on the floor every now and again for her guide.

The clouds rolled in a steady pace across the sky, dappling Max's satiny coat. Mysti raised a hand to cover her face from the blinding reflection of his fur. "You are like a mirror, Max." He glanced at her, then closed his eyes and snorted a response.

The wind blew and a nearby tree's branches scratched against the glass. Mysti shuddered as the sound awakened her memory of her first night in Shifting Plains. She had awoken in front of the shack in a downpour of rain, lying face-up in a deep puddle. Mysti had remembered nothing and crawled on hands and knees into the shelter, shaking and vomiting. For hours she huddled in the room with the plate glass window, the tree's scratching in her ears.

Mysti looked around the now familiar room. The

wooden slats that made up the walls were splintered, and wind escaped between the gaps. Light shone through small openings in the corners of the ceiling. Her slight movements on the floor and Max's breathing were the only sounds. Mysti took a deep breath; the scents in the room filled her with a blend of familiarity and fear.

Max rolled onto his back and groaned. Mysti smiled at him. He wagged his tail against the wall; the window vibrated in response. "You are a good friend, Max." *My only friend,* she thought.

Mysti held her sculpture next to Max in order to inspect it for accuracy. "What do you think, boy?" He glanced in her direction and vocalized a yawn. Mysti smiled as she made an adjustment on her work. "You shouldn't have made that face. It will now be immortalized forever."

Mysti started to stand, using her hands for support, but fell back into a seated position. Max hopped to his feet and walked over to her. She sighed and reached up to grab his fur. He pulled backward, helping her to her feet.

"Thanks, Maximillian," Mysti said and patted him on the head. He pushed his nose into her waist and whined. Mysti stretched. The pain in her joints was a testament to the hours spent seated and unmoving on the cold floor.

She walked into the front room and placed the sculpture on the woodstove among at least a dozen others. "This one is my best yet, Max, don't you think?"

Mysti took her routine walk around the shelter. A side room contained an old bed with a wrought iron headboard. The mattress had long ago rotted away. Mysti gazed out of the bedroom's window. There were no mountains on this side, only flat land with the outskirts of a forest to the south.

Mysti relished the sound of her boots as they struck the old wooden floor. She left the side bedroom and entered the darkest room of the shack. It was furnished only with a small table and empty bookshelf. Orange light filtered through the dirty window and illuminated Mysti's chalk drawings from her earliest days in Shifting Plains. The work looked rushed in her eyes now, almost frantic.

She walked back through the room where she had spent the day and looked for one last time through the wide window. The mountains' colors faded away under the waning daylight. Mysti sighed and pressed her face against the plate glass. Her breath fogged the window. She knew it was time to leave, but departure always left her feeling empty, like saying goodbye to an old friend.

Max grunted from the front door and shuffled his feet on the grainy floor. His red eyes glowed in the evening sun's haze. Mysti leaned over, wrapped her arm around his broad neck and hugged him, relishing his familiar smell.

Max began to growl, and Mysti jumped back when his fur rose and sharpened into spikes. "What is it, boy?" she asked as he pushed her back into the shack.

The wind blew, trapping loose dirt in Mysti's eyes. She covered her face and tried to pull Max in so she could shut the door, but he resisted and barked into the wind. Her heart quickened, and her stomach jumped in response to a stinging scent in the air. It smelled of home, but no home she could remember.

There was a loud crack from above, as if a large piece of the sky had broken away and was hurtling to the earth. "Max!" she shouted just as the wind died; her voice cut into the atmosphere. Mysti peered out of the cabin and saw nothing. Max inched off the porch, his body low to the ground.

Mysti surveyed the tree line and the ground. The grass appeared a dull orange in the sunset. She hopped off the porch and followed Max's gaze. A slow trickle of water had begun to emerge from a small crack in the dirt. It pooled and developed into a puddle of hazy liquid. The ground under the puddle softened and divided into two pieces.

Max and Mysti jumped back as something began to emerge from the crack. Mysti grabbed Max by the scruff of his neck and tried to pull him away from the area, but he held fast, growling and showing teeth.

An arm became visible, and then a feminine head covered in long brown hair emerged from the split in the ground. Large, soaked wings that were mangled in appearance clung to her back. The water drained in moments and left the creature lying in a muddy pool. She screamed and rolled onto her back.

Mysti stepped back a few paces and watched the creature sob on the ground. Max circled the puddle and sniffed. Mysti inched closer, holding her arms around her body, as understanding came over her. "Shifting Plains has a new inhabitant," she whispered to herself.

Max nuzzled the woman. She saw him, screamed, and attempted to roll out of the mud.

"It's okay," Mysti said, leaning over. "He won't hurt you." Mysti patted Max on his head with too much force. He grunted and backed away.

The woman's gaze fixed on Mysti for a moment before she glanced down at her body. She sat in a daze and examined the edges of her wasted skirt. One wing began to twitch. There was a popping sound, and the woman screamed and began to tremble.

Mysti knelt down to her. "Let me help you."

The woman met Mysti's eyes. Her face quivered and a dried blue substance clung to her cheeks. Her eyes widened and she said, "I'll forget who I am. Any minute now."

"Tell me your name," Mysti said.

"Jailyn," she replied and in a rapid motion grabbed Mysti's arms. The woman's eyes were bright, her grip strong.

Maximillian growled as he moved to get between them.

"Please, remember my name. It's Jailyn," the woman said. Mysti noticed her gaze shift to a large ring placed on her left hand.

Mysti nodded and offered a smile. She watched the curious woman, who slumped back into the puddle. Jailyn sobbed with her face toward the soft ground and held the ring tight against her chest.

"Jailyn," Mysti called. The woman did not respond. "My name is Mysti. Why don't you come with me? It's not safe to remain in this place after dark." She took Jailyn's arm and pulled her to a standing position.

Max whined and began walking in a circle, his head pointed upward as he sniffed the air. He pointed his nose to the darkening sky and howled. "Let's go," Mysti said and tugged on Jailyn's hand. She resisted and Mysti said, "We must go now," and pulled with more force.

The two women walked to the edge of the tree line and

stepped onto a path. Max pushed Mysti from behind, urging her forward. Jailyn seemed to sense the urgency and picked up her pace, dragging her broken wings behind her. Max trotted ahead of them and cut back on occasion.

After a few tense moments the trio neared the edge of the forest. A tree to the right of the trail vibrated, and red leaves floated down at the edge of their path's end. "Oh, no," Mysti muttered under her breath.

Max ran to the base of the tree and barked, his sharp claws digging into its sides. "What is it?" Jailyn asked.

Mysti led them away from the path. Her blue skirt caught onto a fallen branch and her pulse raced as she struggled to rip the skirt and free herself.

"A way out," Mysti whispered. "We need a way out." The pair ran, dodging between the tree trunks in the direction of the forest's edge. Something landed with a thump behind them. Mysti ran at top speed and pulled Jailyn with all of her strength. They reached the edge of the forest, and Mysti saw her white boots emerge into the light.

Maximillian jumped high into the air in front of them and reached for a creature as it dropped out of the sky. The creature screamed and kicked at the animal.

"What were you doing in there? You could've been killed!" the creature shouted.

Mysti realized she had been screaming and closed her mouth. "Sams," she said.

Sams flew higher to avoid Max. His white wings beat the air. "Any chance you could call off your mutt?"

Mysti patted her knee and blew the slim whistle she wore around her neck. Max turned away from Sams and padded to her.

"He was just protecting me. Really, you couldn't have announced yourself?" Mysti said as Sams landed on the ground. He dusted his crisp, white suit and smoothed his matching white hair.

Sams stopped and stared at Jailyn. His brow furrowed into a crease. "Who is this woman with you?" he asked.

"This is Jailyn," Mysti said and patted the woman's back.

Jailyn made no response other than to look around with a questioning expression on her face. "Who is Jailyn?" she asked Mysti.

Mysti glanced back at Sams, whose eyes had transitioned to a deep blue. "What's the matter?" Mysti asked him.

Sams' expression lightened, and he inclined his head and said, "She does not seem to know who she is. Better let me get her somewhere safe."

Mysti felt anger begin to swell inside her. "I found her, so I'm responsible for her. There is plenty of room in my house for her to stay."

Sams moved to touch her shoulder and she moved away. "We are going to my house," she said and made effort to hold an impassive expression. Mysti put her arm around Jailyn and moved her forward. Max fell in behind and snapped his jaw at Sams.

Sams flew in front of her again. "I think you should take my advice."

"Let me by," Mysti said and forced herself to resist his beautiful face. He stared at her for a moment then looked away in the direction of the mountains. "All right," he said at last, and stepped aside to let them pass. He gestured to Jailyn's dragging wings. "Those should retract overnight."

"Well, that's good to know." Mysti hesitated, and then thought better of having more conversation and prodded Jailyn forward.

"May I come by to see you tomorrow?" he asked as they walked away from him.

"If you announce yourself properly," she snapped. "And bring a bone for Max."

The smell of food woke her. She opened her eyes and found herself lying next to a window. Light broke through pale yellow curtains and warmed the small, tidy room. She felt at peace; her thoughts were quiet. Rolling over in the small bed, she relished the feel of the fluffy pillow and plush mattress beneath her body.

The door opened with a faint creak and revealed a thin woman wearing an apron. "Jailyn," the woman said. "Are you hungry?"

She rose and looked around the room. She was the room's only occupant. "Me?"

"Yes." The woman nodded and pushed her long salt and pepper hair away from her face. "I'm Mysti. We met yesterday. You are in my house."

"Where?" Jailyn asked.

"Like I said, in my house." Mysti gestured in a circle with a wide spoon.

"But, where is your house?" Jailyn asked and rose from the bed. She looked down at her body, surprised to find herself wearing a short nightgown. The wooden floor was cold, so she stepped onto a bright blue and yellow hooked rug placed in the center of the room.

Mysti watched her with soft eyes, the ends of her mouth lilted upward. "Come on, breakfast is ready. There is a robe and a pair of slippers in the bathroom across the hall. Put those on and come eat."

Jailyn stood still for what seemed like an eternity. Her mind was a blank slate. She walked across the hall on her tip toes, unable to fight the inexplicable urge to be silent. She entered a small bathroom, just as clean as the bedroom, and crossed the space to a small mirror. Jailyn leaned forward and stared at her reflection. She touched her fingers to her cheek. Her face and blue eyes were familiar to her, but only in a vague sort of way. Her appearance was like a memory from long ago that one cannot distinguish as being from an actual past event or just a dream.

"It's getting cold, girl!" Mysti called from the first floor.

Jailyn washed her face with warm water and dried it on a sweetly scented towel. She stepped into the slippers and wrapped up in the robe then descended the stairs.

"Whatever you are making smells good," Jailyn said as she entered the kitchen.

"Have a seat." Mysti gestured to a small wooden table adorned with a royal blue tablecloth and shiny glass plates.

Jailyn sat down and jumped when pain shot up her

back. She placed her hand on her lower back. It felt hot to the touch.

"You okay?" Mysti asked as she placed a plate full of steaming food in front of Jailyn.

Jailyn's stomach growled. "My back hurts. I'm pretty much hurting everywhere, really. What happened to me?"

"I'm not sure, but we will work it out." Mysti sat down beside her and drizzled hot syrup over flat, yellow cakes. Mysti handed her the small pitcher. "For your johnnycakes."

"What are they?" Jailyn asked.

"They are made with cornmeal, flour, sugar, milk, and eggs. Nothing will hurt you."

Jailyn nodded and forced a smile. The cakes did smell wonderful, and the berries that adorned the side of the plate were bright and fragrant. She finished her entire plate and swallowed two glasses of juice.

"I think your, um, animal wants in." Jailyn gestured to the kitchen door. She pushed back her plate and folded her legs into a crossed position in her chair.

"Well, it's about time you came home," Mysti said to the beast as she let him in and placed a plate of food on the floor for him. Mysti wrapped her arms around his neck for a moment while he ate.

She looked up and smiled, "Jailyn, I don't think you two have been formally introduced. This is my best friend here. His name is Maximillian; at least that's his main name. Sometimes he goes by Max or Scrubs."

Maximillian glanced up at Jailyn as if in greeting, then resumed devouring his food. Jailyn thought the animal had a form that was familiar to her, but she could not place it.

He must have weighed at least 200 pounds, and his height reached Jailyn's mid-torso. His white teeth contrasted with his black fur like stars against a night sky.

"I don't remember getting in bed last night," Jailyn said. She smashed a berry with her fork and watched the juices squirt across her plate.

"No," Mysti said. "I guess you don't. You tried to lie down right away and sleep on the floor, but I forced you to bathe and get into bed." Mysti cleared away the plates and began washing dishes. "You just stared during the whole process, like you were stuck in a daydream."

Jailyn rose from the table and walked to stand beside Mysti as she washed dishes. A window above the sink was open, and a warm breeze flowed through the screen. The air had a strange scent to it, like everything else. The breeze teased frizzy strands of hair across her face.

Jailyn left the kitchen, walked onto Mysti's front porch, and seated herself in a wooden swing. She shook the slippers off her feet and pushed herself back and forth. The swing's chains creaked in time with the motion and her eyes felt heavy. She tapped her cheeks with her cool hands in an effort to rouse herself.

Jailyn pushed herself a little higher on the swing then drew her knees to her chest and used her body to maintain the motion. It was a sunny morning, and Mysti's yard teemed with color. Several tall trees surrounded the back and sides of the house. Her front yard was open and divided by a decorative wrought iron fence.

Mysti came outside with a dish rag slung over her shoulder and said, "Why don't you go on back upstairs and rest; I know you want to. They always do."

"What do you mean?" Jailyn asked, even as she walked in the direction of the stairs.

"Anyone who is flung into this world. They can barely keep their heads off the ground. I was the same way." Mysti paused. "At least, I think I was."

Jailyn felt her stomach jump with faint hope. She struggled to hold her eyes open. "So, will you be able to help me? Tell me who I am?"

"Come on." Mysti took Jailyn by the arm at the base of the stairs. "We will have plenty of time to talk."

Jailyn stumbled and pulled herself up to a standing position with Mysti's help. She felt a sob threaten to overtake her. A sudden grief held on to her heart, but she could not place its source.

"It's okay," Mysti said in a quiet voice. "I'll take care of you. Max and I both will."

Jailyn felt the animal meet her midway up the staircase. He pushed against her and Jailyn looked to Mysti, unsure of what to do.

"Hop on his back and take a hold of his coat. He'll carry you." Mysti said.

Jailyn hesitated, and then as she felt her last bit of energy snuff out, she threw her arms around the animal and rested on his back. He climbed the stairs with ease, a steady force in this shaky, strange world. They crossed the space of the small guest room in an instant.

Max approached the bed sideways so Jailyn could roll off of him onto the mattress. Her last sight was that of two red eyes blazing within inches of her face. She did not know why, but his eyes teased at some dim memory in the back of her mind. The faintest recollection of love touched her mind, a warm body against hers. It was a feeling of security found in the most dangerous places. Only, Jailyn did not remember where that place was.

Mysti backed out of Jailyn's room with Max padding behind her across the soft rug, and the two crept down the stairs. Max whined and she patted him on the head, unlocked the screen door, and let him out. She watched Max trot across her yard and break into a run when he passed her garden. Within seconds, he disappeared into the woods behind her house.

Mysti took a deep breath and leaned against the doorframe. Her lavender was growing well, and the plants scented the warm air. Mysti glanced backward in the direction of the stairs, and then shrugged. Jailyn would likely sleep out the day.

Mysti finished the last of the dishes then tossed on a yellow t-shirt and a long cargo style skirt and headed out to her garden. She picked up her basket of tools and carried it to the patch with the most weeds. After about an hour, she became restless and bored with the task, so she left the garden and walked through the small wrought iron gate, across the grassy field behind her house, and stopped when she got to her small goldfish pond.

Sams had hired some workers to construct the small pond for her and then had filled it with round, orange fish. He had insisted that Mysti would love it, and to her surprise one morning, he appeared with two bulky, yellow-skinned men with bad hygiene to help him dig the hole and haul in the water and plants. Sams had referred to them as "trolls" under his breath when describing the two working men, which had made her leery of them, although their behavior toward her was friendly. The one called Fin became enamored with Mysti and complimented her lemonade and her home, and he offered various little niceties until Sams sent her inside.

Sams had been right about the pond. She loved the escape it offered. Mysti ran her hand across the top of the water and the little fish swam to the top in search of food. She sat down on a decorative rock and leaned over to look at her reflection. Her face seemed to be that of someone else. Lines marked the skin around her eyes, and her face's features seemed less defined. Mysti touched her greying hair and noted that it was not as soft as it was when she first came to Shifting Plains. As least, that is what the folks here told her it was. She could only remember as far as her first day.

Mysti removed a blue handkerchief from her skirt pocket and used it to tie up her hair on the top of her head. She lay down on the soft grasses Sams had planted around the pool. Her awareness of all around her dimmed until she became only barely aware of her breathing. As she drifted off to sleep, Mysti's mind began to tingle; it was the strangest effervescent feeling.

Small sounds of swift, light steps on the grass reached

her ears, getting louder as they neared. The sound stopped, and Mysti opened her eyes. Two children stood before her, holding hands. Grins adorned their precious faces. The female child held out a small flower to her and gestured to Mysti's ear. Mysti smiled and took the flower, and seeing that the child had adorned her own dark hair, did likewise.

The male child placed his hand on top of Mysti's shoulder. She looked into his eyes; the crystal blue had a startling effect, though it was not the first time she had seen this boy. Mysti leaned close to him and said, "Hello."

As always, the children said nothing. They stood still and smiled at her. "It's so good to see you both again," Mysti said. "Won't you tell me your names, please?" The boy backed away and put his arm around the girl, who was his near-mirrored image.

Mysti snapped awake when someone kissed her cheek. Her head swam as she returned to full awareness. "Sorry, to wake you," Sams said. "You looked incredibly peaceful. Although, I'll never know how you sleep so well on this hard ground."

Mysti said, "You scared them away."

"Scared who away?" he said.

"The two children," Mysti said.

"I didn't see any children." Sams shook his head. "Like before, you were simply dreaming, Mysti. That is all. There are no children here in Shifting Plains."

"You couldn't possibly know that," Mysti snapped as a feeling of grief rolled inside her stomach. "The boy's eyes are so bright." A dark look crossed Sams' features. He pulled her to her feet and wrapped his arms around her waist.

Sams said, "I'm sure it seems real to you. All dreams do in the moment we are experiencing them."

Mysti looked up at him and stared into his watery blue eyes. She marveled as she had many times before at how handsome he was. The sun shone through a break in the trees and bounced off of his long silver hair, giving him a glowing look.

"Tell me more about these children," he said.

"I've dreamed of them many times," Mysti replied. "Although…only here, by the pond."

Sams shifted away from her and walked around the small pond. Sams smoothed his ponytail and looked at her sideways. "Hmm."

Sams took off his suit coat, revealing a trim waist covered by a tailored vest. Mysti marveled at how a man of his years could be so slender and blushed when he caught her looking at him. She had known Sams for years, but he always created such a magnetic force, despite her doubts about him.

He walked over to her, carrying his coat in one hand. With his free hand, he touched Mysti's face and ran a finger around the curve of her cheek. "Let's go inside," he said.

Mysti shook her head. "Not right now. Jailyn's resting. Don't want to startle the poor thing," Mysti said as she wrapped her arms around his neck and kissed him. "Besides, I remember how I was when I woke up in that puddle. I was so afraid."

There was a flash of emotion behind Sams' eyes. He was so hard to read. "Don't you remember those days? When you found me?"

Sams nodded then and said, "Speaking of your guest…" He withdrew a small bottle from his coat. "I procured this from town. It's supposed to help the…newly arrived. At least, the ones like her."

Mysti took the blue vial and held it up to the light. She rolled the bottle, which revealed that it was an oil-based liquid; its filmy residue clung to the sides of its container. "Okay, thanks."

"How long do you plan to keep her?" Sams asked. He kissed her on the forehead then seated himself on an iron bench. He removed some fish food from the wooden container beneath the bench and tossed it across the pond. The tiny red and orange fish rammed into each other as they raced to the surface.

Mysti stretched and unbound her hair, brushing it with her fingers. "She can stay as long as she wants."

He raised an eyebrow and folded his arms across his chest. She said, "Don't object, please. Sams, I'm so lonely."

He nodded and said, "I suppose Max and I are poor substitutes for another woman's company."

"You know I love you both," Mysti said and failed to suppress a grin. "But, yes, it's nice to have a new friend. I'm going to take her to the market tomorrow. We will need more supplies."

"Yes," Sams said. He shoved his hand in his pocket and removed a small drawstring purse. "Take this. Buy whatever you both need. I'm guessing you won't make enough from selling your plants and art to support you both."

Mysti felt her cheeks warm when she took the purse. She wrapped her arms around him and nuzzled her face into his neck. She relished his familiar smell and warmth. "Thank you," she whispered. "You've always taken such good care of me. How can I ever repay you?"

"You don't owe me anything. All I've ever wanted was to be with you. And you allow me that."

Sams began coughing, backed away from her, and put his handkerchief around his face. Mysti saw that the cloth was dotted with a blue substance before he shoved it back into his pocket. "Well, I guess I better go," he said and went to hug her goodbye.

"Why are you coughing? You've only just arrived." Mysti placed her hands to the sides of his face. She felt tears of disappointment fill her eyes.

"No," Sams said. "I've been here all day. Had business." He coughed again, over and over, unable to catch his breath.

"What if you take this?" Mysti held the blue vial to him. "We can get Jailyn another one."

He stared down at her. Sams' cheeks were drained pale and his eyes bloodshot. "That's for her, Mysti."

"Don't play me for a fool, Sams," Mysti said. "You two are the same species."

He recovered and moved to hug her. "I must go."

"Wait," Mysti said and nudged him away from her. "If you won't tell me about my past, at least tell me where she came from. And you."

Sams said, "Mysti, just be content. After all, we have each other."

"I'll never be content. If you love me so much, why won't you help me? Why have you kept me in the dark all these years?"

Sams squeezed her upper arms and pulled her to his chest. His eyes blazed, their blue light shining into her face. "You are happy here. You are content."

Mysti felt a warmth wash over her as he stared into her eyes. Sams handed her the basket of tools and turned her in the direction of her house. She bid him farewell with a kiss and thought about how much she loved him as she walked away. When Mysti opened the screen door of her home, she found Jailyn staring after him, her brow furrowed and jaw clenched. "Wow," Mysti said. "Your eyes light up just like Sams'."

Jailyn brushed her hair with Mysti's blue comb. She shuddered when she looked in the mirror. A red scar stuck out against her white skin and peeked out several inches from the neckline of her shirt. Her face had transitioned from pale to grey, and her hair lay flat against her cheeks and shoulders. Her second night in Shifting Plains had been almost as dreamless as her first.

"Come on!" Mysti shouted from the kitchen. "We better get going, or all the good produce will be gone."

Jailyn tied her hair back as best she could and took a deep breath. She choked on the air and stumbled backward, landing on the tub's edge and then falling to the floor. Jailyn screeched out a call for help. The room spun, and she wrapped her arms around her head in an attempt to stabilize her vision. She was overcome by a wave of nausea as her body began to shake.

"What's the matter?" Mysti asked, out of breath from racing up the stairwell.

"Everything is spinning," Jailyn gasped, "And…I can't breathe."

Mysti said, "I have something that will help. I'll be right back."

Hot tears ran down Jailyn's face as she sobbed. She thought of how she did not know who she was or who Mysti was or what was happening to her. The single tangible item that followed her through the puddle was a beautiful, multicolored ring on her left hand, which possessed only empty meaning. Her heart ached for someone she could not remember and a life she only hoped she once had. Death seemed like a sweet reward to this madness.

Mysti's boots struck the steps two-by-two, and she dashed into the bathroom. She held Jailyn's face with one hand and held up a small blue bottle. Jailyn held Mysti's hand at bay when she tried to feed her a small amount of the liquid from a dropper.

"What is it?" Jailyn asked.

Mysti hesitated then said, "I don't know, actually. Sams gave it to me. He said it would help you." She placed a drop of the gold liquid on her finger.

"Oh, no!" Jailyn said and forced herself to her feet. The room stopped spinning, but every breath felt like a heavy blanket had been placed over her face. "I don't trust him."

"Why?" Mysti asked. She sat on the fluffy toilet cover

and pushed her hair behind her ears, the small bottle resting in her lap.

"I don't know, not yet anyway," Jailyn replied.

"Look, I know he startled us the other day," Mysti said. "But, he's helped me a lot. I don't know why I am here any more than you do, but I couldn't have made it without him."

"I'll be okay," Jailyn said and forced a smile. "Maybe I just need some fresh air. Besides, you said we needed to hurry, right?"

Mysti frowned at her and slid the bottle into her pocket. The two women descended the stairs in silence. Max barked at them through the screen door. "He's going with us?"

"Of course," Mysti said. "I try not to stray too far from home without him. Shifting Plains holds many dangers."

"How do you know?"

"Sams told me," Mysti said as she locked the door behind them.

"Right," Jailyn said. On impulse, she grabbed a small hat hanging on Mysti's back porch and pulled it down over her stringy hair.

The little group entered a small opening in a forest of tall, slim green trees. Jailyn inhaled and felt her lungs open a bit. Max sniffed into the air and along the ground beside them. Jailyn's heart fluttered in apprehension when his red eyes focused for a moment on her face. He snorted and moved forward, establishing himself at ten paces ahead of them. Jailyn could not understand Mysti's attachment to the creepy beast when he looked every bit the predator himself.

Jailyn studied Mysti as they walked. She was wearing a white shirt, a long red skirt, and rugged boots. Her lengthy salt and pepper hair swayed in response to her steps.

"How much are you planning to buy?" Jailyn asked and pointed to a large crushed velvet sack slung across her shoulders.

"I need to buy enough food for both of us for a while." Mysti looked at Jailyn and offered a warm smile. "I'm so glad you are here, Jailyn. I love Max, but he has difficulty with conversation."

The animal glanced back at them when he heard his name. "Yes, I suppose he does," Jailyn replied.

Jailyn discovered she could not judge length of time in this place. She only knew that she was beginning to feel tired and thirsty. They entered a clearing. Jailyn gasped at the view as Mysti and Max stopped to look around for danger.

"It's so beautiful!" Jailyn said and grabbed Mysti's arm for support. To the left of the clearing, mountains covered in colorful trees strived to reach the skyline. Some areas were darkened by slow, drifting clouds. Golden trees shimmered in the sunlight. Jailyn looked at the sky and marveled at its color.

"It is breathtaking," Mysti said as she stroked Max's head.

A breeze blew across the grasses in the meadow as sunshine warmed Jailyn's skin. She rolled up her sleeve, in hopes the light would bring healing. Instead, her skin began to itch. "That's odd," she remarked as she stared at her arm. "Ah!" The itching turned to intense pain and she struggled to pull down her sleeve.

"What?" Mysti asked.

"My arm started burning," Jailyn said. She placed her

hand over her forearm; it was sensitive to the touch.

"Are you okay?" Mysti asked.

"I don't know," she responded and felt her stomach tense in frustration. "It's just so beautiful here. I thought the light would be good for me." Jailyn pulled the hat down farther to cover her face and wondered at the instinct that had prompted her to grab it.

"I don't know," Mysti said. Her eyes were wide and she was shaking her head. "Maybe we can get some answers in town."

Jailyn glanced back at the colorful mountains as the group reentered the forest. She shuddered and wrapped her arms tightly across her chest, hoping her health would adjust to this place. Then again, maybe her health had been bad in her homeland too.

The trail ended on the outskirts of a small village. As they drew near, Jailyn heard music being played by various instruments. Voices of different volumes rang out, and smoke from cookfires rose into the air. When they came to a tall wooden gate, a lanky, tree-like being approached a small opening in the gate and asked, "What is your intent here?"

"I'm Mysti, Sams' charge, and these are my companions," Mysti said. She patted Max's fur in a soothing manner. "I'm here for the market."

The gatekeeper stared down at them for a moment; his sharp black eyes settled on Jailyn. The tree-bark-like muscles of his pointy face twitched.

"Well?" Mysti said, waving her bag in front of the gate keeper.

"Of course, Ms. Mysti, you are welcome here. Your

guests will have to wait outside."

"No," Mysti said and straightened her back. "My companions will come with me. Unless, of course, you would prefer to speak to Sams about the matter."

"What now?" A male being with dark skin and a squat frame appeared beside the gatekeeper. "What's the hold-up, C?"

"C" gestured to the small group, and the wave of his hand paused at Jailyn's face.

Jailyn glanced down at her skirts and shirt. She could not see anything amiss in her appearance. Mysti glared at the heavy man and said, "This is ridiculous. We have walked a significant way to get here, Mr. Stimes. Will you keep us out all day?"

They exchanged glances and looked at Jailyn. Mysti said, "You two are like children. She should be the leery one; after all, being downwind of you two is like standing next to a garbage heap."

Mr. Stimes bristled and cleared his throat, "Very well. You know how careful we are about strangers."

5

They walked through the town in the direction of an open market. Slim, tall, grey nested buildings lined the streets. Each building appeared to lean downward, giving the walkers below the sensation of being watched. There were small wooden cottages adjacent to a stone road on the hills outside of the market. Jailyn recognized the faint shadow of the mountains behind the cottages. She did not know why, but in her heart she longed to be in those mountains.

Beings of various shapes ambled along the road, weaving in and out of the shops. A short male with a long nose and solid white eyes tipped his hat as he limped past them in the opposite direction. Stores with glass windows displaying their goods lined the streets. In the alleyways, carts in no particular order offered food, jewelry, and lots of things Jailyn could not identify.

"Our first stop, Lady Bug," Mysti said and tugged on Jailyn's arm to pull her into a small shop. Max remained at the shop's door, ever vigilant of their surroundings.

"Good day, Miss." A tiny woman smiled up at Jailyn. Her dingy skirt and cloudy eyes matched the grey hair wrapped into a bun on top of her head.

"Hello." Jailyn stared down at the woman, who hovered below her elbow.

"Is there anything you need, dear?" the woman asked. "I have more to offer than what ya can see on the shelves."

"I don't think so," Jailyn said. "But thanks all the same."

The woman clicked her tongue against the roof of her mouth. "Standin' near you makes my pallor appear flushed. Want something for what ails ya?"

"What do you think 'ails' me?" Jailyn asked. She stepped backward and bumped into a barrel of something being pickled. Juice sloshed onto the floor, but the shopkeeper paid no attention.

"I can't describe how ya feel, but I know you don't feel

well. None of your kind can survive here without…eh, how can I put it? Medicinal supports. At least, not for long and not without sufferin'," the old woman said.

"What can you offer me?"

"Feeling up to a trade, my doll?" The shopkeeper grinned and showed a mouth with few teeth.

"I have nothing to give you," Jailyn said. She saw Mysti out of the corner of her eye, making her way around the store.

"Of course you have something to give me." She leaned in and laid a wrinkled, cold hand on Jailyn's back. "I'll take a feather from one of those wings. A bottle of treatment for each feather you give me."

Mysti approached, carrying a basket laden with fruits and vegetables. "Ms. Bloom, I need to pay for these, please."

Ms. Bloom stomped her foot onto the wooden floor of the shop and shouted, "Son! We have customers."

A giant man entered the shop from a back room. He ducked his head to fit beneath the door frame and ambled to the register. He looked at Max, who growled at him from the store's entrance, and placed a metal two-pronged device on the counter. "I can help you here," he said.

Once Mysti had walked away, Ms. Bloom stated, "Follow me."

"How will you get a feather?" asked Jailyn.

Ms. Bloom shushed her, pulled her into a large room, and closed the door behind them. Jailyn surveyed the room and covered her face to protect herself from the smell. Organic bits floated in jars on shelving that lined the walls. A dark vine with pink diamond shapes along its trunk grew from the floor to the ceiling. Jailyn screamed and backed against the door when the vine moved and slithered onto the floor.

Ms. Bloom jerked her head out of a large, ancient chest. "Oh," Ms. Bloom said. Her belly bounced up and down as she chuckled. "Don't be afraid. That's my pet, Lima. He won't hurt ya."

Jailyn sat on a high-backed, overstuffed chair and pulled her feet up to her knees. The old woman's pet propelled itself across the floor on dozens of tiny legs and moved in her direction. Lima swirled its body around the chair's legs and looked up at Jailyn. Its breath burned hot against her naked ankle. It slithered closer; four little legs alighted on her boot. Lima began to hum a strange little tune.

"Lima!" Ms. Bloom shouted without lifting her body, now buried deep in the chest. "You leave her alone."

Lima snorted as it backed away, and a puff of vapor rose from its nostrils. Jailyn covered her face. The haze burned her nose and made her cough.

"Got it!" Ms. Bloom backed out of the chest and slammed down the lid. She held a shiny tool with two hooked ends.

"What is that?" Jailyn asked.

"Will only hurt a little," the old woman said. She held two fingertips an inch apart. "Just a little."

"Let me see what I get with the deal," Jailyn said. Ms. Bloom frowned and shuffled back to the chest.

Someone pounded on the door; both women jumped in response. Jailyn recognized the sound of Max's agitated padding against the floor, and she opened the door for her companions, which forced Ms. Bloom's squirming pet to backtrack.

"What are you doing?" Mysti demanded. She held Max's fur in one hand and her shopping bags in the other.

"Ms. Bloom wants to make a trade. One of my feathers for a bottle of medicine."

"No," Mysti said and shook her head. She reached forward and squeezed Jailyn's hand, "You cannot give her any part of you."

"Why not?" Jailyn asked. She looked between the two women.

Ms. Bloom's cheeks were reddened. "She needs the medicine, Ms. Mysti," she said and tucked the tool into the folds of her thick skirt.

Mysti looked to Jailyn and said, "There is no need to give away a feather." She glared at Ms. Bloom, held up a small leather purse and said, "I can pay you for the medicine or get the product elsewhere."

"I will only take a feather." Ms. Bloom put her hands in the pockets of her skirt. "Besides, she needs the potion far more than one of her feathers now," Ms. Bloom said and displayed a small bottle filled with golden liquid.

Mysti smiled and winked at Jailyn. "We won't be needing any of that. You see, we already have some."

"You will want more." Ms. Bloom said to Jailyn as she put the bottle away and slammed the lid. She bent down and let Lima slither up her arms to rest across her shoulders. "I can't promise the price will be the same."

"Why do you say I will want more?" Jailyn asked. She pushed her heels into the floor in order to stop Mysti from pulling her back out of the room.

"I'm afraid that depends on things I can't foresee. Like

how much you enjoy breathing easy, or if you prefer to endure pain or avoid it altogether."

Jailyn turned away from the woman and followed Mysti back to the street. "Why did you stop me?"

"It was something Sams told me once. He was in his natural form and I was teasing with him and pulled on one of his wings. He pushed me away, with some force, I may add. He said," Mysti gave a half-smile, lowered her voice, and pursed her lips in order to mock Sams, "'losing a feather in Shifting Plains would be disadvantageous.'"

"Why?" Jailyn asked.

"He didn't expand on why, sorry." Mysti said. She handed Jailyn a large orange melon. "Let's stay together from now on, shall we?"

They walked down the street carrying their goods. The scent of food permeated the air and something familiar made Jailyn's mouth water. She realized that she was both thirsty and hungry.

Mysti handed Jailyn the small bottle of potion from Sams. "The good news, Jailyn, is that we will see Sams soon. You can ask him yourself." Mysti stopped before a food stand to buy them some sweet, fruity drinks. "Don't get your hopes up though. He rarely gives a detailed answer."

The group moved with their beverages to sit in a rundown gazebo at the edge of the market. They each chose a bench, and Jailyn watched Mysti pick several of the small pink flowers hanging down from the structure's roof. Max lay on a step, stretched in the sunshine, and watched the passersby enter and leave the marketplace entrance.

Jailyn took the small bottle from her pocket and rolled

it in her hand. She stared at its contents that shimmered in a small sunspot that eased through a hole in the gazebo's ceiling. Jailyn savored the clean-tasting drink and felt her body awaken with each sip. The air felt healing to her, but she remained in the shade, hoping to avoid a recurrence of the morning's sun reaction.

"What are you waiting for, Jailyn?" Mysti asked.

"I will," Jailyn said. She took another long sip of her drink and shrugged. "I just don't trust Sams, Mysti. And I really don't trust that old lady with the creepy pet."

"Then trust me," Mysti said.

Jailyn returned Mysti's gaze. Mysti was seated cross-legged on the bench. Small pieces of greying hair floated in the breeze and danced against her small face. Max groaned and rolled onto his back to feel the sunshine on his belly.

Jailyn busied herself with stirring her drink then turned around to look at the mountains in the distance. The orange sun began its descent to end the day. Two large, winged animals circled each other in the sky and took turns singing a haunting melody. "What are those creatures, the ones in the sky?" Jailyn asked.

"Sams calls them 'lopers,'" Mysti replied. "Their song makes me sad. I wish they would be silent."

"I like it. I think the sound is soothing," Jailyn said. She watched the animals as they danced about each other. They seemed oblivious of anything else living except themselves. The lopers' feathers were purple, and their wings shimmered when they hit the light.

Max jumped to his feet and barked, breaking the stillness of the moment. Mysti groaned and said, "When will I learn to trust my instincts?"

Two tall, lumbering men walked in their direction. The leading man wielded a two-pronged instrument. Mysti and Jailyn took in their surroundings and exchanged glances when they realized they were trapped.

"Let's jump over the railing." Mysti whispered and pushed Jailyn to the side. Both women hopped over the railing and landed in the dust. Jailyn helped Mysti get to her feet and pulled her in a wide arc in an effort to get past the men and back into the marketplace.

Max closed the gap between the women and the attackers, snarling, drool splattering the ground. One of the men raced forward and attempted to grab Mysti, but she ducked below him then stumbled backwards.

Jailyn's attacker failed an attempt to feign left and Jailyn's fist struck him in the jaw. He laughed and said, "Is that all you got?" The giant man grabbed her by the arms and lifted her at least seven feet off the ground.

"Put me down," she shouted and wriggled to loosen his grip. He tightened his hold, and Jailyn's sides and stomach burned.

"Jack! Look what I caught!" he shouted. His rancid breath made her gag.

"You will put her down now. I know where you work, remember? You know who protects me. You can say goodbye to your mother's store," Mysti shouted. Max remained by her side, holding off the man named Jack.

Jack laughed and whipped the silver instrument above his head in a coiling motion. It emitted a low hum that elevated to a high-pitched whine. He made several jabs at

Max with the prong, but the animal was fast and able to dodge his attempts.

In a swift move, Max tore a chunk out of Jack's leg. He screamed but recovered and shouted at Max, "You are one dead beast!" He wound the silver prong several times in the air and came at Max with a vengeance.

"Run, Max!" Mysti shouted, but the animal would not back down. He snarled, showed bloody white fangs, and pounded his paws against the packed earth. Max's eyes came aglow and emitted a dark red light. Max circled Jack and inched ever closer.

Jack's muscles tensed and he swung at Max, who jumped out of the way and leapt into the air. Jack screamed as blood poured from the side of his face. Max spat an ear onto the ground.

"Someone help us," Mysti shouted. "Don't you people know who I am?" The onlookers kept their distance, most of them small, old, or both.

"Should they?" a voice said behind them.

The giant dropped Jailyn onto the hard ground, which knocked the wind out of her. She heard their assailants' boots hit the pavement as they fled. Jailyn lay still for a moment, unable to breathe. A gloved hand appeared before her face. Jailyn stared at the hand until the fingers snapped and a voice said, "Perhaps I'm mistaken? It just seems logical to me that you would like to get off the ground."

Jailyn took the hand and was yanked to her feet at a dizzying speed. She glanced at Mysti, who was pale and holding onto Max. Jailyn shielded her eyes from the sun as she looked upward into the face of a man in dark clothing.

He stood still, watching her, and she saw her scared, dusty reflection in his sunglasses. The man's eyes glowed red even behind his shades. Jailyn stumbled backward a few paces to put distance between them. She had been handled enough for one day.

"So, Mysti, who is your little friend?" he asked and placed his hand on Mysti's shoulder. Max attempted to push him away from her, but the man whipped Max across the face with a black cane. Max flew into the air and landed with a thud. Mysti screamed, but Max hopped back to his feet, shook off the landing, and padded back to her. The man held out his hand and, with an unseen force, kept the dog at bay. Jailyn watched in amazement as the animal appeared to run into an invisible wall, over and over.

Jailyn glanced over at Mysti, whose eyes filled with tears as she watched Max struggle. Jailyn felt an anger rising within her. "Why did you intervene with our dilemma only to continue harassing us?"

"It's my job to keep our market safe."

Jailyn's stomach twisted at the sound of his voice. She knew this was not the first time she had faced this man before. "Leave them alone. It's clear you are here for me."

The man smiled. "You are housed with Mysti, I see."

"What business is that of yours?" Jailyn asked. She felt Mysti tug on the back of her shirt.

"All business here is mine," he said.

Jailyn looked around. People had been milling about when they arrived, but now the street was empty; even the shopkeepers had left their wares unattended.

The man leaned in and looked into her eyes. Jailyn felt

a hate rise within her. "How do I know you?" she asked.

"Me?" the man asked. He raised his hands in the air and cocked his head to the side. "We've never met. But, I can assure you we will meet again. After all, I know where to find you."

Mysti rocked in her chair, the swaying motion soothing her from the day's events. Max sat at her feet and licked his wounds. An angry red line that ran from his left eye and across his nose would mar his face forever.

When they had returned, Mysti had fed Jailyn a snack and put her to bed. Their journey home was arduous. In the clearing, Jailyn again lost her breath and turned blue for a moment. She had recovered after several tense minutes, and the three returned just as the last bit of the day's light extinguished.

The sound of the lopers grated Mysti's nerves. "Why can't I have just one night on the porch without that sound?" she said aloud and rubbed her aching temples. The birds' song intensified as if to purposefully anger her. It seemed to twist in the air and wind its way down through the forest and swim through the breeze to her home.

Max whined and Mysti stopped rocking. She laid her bare feet on the cool wood and called him to her. He staggered to his feet and placed his nose in her palm. Mysti met his eyes for a moment. Their color was dull.

"I don't know what I would do without you," she whispered. "You have kept me safe all these years." Mysti wiped her hand across Max's head then rubbed her thumb down the bridge of his nose. "I have aged. Have you also, my friend? Or are you timeless like Sams?"

Max wagged his tail against the wood. He placed a paw on Mysti's lap and pushed his large head beneath her chin. "I wish you could talk, Max. I wish you could tell me who I am and what I said when I came out of the puddle. Did I remember something like Jailyn?"

Max abruptly hopped off her lap and barked into the darkness. Mysti rose from her chair and squinted into the front yard. She moved toward the door in case she needed to get them inside.

"It's just me," a voice called from the darkness. Mysti heard Sams open the gate.

She patted Max on the head and motioned for him to lie back down, which he did without hesitation. Mysti returned to her chair and watched Sams approach. He retracted his wings with a pop and returned to the form she cherished. He walked in a brisk pace, never taking his eyes off of her.

He leapt up onto the porch and when he reached her, scooped her up into his arms and pulled her to him. "I'm sorry I wasn't there," he said.

Mysti shoved her face into his chest and breathed in his familiar scent. She felt herself begin to cry, and he held her tighter. "I wish you had been." She sobbed and felt regret claw its way into her chest. She hated her dependency on Sams.

Sams lowered her so that she was flat on her feet. He lifted her chin so he could look at her face. Mysti felt hot tears course down her cheeks. "Zyne was there."

"I know," Sams said. Mysti could see the muscles of his jaws working; the corners of his mouth lowered. He placed her face between his warm hands and, leaning over, kissed her cheek then her forehead, and then her lips.

Sams lifted away and closed his eyes for a moment. "He promised me he would never hurt you."

"He didn't. Not permanently," Mysti said. She stepped back and looked into his face. His blue eyes were filled with tears. Mysti stared at him for a moment then said, "I thought he was going to kill Max."

"We could find you another Max, Mysti." Sams said gesturing to the open air. "There is no replacement for you."

"No," she said, tears resurfacing. "There is no other Max, Sams. He's my companion. Max is there when I have breakfast, work in the garden, go to the market…"

Sams interrupted. "Haven't I also kept you from harm?" He ran his hands through his unbound silver hair and paced to the end of her porch. He stood like a statue with his back to her and stared into the nothingness of the night.

The lopers began singing again. Mysti covered her face with her hands and took a deep breath. The vague scent of her garden reached her nose and brought with it a bit of calm.

After a few tense moments, she called to him, "Sams." He turned to meet her gaze and leaned against the frame of the house. Moonlight enveloped his face; the luminescent quality of his eyes seemed to radiate within the glare. Her eyes fell to his tailored vest, admiring how the clothing hugged his slim waist. She could see his chest rise with each steady breath.

Mysti averted her eyes for a moment to break away from his spell and said, "Why would Zyne promise you anything? Especially about me?"

Sams stood and took measured steps to close the distance between them. His hair fell behind his shoulders as he crossed the porch. He put his hands in the pockets of his pants and stopped less than a foot from her. He gazed into her eyes and she felt warmth cascade into her face and glide down her body. Mysti could feel the muscles in her shoulders release. The air sweetened and refreshed her mind, easing her worries.

Sams wrapped his hand behind her back and pressed her to him. He placed the side of his face to her cheek and whispered in his language. She could not understand what he said, but her knees begin to tremble in response to the soothing tones.

He kissed her cheek and began to speak in words she understood. "I will not fail to persuade those of power in this land, or any other place, if it means keeping you with me. My whole purpose is to keep you safe. And with me."

Mysti was weak and her vision blurred, "Why do you not help me...help me get to my home place if you love me so? We don't even know my real name. At least Jailyn has that."

"We cannot be together in that place," Sams said. "I'm sorry, Mysti. But I would die without you now."

Mysti pushed away from him and stepped back. She put her back to a column for support. "You speak as if you hold me captive! At least tell me how I got here. You owe me that much."

Sams shook his head and straightened his posture. "Come here, Mysti. I mean you no harm, woman."

"No," she said. "Not this time, not until you give me some answers."

"This is your home, here with me." Sams said.

"Shifting Plains isn't even your home!" Mysti said. She walked over to him and put her hands on the sides of his face. "If you linger here more than a day you start to get sick. Please, don't pretend that you leave because you have business to attend to elsewhere. It makes a mockery of us both."

He glared over her head for a moment, then spoke, "It's true that Shifting Plains makes me sick. But haven't you noticed that over the years, I've stayed longer? It's because of you. My antidote."

Mysti shook her head. "Why can't we be together in my homeland?"

Sams grabbed her arms and closed his fingers around them. He moved his face so that his lips hovered above hers and whispered, "You are safer and happier here than you could be anywhere else. Trust me. I know what is best for you."

Mysti felt a familiar quiet envelop her body. She looked into Sams eyes. They were radiant, and she felt he could read her innermost imaginings. Mysti thought of her bed. She recalled the crispness of the sheets, the smell of her quilt, how its weight pressed down on her while she slept.

Sams said, "Want me to take you upstairs?"

She raised her hand and slapped his face with as much force as she could manage. "You will not play games with my mind. Not tonight. I've cowered for years because I was alone. Not anymore. I want answers."

Sams stepped back and covered the side of his face with his hand. He stared at her for a moment, then crossed his arms across his chest, a flat look covering his features.

"Speak to me!" Mysti said. She glanced away for an instant, then turned her body and punched him in the waist. That beautiful and perfect waist had distracted her during many of these conversations. "If you want to continue this relationship, you will be straight with me."

She backed away, clutching her fists. Sams remained still; only redness in his cheeks belied he had felt her assault.

Max stumbled to her. She patted him and felt a surge of guilt when her hand touched dried blood, left over from the afternoon's struggle.

"You are acting like a child." Sams took several steps in her direction.

"Don't come near me," Mysti screamed. She grabbed a potted plant and threw it in his direction. Sams deflected the plant and tried to grab her. She ducked beneath his arm and jumped off the porch.

Mysti raced down her stone walkway and through the gate. Out of the corner of her eye, she saw Max leap the fence in order to follow her. She ran as fast as she was able; small rocks cut into her bare feet.

"This is pointless." Sams popped out of the sky into her path. He placed his hands on her shoulders.

Mysti fought against him and said through clenched

teeth, "Let go of me." Dust kicked up into her face as Max approached at full speed.

"Stupid beast," Sams kicked the animal and said to Mysti, "Would you call him off?" To Max he said, "I'm not going to hurt her, you dumb mutt. Back away!"

"I love you, Sams, but I'm done with you lording over me," Mysti said and found Sams' hand. She dug her fingernails into the skin and was satisfied when he screamed, loosening his grip just enough that she was able to free herself.

She ran in the direction of her shack. Mysti imagined how she might keep Sams out while she was safe inside. Her bare feet found the prickly needles at the edge of the forest. She entered the path and within seconds was in total darkness.

Her steps slowed. A sickening realization washed over her when she realized that even if she could find her way through the darkness, there was no way to keep Sams out of the structure. Mysti's chest heaved as sobs overtook her. A familiar vague longing sunk its way into her mind and heart.

Sams approached her from behind. He chuckled and said, "Why stop now? We could do this all night."

"What must I do to make you treat me as your equal?" Mysti asked.

"You are my equal," Sams replied. "Mysti, don't you realize I'm here for you? It's what keeps me coming back to this place."

She turned to face him and said, "Tell me why you keep me here."

"I knew you and came to love you in your home world.

I sent you here," Sams said. He placed his hand on her back and walked her away from the forest. "In Shifting Plains, we can be together." Mysti did not resist. She let his words sink in. He was finally going to talk to her.

Sams led her back through the gate and across the yard to her garden. They each sat on one of the stones placed around the small goldfish pond. Mysti watched Sams as he withdrew a thin leather strap from his pocket and tied his hair back. The lopers were silent; the only sounds Mysti could hear were those of the tinkling waterfall at the edge of the pool. Max padded to the pond and took a deep drink. He snorted in Sams' direction, then lay at Mysti's feet.

Mysti's thoughts began to race when Sams remained silent. He stared at the water, not even glancing in her direction. She forced herself to ask, "So, you brought me here?"

He sighed and traced his fingers over the water. The bright scales of the fish glowed in the moonlight as they swam near the surface. "Yes. I had known you for years. My love for you did not wane with the passing of time. Mysti..." He met her stare. "I have no doubt that I did right by you."

"How is that? Did I have family, friends? What do they think happened to me?"

"You would be dead now if I had left you in that world. You had family. But, they placed you in peril. I could stand for it no longer."

Mysti shook her head and tried to think through her fears. She thought about her dreams of the children and felt her heart bang against the inside of her chest. Despite her best efforts to steady her voice, Mysti's tone wavered. "Did

I have children?"

He looked away from her and spoke to himself in his language. He remained turned away from her and said, "No."

She relaxed somewhat and asked, "Will you ever take me home?"

Sams shook his head. "There is nothing for you there."

Mysti gasped when he dropped to his knees in front of her. Tears streamed down his face. "I'll take you anywhere you want to go in this world. I'll find a way to stay in Shifting Plains longer. Whatever it takes to keep you happy." He took her hands and wove his fingers through hers, "The only thing I won't do is return you to a world that will snuff you out before your time."

Mysti smiled at him and kissed his forehead. He wrapped his arms around her waist, pulled her to him, and kissed her. She returned his kiss and, for the moment, was grateful that at least after so many years he had begun to talk to her.

"Why did you wait so long to tell me?" she asked.

"I've wanted you to have a new start here. One without memories of your past life. No fears, just a feeling of comfort with me."

"Did I love you back?" Mysti asked. "When we were in my home world?"

"Yes," he said. "I'm sure of it."

Jailyn woke up to the smell of breakfast cooking. Her body felt like a raisin, withered and dehydrated. She dragged her feet step-by-step across the hall into the bathroom. Jailyn grimaced at her own reflection. Her face was ashen. Wrinkles adorned her forehead, and her lips were white and thin.

She soaked in Mysti's hot bathtub until she could no longer ignore her hunger. Jailyn dressed in loose jeans and fitted cotton shirt, then descended the stairs with care. When she was halfway down she was able to view Mysti's front yard through the window above the doorway. The landscape seemed to mock her. Sunshine reflected on the surface of the goldfish pond. Mysti's garden seemed to have flourished overnight. Tall blue and yellow flowers swayed in a light breeze.

"Well, look who's up!" Sams stood at the bottom of the staircase, a steaming cup of tea in hand.

She turned to go back upstairs, but Mysti approached and said, "Come eat. I promise, Jailyn, he won't bite."

Sams stepped into the kitchen and paused to smooth back Mysti's hair when she passed. Jailyn watched Mysti smile in response to his touch.

Jailyn took a place at the table opposite Sams. Mysti patted her on the back and handed her a bowl that contained a mixture of nuts and berries. She then placed a basket of warm bread on the table. Sams removed a small bottle from his pocket and swallowed the contents. Jailyn took a bite of her berries and kept her eyes on the man sitting across from her.

Sams held up the empty bottle and said, "You should be drinking this as well." He grabbed a slice of bread and spread strawberry jam across the surface. He took a bite and smiled at Jailyn. "You look terrible. You will only get worse, you know?"

Jailyn looked down at her bowl. Her fingers trembled. She was hungry, but the berries and fresh juice failed to revive her. She watched Sams. He ate his bread and surveyed Mysti's every move. Mysti joined them at the table by seating herself in Sams' lap.

Mysti looked at her and said, "Please, Jailyn. Won't you try it? You look awful, especially considering you slept almost ten hours."

Jailyn removed the small bottle she had carried with her for days. She looked at Sams and said, "I don't trust you. How do I know this won't make me sick?"

Sams shrugged, "We are the same species. If you want to continue feeling like a dishrag, by all means, don't drink the potion. It's all the same to me." Jailyn watched Mysti frown in his direction, and Mysti whispered that he could be kind or leave.

Jailyn ate her berries, then excused herself and went outside to the porch. She sat in the rocking chair, but was forced to sit still because the rocking motion made her nauseous. After several moments, Mysti walked onto the porch holding a small bag. She wore a long skirt that breezed in the wind, a light scarf around her neck and a wide-brimmed hat on her head.

Sams hopped off the porch and walked across the yard to stand in the shade. He donned a hat as well and had put on a light long-sleeved jacket. "Sams is finally taking me to the mountains."

Jailyn felt a leap of hope in her chest. "The mountains?"

"Yes," Mysti said. She held up one finger at Sams and he nodded understanding. "Jailyn," Mysti whispered. "Sams finally disclosed some things to me last night."

"Oh?"

"We had a bad fight. But, the drama was worth it because he confessed to bringing me here to Shifting Plains."

Jailyn let her mouth drop open. "What?"

"I'm really hoping to get more information out of him. He's feeling a little guilty right now, so he has finally agreed to take me to the mountains. I've heard talk in town about a beautiful waterfall there."

Jailyn nodded and said, "That sounds nice."

"Do you think you will be okay if I leave you alone for the day?" Mysti asked. She slung her bag over her shoulder and said, "I've left you some lunch on the counter. And I can leave Max here if you'd like. I think he needs his rest anyway."

Jailyn nodded and said, "I will be fine. You've babysat me enough." She watched Mysti descend the porch steps, then hopped up from her chair and grabbed her wrist. "Do you think you could take me to see that waterfall another day? Could we take a trip to the mountains?"

Mysti laughed and hugged Jailyn, "Of course!"

Jailyn watched the pair leave. Max shuffled up beside her chair and whined as he watched Mysti fade from their sight. She looked over at the black beast, who returned her gaze. From her seated position, their eyes were parallel. "You are one big pet, Max," Jailyn said. He leaned closer to her, his breath on her face. She decided against petting him.

She rose from her chair and walked to Mysti's pond. The fish moved with ease under the cool, clear water. Jailyn sat on a smooth rock and ran her hand across the dark green grasses. Her fingers stumbled upon a clear cylindrical object. She picked it up and felt a surge of power race across her hands. She walked to stand beneath a shade tree to examine her find.

There was a tiny engraving of a bird on the object. "Where did this come from?" she wondered aloud. Her hand tingled, so she put the clear piece in the opposite hand. It too began to feel prickly, as if the blood had momentarily been cut off and was now returning to the appendage.

Jailyn held the object to her ear and dropped it to the ground. She retrieved it at once and held it to her ear again. There was a gentle humming vibration that tickled her ear. She slipped the object into her pocket, but not before double-checking to ensure the pocket was secure and without holes.

She resolved to go on an adventure of her own for the day and returned to the house. A few nights before, Mysti had told her about her own arrival to Shifting Plains and the little shack that had both comforted and haunted. Jailyn had a strong desire to see the place where they had each entered Shifting Plains, but she held small hope it would provide any answers.

After retrieving a container of water and bagging her lunch, she left to go for a walk to the shack. "Wanna go, boy?" she called to Max. The animal snorted and lay down on the porch with his back to her.

"Suit yourself," she called. She snatched a wide-brimmed hat and Mysti's gardening gloves to cover her face and hands. When she shut the gate behind her, Jailyn turned back to look at Mysti's house. The structure stood tall in the day's light. The sun brightened the blue shutters and lightened the white paint that covered most of the exterior. The rocking chairs and porch swing lilted in the breeze. Max lay unmoving on the porch. Jailyn wondered if she would be here forever. She hoped not.

Jailyn touched her pockets to ensure the potion bottle lay in one side and the clear wing-engraved object lay in the other. Once satisfied that she was prepared, she set out through the forest.

As the thick trees blotted out much of the sunlight, the air was cool and damp. Mysti's boots were too big for Jailyn's feet, so she stumbled a few times on roots hidden beneath the foliage. The path forked, and for a moment, Jailyn worried that she had chosen the wrong direction. Just as her heart began to pound in her chest, she emerged from the path into the clearing.

She walked up a hill covered in yellow flowers and abuzz with small pink birds that jumped from plant to plant. One of them hovered at the side of her face, and she heard its tiny wings flapping. Jailyn put a hand out to the tiny creature. The bird chirped, touched the palm of her hand in an instant, and then flew away.

Jailyn picked a few of the flowers and breathed their scent in deeply. She bundled them in her hand and crested the hill. Just below her in an open valley, set before the glorious mountain range, was the little shack Mysti had told her about. She smiled to herself and after a quick survey of the land below her, jogged down the hill. She was able to stop herself from falling at the bottom but dropped a few of her flowers.

She stepped onto the porch then turned back for a moment to survey the land behind her. Jailyn wiped dust away from a bedroom window and looked inside. She could make out art on the wall and to her left, small sculptures on a wood stove. It was exactly as Mysti had described it.

Jailyn hovered at the door of the shack for a moment and felt a pang of regret. She hoped Mysti would not feel her privacy had been invaded. She decided to apologize later if that was the case and walked into the shelter.

In the front room, Mysti had left at least a dozen small sculptures. It was clear that Mysti's skill was improving, as there was a progression in the clarity of the details in each piece. Jailyn held one up to the light. "Max," she whispered.

Jailyn walked into the back room and gasped when she saw the view of the mountains through the plate glass window. Mysti had mentioned the window, but had not spent enough time on the details. Jailyn put her hands on the window and leaned in, letting her nose touch the pane. She pressed her eyelids together to enhance her vision and was surprised to see a tall, sharp-edged structure pressed against the mountainside. She wondered at its purpose.

The mountains seemed to call to her, as if they were her home. She shook her head. "Your home is far from here. You can feel it," she said to herself. Still, Jailyn could not tear herself from the window. The clouds rolled across the sky, creating blotches of light and dark on the colored trees. The sun was high in the sky when she heard her stomach growl.

Jailyn walked about the shelter as she ate her food. She cracked open the door, and once ensuring it appeared safe, stepped onto the porch. The air was warm, and she took a deep breath. Right away, she began to cough and sputter so violently that she had to spit her food out for fear of choking.

Her eyes burned and she stumbled off the porch, falling into a heap onto the ground.

"Are you okay?" a small voice said.

Jailyn forced herself to a standing position and stepped back onto the porch. Through her blurred vision, Jailyn could make out a small female figure. She sputtered again and said, "Wait here." She went inside and raced to get a sip of her water from the back room.

Jailyn returned to the porch. The little girl was seated on the porch steps. She smiled at Jailyn's approach and stood, smoothing her blue sundress in the process.

"Hi," she said and offered to shake Jailyn's hand.

Jailyn moved as close as necessary to shake her hand, then stepped back a few paces. The girl watched her. Jailyn tried in vain to read her face, but it was devoid of any telling emotions.

"My name is Lacey. What's your name?"

"I'm Jailyn." She stared for a few moments at the little girl, who began to wring her hands while she waited.

"I live at the base of the mountain." Lacey walked around the front of the shack and pointed behind it. "The one over there."

Jailyn thought about how much she wanted to see the mountain. Her heart quickened and she asked, "Have you always lived here? In Shifting Plains, I mean."

"Sure," the girl scrunched her nose. "But you haven't always lived here, have you?"

Jailyn forced a smile, "I guess that means I look quite the tourist."

"No, not at all. I just hear things where I live, that's all," Lacey said with a wide smile. She was missing her two front teeth. Her short, straw-colored hair surrounded eyes as dark as midnight. "Wanna see where I live? I have a short cut. Only I know about it."

Jailyn hesitated. "Could I be back here before nightfall?"

"Oh, yes. If we go now, you can be home before it's time for dinner."

Jailyn asked, "Is there a waterfall near where you live?"

"It's a little out of the way, but we can take a detour if you want to see it."

"No, that's okay, I'd actually prefer to avoid it," Jailyn said. "Will your people mind my showing up?"

Lacey looked at her and winked, "Oh, they are boring. Why don't I just take you to where I play? It's lots of fun." The girl took her hand and led her behind the shack. When they reached the bottom of a hill, there was a small parting in the tall grasses.

Jailyn watched the girl in silence for a few moments. Lacey hummed a tune with no recurring theme and stooped once in a while to touch the ground with the tips of her fingers. She glanced back at Jailyn and giggled even though there was no obvious amusement. Jailyn's stomach jerked in nervousness, and she wondered what path she had stepped onto with this little Shifting Plains native.

The pair made their way down a steep incline through a wooded area. Lacey took Jailyn's hand when they entered a small clearing and had to cross over a wide creek. "Just follow me and you won't get wet."

When they reached the creek's center, Jailyn paused and pointed to the mountain. At the base, she could now make out the individual leaves on the trees. "On the side of the mountain, are those cabins?"

"Yes," Lacey said. "But, that's not where we are going. I'll be taking you up to that tower." She gestured to the industrial black structure Jailyn had seen earlier from the shack's window. The building seemed to reach for the sky.

When they reached the sandy bank, Jailyn began to cough. She sat down in the rock laden sand and tried to catch her breath. Her hands turned cold, and the sunlight stung against her skin.

Lacey knelt down and met Jailyn's eyes. She stretched her hands out to Jailyn and sang, "*Come, come, my little friend. We are together until the end.*"

"*You and I, me and you, being without you makes me blue.*" Jailyn surprised herself by finishing the little tune. Lacey pulled her up from the ground with so much force that she almost fell forwards. "You are strong for such a little thing."

Lacey smiled and nudged her toward the cluster of trees at the base of the tower. "That's an impressive structure," Jailyn said and paused when they reached the building to look up. She could just make out the top of the tower, which had tall spires on each corner.

"Wait until you see the inside. That's where the fun is." Lacey smiled. "You aren't the easily scared type, are you?"

"I'm not sure if I'm skittish, but I am sure this feels like a bad idea."

"There's no fun in life if you never do anything that scares you," Lacey said.

When the pair reached the structure, Jailyn watched Lacey scan the area behind them and asked, "Are we allowed to go in here?"

Lacey placed her ear against a circular lock and turned it until there was a click and the metal gave way to create an oval door. She dug a torch from beneath a nearby bush then took Jailyn's hand and pulled her into darkness, shutting the door behind them. Lacey reached into her pocket, took out a small stick, and then scraped it against the wall. A bright red flame lit the area and illuminated the narrow, twisting stairwell.

Jailyn sneezed a few times in the damp air as they ascended. She could feel bumps rise on her skin and a chill flash down her spine. "What is this place?"

Lacey placed her fingers over her lips and whispered, "Must talk softly. We don't want him to hear us."

Jailyn felt her neck muscles tense. A faint blue light emerged and shone on the stairwell, then on Lacey's face when she turned back to look at her. "Turn down your eyes, Jailyn!"

"What?" Jailyn paused and held her hand in front of her face. Her eyes were glowing blue. "I'm not sure how to. Maybe we should just go back."

"No," Lacey snapped. "We haven't gotten to the fun part."

"Which is?" Jailyn asked.

"The man who lives in this tower keeps his treasures locked away here. They are lots of fun to look at." Lacey paused and placed her hand on Jailyn's shoulder. "We don't want to see him though. He's so scary, just the sound of his voice makes you want to run away and scream. The sight of him makes grown men wet their pants."

Jailyn glanced back in the direction of the tower's entrance. The light from her eyes alone would not be enough to guide her down the steps.

"You said you were bringing me to the place you play. This is where you play?" Jailyn asked. Lacey shrugged her shoulders and resumed climbing the stairs.

They approached what appeared to be a dead end. Lacey knelt down and placed her hand on a piece of ground adjacent to the smooth interior wall. There was a *click* and a chunk of the wall shook, then swung inward, making just enough space for them to pass through.

"Wait," Jailyn said to Lacey. "Tell me more about this

man. Who is he?"

"He's the Darkness. Black hair, black eyes, black soul. He even dresses in black."

"How old is he, then? Is he a young man or an old one?" Jailyn asked.

Lacey held the torch close to Jailyn and examined her face. "I'm not sure. Maybe somewhere in the middle. Like you." Lacey took her hand and pulled her into a small, open space.

Jailyn grabbed Lacey's arms and squeezed. "Is this man named Zyne?"

Lacey smiled, "That's the one."

"Oh, no. I've seen enough of him to last a lifetime." Jailyn stumbled in her effort to get out of the tower, but Lacey raced ahead of her and cut between her and the stairway.

"I'm leaving whether you want me to or not, little girl," Jailyn said through clenched teeth.

"Do you want to know about where you live or don't you?" Lacey grabbed Jailyn's wrist and, with overpowering strength, pulled her back through the opening. When they entered the area, a strong sense of familiarity washed down Jailyn's back. She slunk down the rock wall to seat herself on the cold floor. She folded her knees into her chest and felt something on her face. Jailyn wiped her cheek with her hand. It was damp with tears.

"Why are you crying?" Lacey asked in a whispered voice. She stood unmoving, the shadows of the torch's flames flickering across her tiny features.

"I feel such grief," Jailyn said. "I don't know why. As soon as we walked through that opening, it hit me like a breaker from the incoming tide."

"That doesn't make sense," Lacey said, her voice wavering. She stared down at Jailyn and said, "This place is new to you."

Jailyn pushed herself to a standing position. She placed a hand over her chest and felt her heart race beneath it. A faint whisper reached her ears. "*Jailyn. Go.*"

Lacey bit her fingernails and watched her from the corner of the small space. Jailyn returned the small child's gaze and walked to her. She pushed Lacey's bangs out of her eyes with a light touch. Lacey jumped back and said, "We should get moving."

Jailyn asked, "How do we know one another?"

"We don't," Lacey said and walked away, forcing Jailyn to catch up to her or be left in complete darkness.

The pair emerged into an open dimly lit circular area that contained six small rooms. Three were dark inside and appeared empty. The remaining spaces had occupants. The lighting in these spaces varied; one was bright as if lit by the sunshine. Jailyn looked to Lacey and whispered, "This is where you play?"

"Sometimes," Lacey said with a smirk. "It's pretty fun."

Lacey placed her torch in a holder at the room's entrance and nudged Jailyn toward the outer enclosure. Jailyn stopped about three feet from the glass. A large brown-furred beast was lying on a tattered blanket. It rose to its paws and sauntered over to greet them. The creature stared at Jailyn with golden eyes and placed his nose on the glass that fogged in response to his breath.

Jailyn longed to touch the beast's fur, to run the coarse

hair through her fingers. It leaned closer and emitted a low whine. She felt a catch in her chest. He was like Max.

Lacey pulled on Jailyn's shirt sleeve. "Wanna feed it?" She lifted her hand to Jailyn. It was filled with slim slices of dried meat.

"How?" Jailyn asked, taking the meat.

"Like this," Lacey opened a small trap door at the bottom of the glass. The beast glanced down at the opened door, then back at Jailyn. It snorted and pounded its front paws against the ground.

Jailyn took the meat from Lacey and fed it to the animal. Its whiskers ran across the top of her hand and she snatched it backward.

"Don't worry. He won't hurt you," Lacey said. She then put her tiny hand inside the enclosure, and the animal purred and rubbed his nose against her palm.

"Why is he in here?" Jailyn asked.

"He was one of Zyne's guardians. He failed to catch an escapee, so Zyne put him in here."

"When will he let him out?" Jailyn asked. She placed her hand against the glass. The animal leaned against it, eager for contact.

Lacey looked down at her hands and said, "Never. Disappointing Zyne will be anyone's last action." She emptied her pocket of beef, patted the animal on its head, and shut the trap door. The beast moaned and turned its head to the side. As they walked away, it followed them to the farthest reaching corner of its cell.

The middle cell held a large winged creature. It looked to be starving and paid them little attention, even when Lacey drummed on the glass. It glanced at them with its remaining eye and hissed, then turned his back to the pair. His once feathered back was now naked except for one lone feather still clinging to his emaciated skin.

The pair moved to the sunlit cell, and Lacey said, "This one is my favorite."

Soft grasses covered the floor and a tall, wide flower-covered tree stood in the middle. A tiny blue-skinned creature was seated on a wooden swing, hanging on a low lying branch. Pink flower petals tossed about in a warm breeze. The creature wore a silver dress; its skirts glided across the ground.

Jailyn knocked on the glass and waved. The creature made a startled noise and looked around. After a few moments, she resumed swinging. "She doesn't see us?" Jailyn said. She stepped a few paces backwards and admired the beauty of the small room.

"No," Lacey said. "She is forever trapped in the illusion that she is still safe at home." Lacey opened the trap door and shouted in, "Helloooo. How's the weather in there?"

The little creature hopped off the swing and began to cry out, "Avo, is that you?" She raced around the tree and looked up into its branches. She ran to the front of the glass with blinded eyes and shouted again, "Avo, where are you?"

Lacey started to shout something again, but Jailyn grabbed her arm and pulled her away, shutting the trap door. "You stop that right now, young lady." Jailyn twisted her arm upward and was surprised by how reflexive the action felt.

"Let go of me!" Lacey shouted and twisted her arm out of Jailyn's grasp. "I don't know who you think you are, but…"

Jailyn waited for Lacey to finish her sentence. When she did not, Jailyn stated, "Entertainment is no excuse for cruelty. You are old enough to know that. Besides, you clearly shouldn't be spending time in here. Waiting for this Zyne character to catch you here and put you in one of these cells."

"Oh, he wouldn't do that," Lacey stated and smiled up a Jailyn. Her dark eyes turned red, and she laughed in a throaty voice that was out of place for a young person. Lacey gripped Jailyn by the wrist, twisted the skin and whispered, "He loves me. More than anyone in my life has ever loved me." Without releasing her hold, Lacey pulled Jailyn outside of the room and back to the staircase. Instead of descending, she pulled them upward.

"I've seen enough, Lacey. Let's go back," Jailyn said and tried to resist the little girl's ferocious pull.

"I think the man in here would like to meet you. This part will be the most fun of all," Lacey said, her eyes a bright red.

They entered a room where a tall, slim dark-haired man was tied to a spire. Dried blood clung to his body, and he hung limp against his bindings. He appeared the same age as Jailyn. He raised his head and when his eyes met hers, they widened in horror. He shouted, "Jailyn, it's me, Nathan!"

Jailyn backed away and looked at Lacey, "How does he know who I am?"

Lacey did not respond. She took something out of her pocket and tossed it inside the man's cell. White, winged creatures flew against him and bit his skin. The man screamed from the pain and uttered words in a language Jailyn did not recognize, but she felt their dark intent.

She looked down at Lacey, whose face was no longer that of a little girl, but contorted into something else.

Jailyn looked back at the man, whose intent stare woke something in her. A picture of a smoke-filled colorful room flashed in her mind and then dissipated. She grabbed a torch from the wall and raced down the stairwell. Jailyn heard small feet padding after her. "Jaaillynn, let's keep playing."

Jailyn tripped down a few steps and landed on an open platform. She retrieved the torch and ran. She shut out all thoughts of anything save the fresh outdoor air.

Jailyn saw the door ahead of her and slammed her body into it. She screamed as she used all her available force, and once she reached the outside, she tossed down the torch and raced for the creek. She risked one glance backward when she crossed the water. A woman in leather watched her from the bank with a wide grin.

9

"Jailyn, wake up!" Jailyn opened her eyes and looked around. Her heart pounded in her chest as she tried to get her bearings. Jailyn was in the shack, lying on the floor. Mysti stood over her with a lamp. Otherwise, it was dark. Stars shone through the window. A vague painful memory of traveling to the mountain lingered in her mind. As she concentrated on a remembered string of events, the memory drifted away like wood smoke rises into the air.

"I'm...I'm sorry," Jailyn said and struggled to her feet. "I must have fallen asleep."

"When I got home and realized you weren't there, I was so worried. Max tracked you here," Mysti said. "How ever did you find this place? The directions I gave you were so vague."

Jailyn leaned against the wall. Her vision blurred. She gripped the wall as the room started to spin. "You must take this potion," Mysti said and removed the vial from her pocket. "I'll not stand for this any longer. Sams told me it's amazing you've lasted this long."

Jailyn took the bottle and rolled it around. She looked at Mysti, holding her lamp and Max behind her. "Okay," she said. "If you are certain it will be okay."

Mysti nodded and Jailyn downed the potion. It had a sharp, bitter taste, but she forced herself to swallow. After a few moments, Jailyn began to feel energized. She hugged Mysti then hopped off the porch into the night. She raced around in wide circles in the grass and breathed deeply, relishing the absence of the nagging cough.

When her legs began to shake, Jailyn slowed to a walk and returned to the shack. Mysti leaned against the door and stared at her with one corner of her mouth turned upwards.

"Mysti," Jailyn asked. "Where do you get the ideas for your art?"

"From dreams mostly." Mysti stood; her eyes darkened.

"Will you tell me about them? Especially the drawings on the wall," Jailyn asked and opened the door for them.

Mysti led the way with her lantern. It was muggy inside the shack and smelled of old, rotting wood. The shadows of their figures created an eerie ambiance.

Mysti held the lantern high to illuminate a crude painting of a large black bird. The image spanned the height of the wall. Its feet seemed to perch on the floor, and its beady eyes turned toward the window, as if watching for someone or something. "This was my first drawing. It came to me from a memory. At least, I'm pretty sure it was a memory."

"This bird intrigues me the most. It reminds me of home," Jailyn said. Mysti looked at her with a raised eyebrow. "Not of this horrid place, of course, but of my home. Maybe yours, too."

The two women stared at the painting. On each side of the bird stood a child of the same stature, one female and one male. "Tell me about these two?" Jailyn asked. She approached the wall and ran her hand across the female child's long ponytail.

"These paintings represent my biggest source of frustration," Mysti said. She placed her hand on the male child and smiled. "I've dreamed of these children several times. They both have hair as dark as tar and eyes the color of the sky on a clear summer day. They were so beautiful, Jailyn. In all the dreams, they stayed for a few silent moments, never saying a word."

Jailyn's thoughts raced. She pulled her fingers into fists, trying to suppress a tingling feeling in her hands. She noticed for the first time a strange scent in the air. It was like rotting meat lying below a hedge covered in sweet smelling flowers.

Jailyn reached into her pocket and withdrew the glass

sphere. "Mysti, I found this on the ground, next to your goldfish pond."

"Oh!" Mysti said and clapped her hands over her mouth. "Sams will be so glad you found it! He carries that with him wherever he goes."

Jailyn handed the piece to her. "Have you seen this?"

Mysti rubbed her finger across the engraving of a bird and held the piece next to the lantern. "It's a raven."

Jailyn took Mysti by the shoulders and turned her to the painting. "So is that."

Mysti shook her head and squeezed the object in her hand. "But what does this mean?"

"I think you are remembering," Jailyn said. "In fact, I think I'm remembering also. Earlier, a little girl took me on a walk to a tower by the mountain. I can't recall much else."

"Sams said there are no children in Shifting Plains," Mysti said and began pacing the length of the room.

"Does Sams know about this place?" Jailyn gestured to the shack.

"No," Mysti said.

"Why not?" Jailyn asked, placing a hand on Mysti's arm to gain her full attention.

"I don't trust him enough. Not with this," Mysti said. She began to cry again. "I'm so trapped. He's so good to me most of the time. I managed to get him to confess that he brought me to Shifting Plains, but he was quiet today. He swears that I would have died in my homeland, but something just doesn't feel right to me." Mysti gestured to her heart. "It doesn't settle here."

Jailyn took the piece from Mysti and examined it in the

torchlight. Her fingers tingled, and it seemed to warm in her hand. She tossed it up in the air a few times, each time a bit higher. Something occurred to her.

"Let's go outside." Jailyn grabbed Mysti's arm and pulled her outside. "Quick, bring the lantern here." She was not quite satisfied with the light, but decided to try anyway. Jailyn tossed the piece in the air. When she did, a string of unfamiliar words left her mouth. As soon as Jailyn closed her mouth, the cylinder transformed into a long, thin sword. It landed in her hand, and her fingers closed around it.

"I'll take that." Sams dropped from the sky. "You!" He pointed to Mysti. "Go inside. Do not come out until I tell you it's safe."

"Hello, Sams." Jailyn raised her weapon.

Sams stared at Jailyn, and she watched the color drain from his face.

"Perhaps you shouldn't have given me that potion. I'm beginning to feel quite new," Jailyn said. "And I'm starting to remember you." She pointed the tip of the sword in Sams' direction.

"Well, well. So, it's true the apple doesn't fall too far from the tree, eh? A family of failures." A thick knife appeared in Sams' grasp.

"What do you mean?" Jailyn demanded.

"Clara was supposed to seal your mind so nothing could re-open it. Of course, who knows? Maybe she did a shoddy job. It could flicker out any moment." Sams flapped his wings and hovered several inches above the ground.

"I'll cut you down, Jailyn. It will be easy for me," Sams said.

Jailyn slashed at Sams, but he darted away from her. Searing pain shot across her back as her wings struggled to open.

Sams landed on the ground just out of her reach. "Fighting me without wings is futile. You aren't even a match."

Mysti raced to Sams and pulled on his arm. "Please stop this madness. I'm sure Jailyn will give you back your sword. Let's go back to my house and talk it over."

A loud, shrieking sound pierced the night. All three put their hands over their ears. Max howled and ran in no particular direction. The sky appeared to crack open. Many lines streaked the dark sky to reveal a lighter lining on the outside. The sound elevated, trees popped, and the shack began to quake.

"Mysti!" Sams yelled and threw his arms around her. Max stood next to them and barked at the sky. The night lifted as the inner membrane peeled away, leaving a pink-tinged illumination.

Jailyn looked at the torn sky and clawed her chest in the midst of a sudden pang of grief. Her ring became white hot, burning her finger, and flashed a brilliant light that forced them to briefly shield their eyes. "Nathan!" she screamed into the sky, then fell into a heap on the ground.

The ring dimmed, leaving Jailyn's mind swirling with disjointed memories. Jailyn recalled her daughter, Clara, as a teenager slamming the door in her face; she remembered baking cookies in her kitchen on a rainy day, and thought of her husband's smile at their wedding. She sobbed when the images of her husband's death poured into her mind and those of her own defeat at the hand of their daughter.

Jailyn caught movement out of her left eye and saw Sams stumble toward her, struggling against the shaking earth. Jailyn lifted herself to a crouched position and raised her sword. She felt the Faith fill her weakened body and renew her strength. Jailyn winced when her wings repaired and popped back into position.

Mysti's voice was dim in the wind. "Please stop this fighting and let's get inside." She held on to Max for stability.

Jailyn dodged past Sams and ran to Mysti. "I remember." Tears filled her eyes. "I remember everything. About me. And about you. Sams is no friend."

Sams shoved Jailyn with such force that she slid across the grass and under the shack's porch. The sword landed out of her reach. He clenched his teeth and gestured to the sword and then to Mysti. "These are mine."

"Not anymore," Jailyn said. The glow from her eyes illuminated the night. Words from an unknown language bubbled out of her. She rolled away from the shack and kicked Sams in the face. Jailyn retrieved the sword and slashed at Sams, who attacked her from above.

Sams failed to see Max rush him, and he dropped his knife when the beast tore at his leg and pulled him to the ground. Mysti cried in the distance and called Max to her. Seizing her chance, Jailyn seized Sams' weapon and pierced his shoulder with it. Using all of her remaining strength, she buried it deep into the ground, pinning him. He screamed in pain and struggled to break free.

"Mysti, we must go now." Jailyn grabbed her by the arm and pulled her to the edge of the tree line.

"No," Mysti said. "I won't leave Sams here. I don't know who to trust, but I've known him longer. You seem to have lost your mind."

"Quite the contrary," Jailyn said. "I've recovered it. And I'll help you recover yours, but you must come with me."

Sams said, "Mysti, she is dangerous." His blood pooled on the ground as he wrestled to free himself.

"Why don't you call her by her real name?" Jailyn said.

"What?" Mysti said. She looked between Sams and Jailyn. Max stood at her feet, displaying his teeth.

Jailyn glanced at the tree line then back at Sams. He was beginning to ease the knife from the dirt. "Max, go stand over him." The animal glanced at her, then seemed to understand and moved to glare down at Sams with bared teeth.

Jailyn beckoned to Mysti. "Quickly, follow me." Jailyn led her into the room with the wall painting. She held the lamp near the image and met Mysti's wide eyes through tears in her own and said, "I know who you are, Lilly Raven."

"What?" Mysti took several steps backward.

Jailyn gestured to the wall. "Look at your painting. When you first arrived, some part of you remembered. This raven is your family's symbol. It's everywhere in our city."

Mysti said, "How do I know I can trust you? Believe anything you tell me?"

"I'm not sure how to prove to you that you can, and we don't have long." Jailyn lowered the lamp and placed it to the side. "Do you want me to tell you what I know?"

Mysti wiped tears from her face and nodded. Jailyn's words raced together. "You belong to the powerful Raven family. Your people are charged with concealing the existence of the supernaturals, as well as creating weapons for the Illumin force." Jailyn gestured to herself. "I'm not on the force, but I'm an Illumin and so is Sams."

"He is?"

"Yes. But, you knew he and I were the same, didn't you?" Jailyn said. "I have to get you back home. Mysti…" Jailyn touched her friend's hand. "You disappeared from your family years ago. The Illumin force searched for you, but it found no trace."

"But, Sams said I would die in that world. He said he brought me here for safety."

"Who you decide to believe will be up to you." Jailyn shuddered as the wind picked up and whistled through the dilapidated structure. Now that she was herself again, the stench in the air was overpowering.

Mysti stood and paced in front of the raven. "Jailyn, did I have children?"

Jailyn placed her hands on the drawing of the female child. "Yes. You have twins – a boy and a girl named Hunter and Katy."

Mysti stepped back and viewed the pictures for a moment. She began sobbing and ran to Jailyn, throwing her arms around her. "Those dreams I had must have been memories."

"I want to get you back to them, and I think there is a doorway back to our home, near your house," Jailyn said.

Mysti nodded and turned to survey the room. "This place has been so special to me for so long." She ran her hands across the small sculptures and placed one in her pocket. "I'm ready."

They stepped onto the porch and were relieved to find Sams still pinned to the ground with Max hovering over him.

"Mysti," Sams said. "Don't believe anything she says. You know me. You know us."

"No, don't call me that name anymore," Lilly said. She wiped tears off her cheeks. "I'm going to go back and see for myself. If I do have children, you have made the most grievous error by lying to me." She called to Max, and the three ran into the forest.

They raced up the flower covered hill toward the forest. Lilly sobbed and followed Jailyn as best she could. Her heart felt broken.

Jailyn led them through the trees. It was illuminated by the sick pink light of the strange new sky, and every tree seemed to hide a monster.

Through sobs Mysti choked out, "I hope we can make it. I've never been through the woods at night."

"We will make it," Jailyn said and clasped Mysti's hand. "But we must run."

"How do you know how to get us out?" Mysti asked.

"My husband, Nathan, told me how the portals are created. He used to travel here on occasion. Shifting Plains is for his people, after all. No more questions, just run."

The pair emerged from the tree line. Lilly made for the

house, but Jailyn said, "No, wrong way."

"Where?"

"To the goldfish pond," Jailyn said. "That's where he put the doorway between our worlds. It explains why your dreams of the children always happened there."

They paused at the water. Jailyn looked at Max. "Tell him goodbye, Lilly."

A sob caught in her throat. Max whined and wagged his wide tail from side to side. "Can't he come?"

Jailyn said, "This is his world."

Lilly said, "I've lost so much today. Sams may kill him if I abandon him." She gripped the animal's fur coat. Jailyn's breath was racing as she glanced between Lilly and the forest.

"Okay, but I can't promise he'll make it. I don't know the strength of this portal. Hold on to me and step into the water," Jailyn said.

Lilly lifted her skirts then dropped them once she realized the futility of the gesture. She glanced back in the direction of her house and imagined how it looked in the darkness.

"Are you ready?" Jailyn asked.

Lilly's throat felt closed in grief, so she nodded once. Jailyn grasped her hand tightly then sank her free hand into the water. She closed her eyes and spoke in strange words that were soothing to Lilly's soul. The water began to bubble and rise. Lilly's fish died and floated off the pool's surface onto the dry ground. Max circled in the water and smelled the carcasses.

"Hold on," Jailyn said.

The water bubbled higher and higher and enclosed them. Fear gripped Lilly when water crested her chin.

"Don't fear, but hold your breath," Jailyn said.

Lilly felt her body float in the water for a moment, and then it submerged and spun out of control. Her heart pounded in her chest and her lungs begged for air. She felt a push behind her before she flew into open air and crashed onto a cold, hard surface.

"Oh, wow," Jailyn moaned at her side.

Lilly coughed and sputtered and rolled onto her back. She ran her hand across the flooring. It was smooth and cold. Her eyes begin to clear and adjust in the dim lighting of where they had landed, and she turned to her side. They were in a room with paintings on the wall.

Jailyn rolled from her side onto her back and coughed. "I think we made it."

"Where are we?" Lilly asked. She sat up and struggled to her feet. Her heart felt sick when she realized Max was not there to help her rise. She then heard a whine and saw Max in the corner of the room. His tail wagged against the floor when their eyes met, but he did not rise.

Jailyn glanced at him and said, "We will tend to him. Come look at this. Now."

Lilly stood next to Jailyn, who faced the painting on the nearest wall. She touched the surface and felt moisture. Lilly moved her face closer to the painting and felt her chest tighten.

Jailyn sighed, "Sams is brilliant."

The two women stood silently for several minutes staring at the beautiful painting. It was encased in a golden frame and depicted a two-story white house with blue shutters and protected by a wrought iron fence. Its wide porch was as familiar to Lilly as her own hands. "I was so close. All this time."

"He kept your doorway right here at his workplace." Jailyn shook her head. She wrung her soaking shirt sleeve onto the floor and said, "Let's get you and Max home, my friend."

"Welcome back." A male voice echoed in the cold room. Sams stood in the doorway in his blood soaked suit, holding his knife.

Jailyn withdrew her sword. "You have lost, traitor."

Lilly glanced between them. Each did not appear in any condition to fight. She said, "As angry as I am with you Sams, I am done with death today. It's over; just let us pass."

"We are dead already if we don't have one another," Sams said. "You will be with me today. Whether we are together alive or dead will be up to your friend here."

Sams moved into the room and began to circle Jailyn. His eyes appeared aflame and sweat beaded on his face and neck. He glowed blue as he transformed into his true Illumin form. He flew to the ceiling and pushed off with his legs, his weapon aimed at Jailyn.

Jailyn dodged Sams, and he crashed into the wall. In a swift move, he rolled onto the floor and flew into the air. Jailyn slashed her sword against his face, and the tip opened skin on the side of his nose.

Sams recovered and deflected Jailyn's sword with his knife and grabbed her neck. He flew them into the air then dropped her onto the hard marble tile of the museum's floor. A sickening crack and scream spoke of a broken bone. Jailyn's leg twisted beneath her.

Lilly screamed and ran to her, but Sams pushed her back against the wall. "I will have you back in Shifting Plains before you know it, sweetheart. You will be home safe in your bed."

Lilly said, "You can't make me forget your behavior today."

"What you remember is up to me. You should be appreciative that I'm still fighting for you after this betrayal."

"You have lost your senses," Lilly said. She looked at Jailyn, who struggled to lift her sword.

"Just one last detail and we will be on our way," Sams said. He crossed the room and raised his knife in the air. Jailyn swiped at his knees with her sword, but he jumped away. He kicked her wrist and her weapon slid across the floor. Sams raised his knife and swung to sever Jailyn's head, but just as it reached her neck he was knocked across the room, his body buried inside the sheetrock.

Lilly screamed when the huge man retrieved Sams from the wall and tossed him across the room once more. A second winged creature caught him, threw him to the floor, and shoved her boot in his throat.

Jailyn's face was white and tear-soaked, her body crumpled on the floor. "It's okay, Lilly," she whispered.

The huge being crossed the room and approached Lilly. She met Sams' eyes for a moment; his face creased in defeat. The Illumin standing over her altered into his human form and offered his hand. "Mrs. Raven, would you like me to take you home now?"

Katy woke to the smell of johnnycakes and bacon. She smiled and thought of her mother. Nila had not made that type of breakfast in years, and Katy wondered at the special occasion. She sat up in bed and gazed out of the window of her old bedroom. The surface of the pond reflected the early morning sun as the ducks rested on the dock. It was such a mixture of sadness and comfort waking in her childhood home.

Katy rose from the bed and walked to the window. She looked down and was surprised to see D'Nas's car parked in the driveway. Katy picked up her cell phone to verify the early time, and a sick feeling washed over her.

She tossed on some jeans and a t-shirt and headed for the stairs. On her way down, she glanced out of the tall window that opened to the back yard. A large black animal lay between her father's Dobermans. "Dad," she called. "Dad!" She raced down the steps and into the kitchen.

"It's a bit early to be screaming through the house, young lady." Darrus emerged from the dining room holding a plate of food. His eyes were red, and he looked as if he had been awake all night.

"What's going on? Why is there a Shade pet with our dogs?" Katy asked. Her heart raced when she closed the distance between them. "Have you been crying?"

"There's no need to panic." Darrus set his plate on the counter and said, "Something wonderful has happened."

Darrus steered Katy to a small window seat at the edge of the kitchen and nudged her so she would sit.

"What happened?" she asked. "I saw D'Nas's car in the driveway."

Her father's eyes filled with tears as he choked back a sob. Darrus stepped to the side, revealing the entrance to the dining room. A woman with long salt and pepper hair peered at her from behind the doorframe.

Katy's heart pounded in her chest. "Who are you?"

The woman took a step and emerged into the kitchen in bare feet. Her long skirt drifted around her ankles. The scent of lavender wafted across the room and Katy felt time stop. "Mama!"

Her mother ran across the room and pushed Darrus to the side. "I'm so sorry. I'm sorry that I've missed your life." She sobbed and held Katy's neck in such a tight grip that she was unable to speak. Katy glanced at her father. Her emotions soared with hope and uncertainty.

"Katy," Darrus said. "Sams kidnapped your mother and held her captive in Shifting Plains all those years. She escaped with the help of another trapped Illumin. D'Nas found her at the museum and kept Sams from taking her a second time."

Darrus wiped tears from his face with his sleeve then nudged Lilly from Katy. He put his arm around Lilly's shoulders and took Katy's hand. "I know you have a lot of questions, honey, and we will get to them. The important thing is that your mother is alive. And she's never leaving again."

Katy looked at her mother. Her face had aged, but her eyes were the same. Katy hid her face from her parents and sobbed. After all these years, her mother was alive and well. And home. She looked up when she sensed D'Nas's presence. Katy jumped from the window seat and ran to him.

He caught her mid-air and wrapped her in a tight embrace. "You are the best boyfriend that ever lived," Katy said.

He kissed her cheek and lowered her to the ground. "I will gladly accept this position if your parents will allow it. Especially after what has transpired."

D'Nas and Katy looked to Darrus and Lilly. "You are still on close watch, son, but I think you've earned some trust around here. Don't you, Lilly?"

Lilly nodded and took Darrus's hand. "My first order of business will be to find Hunter and complete this family for good. No more missing pieces."

by
Jason Craft

1

Muffled battle sounds thumped against Hunter's skull. He pulled his face out of the dirt and spit up grainy sludge. His own blood pooled around him, creating a slimy mess. When he turned his head to look around, Hunter's neck protested with sharp pain. Shades and Illumin flew overhead, launching into each other all around the cabin where Matt used to be locked away. Roaring winds swirled the surrounding trees into a frenzy that stung his ears with their growling.

Katy called his name in the distance. He lifted his spinning head to watch the tail lights of a car speed away. He pushed himself off the ground. Pain shook his arms, but he held strong. With a violent cough, he expelled more blood into the dirt.

A pair of leather dress shoes landed in front of him.

A harsh voice spoke down to him. "The cruel ends with which we meet are set by our actions in life, Hunter."

"Katy," Hunter managed through the blood choking him. "She found me."

The shoes slammed into his side, rolling him onto his back. Astrous peered down at him with blazing red eyes.

Thick black lines cracked through his grey skin. Rolling blackness highlighted his form, letting the night know who owns true darkness.

"Where will they take my relic?" Astrous demanded.

"They'll guard it now, at the mansion. Safe from both of us."

Astrous hissed at him and moved his foot onto Hunter's throat. "I may still have use of you then."

Thomas walked up with a limp. "His own sister left him for dead. They'll never trust him again. Just leave him to bleed out."

The outlines of the two Shades grew dim. Hunter forced himself to speak.

"M..Matt," Hunter stuttered. "Whe...Where is he?"

"We lost him in the melee," Thomas answered.

"He wore the relic for too long. Now, he's transitioning into one of you."

Astrous growled and pulled Thomas away. "It should have been us controlling him, not the other way around."

They walked away from Hunter.

"T...Thomas, don't leave me here," Hunter begged.

Thomas paused for a moment until Astrous shot a warning glare his way.

Hunter tried again. "You need me...your weapons won't..." His voice trailed off with his fading thoughts.

Footsteps crunched leaves and pine needles all around him. A few quiet voices filled the air, dying off until only silence remained. The wind rustled the trees again, calming him. Darkness clouded his vision, and he gave in to its gentle pull.

He awoke in a green field underneath a sky filled with more stars than he thought possible. A dense tree line surrounded the clearing hundreds of yards away in every direction.

"Hunter?" someone asked in the distance.

He turned around to see Katy running toward him with a smile lighting up her face. Despite their recent disagreements, he smiled back and ran to her. Just before they collided in a hug, long claws grew out from her fingernails. He tried stopping, but it was too late. Pain stabbed into both his sides as she dug into him.

"What are you doing here?" Katy demanded of him.

"You left me!" he shouted back.

Katy's hair morphed from straight, jet-black to wavy auburn. Her face contorted into a scowl that altered her gentle features into pure anger.

She shook him and slammed him back into a solid wall. His back screamed out in pain, tearing down the hazy veil.

"What did you do with Matt?" Clara yelled, holding him up against the side of the cabin.

"I...I did nothing. It was Katy, she brought the Illumin. Astrous couldn't hold them back."

"Lucky I found you then. You're coming back with me."

She dragged him to a black van flanked by several Shades. With every step, he felt like knives were ripping through his body. Seeing just how much blood caked his arms, he fought to hold on to consciousness.

"Can you stand?" someone asked Hunter.

He squinted to see, but it was too dark. What felt like pulsing thorns inside his head slowed him down. Instead of speaking, he lifted his arm. A hand grabbed his wrist and yanked him to his feet. A rush of blood and pain shocked him into noticing his surroundings.

They were in downtown Shreveport at night. That was the most he could make of it before the pounding in his head threw him off balance again. The ground rushed up at him until a thin arm slid around his stomach to stop his fall.

"Like any drunken frat boy, you're going to make it," Clara said.

She led him on a stumbling path to a set of glass doors with the words "Mandrake Tower" etched into the glass. Now he was really in trouble. For a brief moment he thought about trying to run, but the pain crushed his thoughts again. Clara pulled him into the elevator and hit the highest button.

"Your daddy can't protect you now," Clara said, laughing quietly.

"I don't need him to defend myself anyway," Hunter replied, standing as tall as he could.

"You could have used him to rescue you back there. Seems we Shades are the only friends you have left."

He looked down and felt around him. Padded gauze clung to the tender parts of his flesh.

"So, you already identify with them?"

"It's who I am. Why shouldn't I?" She smiled as the doors slid open.

Clara grabbed him by the elbow and guided him through the dark. They wound through a hallway until exiting into a room that peered out into the city's skyline. Most of downtown was relatively dark except for a few office lights that dotted the sides of the buildings.

Even with the dark backdrop, Hunter easily made out the silhouette of Zyne in the corner of the huge window. Some of the pain and wooziness from the van returned to him. Zyne looked straight at him; Hunter didn't need any light to make out his expression.

"You gambled too deep, Hunter," Zyne began. "I once thought that no Raven would betray his own blood, yet you went all in with Astrous and nearly handed him your cousin."

"I had Astrous under control; the rest was all Katy's fault."

Clara stepped away from Hunter as Zyne drew near. A twisted smile bent his face into a frightening image. Fear curled around Hunter's heart, but he held his ground even as the room continued to spin around in his head.

"You had no more control over him than a lab rat has over a scientist's maze. You scrambled around, pressing the right buttons so you might get a few scraps of cheese."

Zyne clamped his hands on Hunter's shoulders. Hunter wanted to shove him away but thought better of it.

Zyne continued, "I have a choice to offer you. If you want, I'll throw you back on the street and you can deal with the fallout from betraying your family while simultaneously failing Astrous. I'm sure Astrous would sic his dogs on you, and I can't imagine why your father would stoop to defend you."

Hunter cringed at the thought of Ginger and Peach running at him to tear his limbs apart.

"Or," Zyne interrupted his thought. "You can follow me."

"Guess I'll have to be your lab rat now," Hunter said, suppressing his fear. "Not really much of a choice."

"Look out the window," Zyne said, motioning behind him. "You've made it through your pointless mazes and are at the top of the city. I want to give you the opportunity you've always craved. You would have been little more than a gun runner for Astrous, but I bring you a chance to end our struggle with your people."

Hunter shook his head. "Don't mistake me for an idealist. Weapons are my art, and war is my canvas. If you want my help, it comes at a high price. Though, I'm sure you can afford it."

Zyne's smile faded. He grabbed Hunter by his shirt and kited him to the window. Grabbing Hunter's wrist, Zyne pressed his hand against the cool glass.

"Feel that?" Zyne asked. Hunter just stared at him, not knowing what to do. Inside him, his heart pounded, threatening to race away. "Of course you don't. Clara, what do you feel?"

Clara walked up beside them and put her hand on the glass. "Thousands of souls living with an unknown fear hanging over them. The world hidden from them by you Ravens unsettles their subconscious."

"That is your opportunity, Hunter," Zyne explained.

"All the people of this city are crying out for the ignorance to be lifted from their eyes. They want to follow the truly powerful beings that can lead them into a new and glorious era."

Hunter backed away from them. "Now you sound like a mad scientist straight out of a comic book."

"Except I'm not mad," Zyne said, creeping toward him. "I will free the people of this city and we will be its new leaders. All the world will see us and flock to join in our power. This is the ground floor, Hunter, and I'm offering you a seat. We will need your weapons, but more than that, we need your commitment to our vision. You can be the leader that your family rejected."

Hunter raised an eyebrow at him. "How are you going to do this?"

"This arrangement starts with trust because I can't tell you everything," Zyne said. "But, we will need to get your uncle back on my side. I need you to text him right now and tell him you are coming to see him."

"What? Tonight?"

Hunter backed away. Clara lunged at him.

"Where's your phone?" She breathed into his face.

"Front pocket."

Her fingers dipped into his pocket and came back with his phone.

She folded his hand around it and said, "Send the text or I'm throwing you on the street."

Hunter sent out a hurried text with Clara still breathing down his neck. "Done," he announced.

"Good," Clara said. "Let's go."

They dragged him back to the elevator in silence. Hunter hoped Daniel would understand the trouble he had fallen into this time.

Clara dragged the purple zebra-striped rug over to the perfect spot. Kneeling on its thick shag, she smoothed it out and lay on her back. Colorful streamers bounded across the Hooka Palooka's ceiling once again. She smiled at her work, thinking of how proud her mother would be right now.

In fact, her mother had lain in the exact same spot when Clara pierced her heart with her own sword. Clara wondered what it must have been like to have your last sight be of your own child stabbing you in front of such a whimsical background.

The memory came alive as she lay there in her mother's place. Reliving her mother's final moments, Clara watched her past self point her mother's sword down at her chest. Clara stared up from the floor at her own face, hidden by more than those ridiculous, oversized sunglasses. A veil clouded everything, keeping her senses as dark as those lenses. Even in her final moments, her mother held on to Clara through the end. The living memory continued with Clara's past self thrusting the sword down into her chest.

A cold pain shook Clara out of it, and she rolled up onto her side. Panting for breath, she reminded herself that that was the moment she had come into her own. When her mother fell down into the Shifting Plains, Clara was free of the power that had consumed her life.

Standing up, Clara returned to her rearranging project. She would have to move the rest of the room around to get ready for tomorrow tonight. The Hooka Palooka's reopening looked to be one of the biggest events in recent Shreveport history, or, at least, she hoped it would be. It was nice to lose herself in the venue's affairs for a little bit.

She heard a knocking at the back door. She made her way to the hallway leading up to it and felt Arthur's strong, dark presence standing behind the door. She imagined her father had felt the same thing when she barged her way into this place to claim her freedom.

Her father had had no idea what would happen when he turned that handle. If only he could see her now, following the source of her power, he would be proud. Or, at least, his old self would be proud. The being that her mother degraded him into would think she had gone too far. In time, after his reconditioning in the Shifting Plains, he would return to her with pride in his eyes.

Shaking off the déjà-vu, Clara moved toward the door and opened it with a wide smile.

"Arthur!" she exclaimed and threw herself at the man dressed all in black for a kiss. "How did it go with Hunter and Daniel last night?"

"Daniel's gone rogue. He threw us out of the shop."

"What?" Clara led him inside to the halfway arranged main room. "How will we keep Sams in check?"

"Hunter should be enough for that. I don't think Sams will go too far once he knows I hold him. Plus, I know how we can keep tabs on Daniel without lifting a finger."

"Oh yeah?"

"Yeah, apparently Gabriella's been running solo now that D'Nas is spending so much time with Katy Raven."

Clara smiled. "Playing the family's allies against each other. I like it."

He winked at her. "It's what I do. Now, are you ready for another lesson?"

"Sure, I guess," she said, putting her hands on her hips. "It's not like I have anything else to be doing tonight."

Taking a brief look around the disordered room, he shrugged his shoulders. "Looks good to me."

She shook her head. "Alright, just make it quick."

He smiled and offered her his hand as if they were about to dance.

"You know I don't have enough rhythm for that."

"With me you do."

Chasing away the flutter in her stomach, she placed her hand atop his. In a smooth motion, he pulled her into a typical ballroom dance and swept her around the room. She had never been good at dancing, but with Arthur she could do anything. His dark eyes reflected the best of her aspirations.

Arthur led her all around the empty space of the room without saying anything. She closed her eyes and followed his steps without even trying. When he moved, she knew how to follow. He spun her out, and she twirled around without putting a foot out of place. She dashed back inside his embrace and assaulted his lips. His power surged through her again just as potently as the first time.

He smiled, cupping her face with his hand. "Now are

you ready to learn?"

"Only from you."

He interlaced their hands and stepped back. "The Shifting Plains is always below you, ready for you to use its power. You just have to know how to dance with it. Just like I just pulled you around this room and directed your movements, you need to do the same with whatever power you pull up. Now, let's start with the tendrils."

He knelt down and she followed him. Pressing her hands into the cold floor, he stared into her eyes. "Your father and I built a replica of Mandrake tower in the Shifting Plains. On its sides we cultivated a snake-like plant that we use to create our tendrils. Push down and call them up. Give them direction and you'll be able to command them with as much dexterity as I."

"How do I call them?"

"Offer them what they desire–pain. Once connected to the Shifting Plains, emotions will feel more tactile. It's difficult to explain. You have to try it." He nodded to the ground.

She felt her eyes widen. "Like now?"

"Yes. Just push down."

Clara breathed in and felt the strength pulsing from him. She pushed down against the ground and felt it give way like cracking glass. A burning world of heat swirled around her eyes. Frightened, she pulled back, but Arthur kept his grip on her hands.

"Fear is for your enemies," he instructed.

Confidence renewed inside her. She continued falling into this world below. The physical room faded around her until it felt like she floated in a bed of snakes. Slick and oily, they swarmed around her, threatening to pull her deeper. Still holding onto Arthur's strength, she grabbed a handful and pulled back.

"Now, surge your pain from the world around you through them," he hinted.

Just as he suggested, emotions felt like physical properties of the Shifting Plains. Pain was all around her. She latched onto it as she floated into the black sky. It felt like her fingers slid against jagged sandpaper all the way back into the Hooka Palooka.

Colorful walls rose around her as she returned to the Earth; however, three black tendrils stuck out of the ground. They desired pain above all else and waited on her command. Trying to look up at a target, she felt darkness pressing against her. It smothered her against the cold floor.

Without thinking, she screamed and thrust her hands in the darkness's direction. The tendrils charged and wrapped up their target. The pressure against her lifted, and she rose to her feet, willing more pain into the tendrils. Squeezing her hands against the air, she watched the tendrils strangle her target.

"That's it! You've got it!" the darkness yelled.

Surprised, she watched the darkness push the tendrils away from it and force them back into the Shifting Plains. The world solidified around her again with a rush of senses. She stumbled backward and fell onto a soft couch. Covering her face with her hands, she waited on the room to stop spinning.

Someone slouched on the other end of the couch. Her

memory caught up, and she realized what just happened. She had attacked Arthur! Jumping on top of him, she went to apologize, but he cut her off by putting a finger on her lips.

"This is why I'm here for you, to guide you through these difficult challenges. Now, just rest and get your place here back in order. I have someone else who needs my help."

She bent down and kissed him as fading vibrations moved through her body.

"Oh," he said when she pulled away, "I've made dinner reservations tonight at the Arch to celebrate your reopening."

She smiled. "Going to introduce me to the high profile crowd?"

He shook his head. "Nope. I just think the place is romantic, and you know how much of a sucker I am for romance."

Laughing, she bent down to kiss him again. "Until tonight then," she whispered.

Hunter stirred from his weird dreams, trying to remember where he was. The clean room spinning around him held only the leather couch he lay on. He stretched his arm and felt the pain shoot all the way up through his shoulder. Everything hurt worse than the night before.

As he sat up, a rush of aches crawled through him. He shuddered and pushed on his temples to steady himself. The room slowed down, and he saw that the only light was coming from a single window behind him.

Reaching up, he gripped the edge and pulled himself to it. Downtown Shreveport fanned out below him in all its drab normality.

"Mandrake Tower," he said to himself, remembering yesterday.

Nothing hurt worse than his sister's betrayal. Zyne should have started with her when he talked about which Raven first betrayed their own blood. She was the reason he was trapped here instead of building his own empire.

A sharp knock on the door turned him around. Zyne entered with a smile.

"Morning, ready to start your new job?" he asked with entirely too much energy.

"Yes," Hunter replied without enthusiasm.

"Good. I would give you some time to heal up, but I can't spare any. Besides, I can almost taste your desire for revenge. Prove your worth to me and you will have it. We can bring Astrous to his knees and force your family to see reason."

Hunter looked down and saw Zyne clutching a stack of papers. "What's that?"

Zyne held them up for him to see. "These are just the few forms we need to get you on our books as an official employee. Consider it your sign of good faith. Now, come with me."

Hunter followed him out of the room down a bare hallway to the elevator. They rode it down a few floors and stepped into a round lobby with quirky furniture spread out all over the place. Several people who looked like they were in their twenties hung all over the furniture, talking to each other or tapping away into laptops.

"This is our temporary residential floor for any employee needing to stay overnight."

Hunter tried not to imagine how pitiful he looked. The occupants tried politely not to stare as he followed Zyne past the lobby and down one of the hallways to the left. They passed several rooms that held wooden bunk beds and computer tables.

The hallway ended in a large window. Zyne pointed out the last room on the left and nodded for him to enter. It seemed larger than the ones he passed on the way here. A single double-sized bed lay against a dark headboard on one wall while the other was covered with posters of various graphic novels and characters. A large wooden desk was shoved against one of the other walls and looked out of place.

"This one is free for now. Bathroom's right through there," Zyne said, pointing to another door toward the back. "Get cleaned up and meet me up at the U-Club."

With that Zyne disappeared, leaving Hunter to wonder what he had planned. It didn't matter at the moment, as a hot shower seemed like the only thing he needed.

Hunter tried to look comfortable in the new set of clothes left for him. They fit perfectly, but knowing Zyne had been planning this unsettled him. He wouldn't let himself be used again. This was his game, and he would tip the odds back in his favor.

A huge mural of the Milky Way galaxy spread out on the wall behind the hostess stand. The words "Universe Club" stretched out along its center. Other galaxies made smaller shapes all along the wall leading to the dining area of this youthful place.

"Welcome, Hunter," a hostess with long blonde locks said.

"Know my name already?" He flashed a grin her way.

Her cheeks grew a bit red. "Mr. Zyne is waiting for you to join him. This way."

She turned and he followed her down the darkened hallway until it exited into the main dining hall. The place was mostly empty, but a few people ate their breakfast and talked excitedly around the bright tables. The tinted windows kept the sun from setting the room alight with piercing color.

"And here we are," the hostess said, waving him to take his seat in front of Zyne.

"Please," Zyne said. "Order anything you want. No charge for you."

He picked up the menu and flipped through it, looking for something hearty with eggs and pancakes.

"All on credit, right?" he asked.

"I'm not cheap like Astrous, Hunter. If I keep you from reaching your potential, then we both are too weak to build our new future in this city. Now that you've helped get Daniel back in play , I need you to set up some other very important pieces."

"So, I'm your new errand boy?"

Zyne's eyes narrowed at him. "Not necessarily. My company has plenty of open software developer positions at the moment. You ever done any large-scale development with Java?"

Hunter rolled his eyes, seeing just were this was headed. "No."

"Have any scripting experience? Linux admin experience? Networking?"

"Nope."

"Do you even have a useful degree?"

"Business degree, but my true talents can't be validated by an expensive piece of paper," Hunter said, leaning forward. "Put me to use and give me something to do besides running around doing nothing."

Zyne huffed at him. "If you can't even perform a few simple tasks, how can I trust you with more responsibility? Right now you're just some rich kid with an important daddy who still has yet to understand how the world really works."

Hunter stood up in protest, but held his words back. Zyne just stared into him with his dark eyes until Hunter eased back into his chair, giving up. His family didn't want him; they even actively moved against him.

"I'm short on friends, so I'll let this play out, Zyne, but if you want me to fit into your scheme, I'll need more than this."

A young man dressed in a blue shirt walked up to take their orders.

"You've used up the last of my patience, so enjoy your breakfast. That's the only charity you'll get from me today. The rest you'll have to earn. I'll let you know when I need you to do something."

Zyne walked away, leaving Hunter to face a confused

waiter.

2

Clara took Arthur's proffered arm as the valet drove off in the car. They stood before a large brick archway with the words "The Arch" inscribed in gold on its front. Each inner brick of the archway was coated in golden paint that shimmered in the evening sun. She slipped her hand through the loop made by his elbow and followed him to the pair of tall wooden doors at the main entrance.

To their left, a line of people wearing typical nightclub attire hugged the wall leading up to a side entrance of tinted glass doors. A neon sign flashed the word "Stonegate" over the head of the bouncer who guarded the door. The bouncer took his time to look over those in the front of the line before he let a few of them pass. Clara watched him hold up his palm to stop the next hopeful group for inspection.

"Must be new," Arthur said to her, guiding her back to the other entrance.

A doorman greeted them and let them inside. They both smiled and moved up to the hostess.

"Reservation for Arthur Zyne, please," Arthur said.

"Right this way," the hostess replied with a jealous smile aimed at Clara.

The hostess took them through a winding trail to a dark spot in the back. The dark brown leather of the crescent-shaped booth was padded just right for Clara; she didn't sink down too far away from the table. Two menus enclosed in black booklets sat next to silverware wrapped in black silky cloth. With another smile, the hostess resumed her place at the front of the restaurant, leaving them to await their server.

"Welcome to my private booth," Arthur said, spreading his hands outward.

"Looks nicer than I pictured. I figured most places this fancy would just dress up their plastic with expensive trimmings, but…" She pushed against the heavy table that didn't budge. "Their tables don't even wobble. Shows they care about the little things."

"Only the best for you."

Their waiter appeared to take their drink and appetizer order. They placed their orders, and he left them alone to dive back into conversation.

"Remember how we used to laugh at people running in here to spend their money on such temporary pleasures?" Arthur asked.

"We?" She scrunched her face at him. "Oh, you mean me and Drake. That's still a bit weird for me to think about. Drake may have been some form of you, but far different from the Arthur that I've come to love. I'll always keep the two of you separated in my mind. Guess my human upbringing really left its toll."

"I wouldn't have it any other way."

She took a deep breath to remember her parents. They were trapped down in the Shifting Plains with no hope of escape unless they saw the world in the same way as Arthur. She held out little hope for her mother, but her father might come back to her.

"Where is my father? Right now, I mean," she asked.

Arthur swallowed to give a little thought to it. "I imagine he has climbed down from the tower and is scrambling after your mother."

"Ready to order?" the server interrupted, placing a steaming plate of stuffed artichoke hearts on their table. They gave him their dinner orders, and he was off again.

"Excellent tea," Clara said, sipping her sweet tea.

Arthur's deep eyes saw into her worry. "We will get him back, baby. Just give him time to reconnect."

"That's the one thing I now have the most of, but that doesn't make waiting any easier," she said after another gulp of tea.

"You felt it the last time you were down there. The memory of your teen years...he knows what he is missing, and he won't abandon you again. We've both seen it. You parents will reunite against us. That's when we can pull him to us again."

She smiled, noticing the twitch in his left eye. He really did care about her father.

"Every time I try to stare into the future, it just looks more like a jumbled mess of what I want to happen and what actually could happen. The first time I saw it in your office was the clearest I've ever seen. Now things are too dark."

"And I'm afraid they are only going to get darker for us." He reached out and grabbed her hand. "Trust me. Especially now that I have Hunter, my plan will pay off. I know you just want to dive into this supernatural world you see around you, but you need to take it slow. Besides, don't you have enough to deal with with your reopening of the Hooka Palooka?"

Her anger flared a little. "What? You don't think I can handle more than you are giving me?"

"That's not it at all. You are the first and only of your kind, Clara. I just want you to find your place without sacrificing who you are. You were raised by two supernatural beings who made you think you were human. It will take you some time to sort through that quarter-century of influence."

"Maybe," she said, feeling he was right. "At least I can run a better club than this 'Stonegate' or whatever that was."

"Yeah that was kind of weird. I don't really want to see a bunch of clubbonites at my fine dining establishments."

"Want me to deal with them like you dealt with my mother?"

He smiled. "That's probably just what that place needs, but you need to keep your profile low. Don't bring any Illumin down on you unless you have to."

She rolled her eyes with a mocking smile. "Whatever you say, boss. Tomorrow night's reopening is going to be big enough to put that place out of business anyway."

Their server returned with steaming plates of food that they sliced into. Both of their steaks were tender and juicy. Clara had never eaten anything so exquisite. This high life was definitely something she could get used to.

For nearly two full days Hunter did absolutely nothing

but traverse the pathway from his bedroom to the elevators. And even then he only went up a couple of floors to get food from the U-club. He tried talking to a few people, but he couldn't really follow their tech-fueled conversations.

"Yo, Hunter!" someone called out from outside his room.

He rolled off the bed and went to see who it was. It was the guy with the thick glasses and unkempt hair. His name was Jimmy, if Hunter remembered correctly.

"What?" Hunter asked him.

"The big man up top wants you to join him," Jimmy replied.

"Why didn't he just come down and tell me?"

"Don't know. He just said over chat that since I was bunking next door to you to tell you to get up there."

Hunter rolled his eyes and headed for the elevator. "Thanks," he said with a passing wave.

He made if off the elevator and walked straight into Zyne's office. He slouched in the chair as if he were back in high school and had just been called into the principal's office. Zyne looked out though his office windows, his back turned to Hunter.

"It's time to move," Zyne said. "I hope you've rested enough."

He turned around to face Hunter with his black eyes.

Hunter shrugged. "Yes. Just tell me what you want."

"I've got a contact you need to meet today."

"Who is that?"

"He is my inroad to securing the city. After you meet him you'll understand why. We've had an uneasy alliance these past few years, but I finally delivered on a long-standing promise."

Hunter stood up. "Great, I've got to get out of this building before your army of delusional nerds drives me crazy."

Zyne laughed, handing him a sticky note. "You are a bit useless around here anyway. Jimmy mentioned you've been restless lately. Here is the address."

Reading it, Hunter must have let the surprise bleed through his face.

"That's right," Zyne said. "Not everyone your family knows is safe from my reach."

Hunter spun around and almost ran for the elevators, the anger building up within him.

Hunter pulled into the nearest parking spot and threw his borrowed car into park. For the third time, he scanned the lot for any vehicles he might recognize. He didn't see anything familiar. Darting inside, he strode up to the reception desk.

"I'm here to see Sams, please."

The well-dressed man looked at him in surprise. "Certainly, Hunter. Your father was just here the other day for our Aztec opening." He picked up a phone behind the counter. "Hunter Raven to see you." He hung up the phone. "He'll be right out."

"Thanks," Hunter said, hoping his dad wouldn't find

him here. Maybe he was being a little too paranoid.

Hunter took a minute to look around at the art hanging on the walls in the foyer. They were mostly paintings of rustic scenery. One with a bear climbing over a mountain caught his eye. The sunbeams peeking from behind the mountain looked too real to have been painted, yet he saw the artist's masterful brush strokes right in front of him.

"I find it sad that the bear will never summit the peak and see that sunrise." A voice interpreted the painting.

Hunter turned around. Sams looked at the painting, his aging face twisted with corruption. White hair hung down to his shoulders as a vestigial symbol of Illumin purity. Today, Sams would confirm all Hunter's suspicions about him.

"You have a more private place to talk?" Hunter demanded.

Sams narrowed his eyes. "Sure, right this way."

He led Hunter down the hallway to the right and into a glass atrium with a couple of empty chess tables wedged between brown leather chairs. The parking lot lay beyond the windows on one side and a garden with short walls of flowers lay on the other. A brass statue of a man painting on a canvas sat in the garden.

"This is about as private as this gets, Hunter. I'm sorry to see you today. I had hoped Zyne's courier wouldn't be someone I knew." Sams flashed a look of pity.

"Don't look at me like that, Sams. I always knew you were dirty. I'm glad to see how right I was. How long have you been plotting with Zyne?"

"Longer than you've been alive. I set this museum up so I can justify to myself why I'm here."

"You know, I guess I really don't want to know why you chose to betray us and join Zyne. Just give me whatever he wants, so I can go back and figure all this out."

"That's probably wise. You're just the pawn anyway." Sams led them farther into the museum into a room filled with various brass sculptures depicting unique aspects of the life of a cowboy. "Wait here."

Hunter fumed while staring at a sculpture of a group of cowboys running down a lone Native American. There was probably some meaning he could read into it but chose not to. Making up pointless explanations for art unnerved him.

Sams returned with a thick cardboard cylinder. "This is what you need to carry back to Zyne. Make sure you don't let anyone else touch it, and don't take it out of this package."

It was much heavier than Hunter expected. "I don't even want to know what weighs this much."

"It's just brass, Hunter. The material isn't what makes it special. This whole room is full of brass, but what you have there is how Zyne and I will move our plan forward."

"So, you are in on it."

"Oh, yes. Can I trust you to not tell your father?" He smiled. "By the way, he is looking quite healthy for someone who had been drugged for two weeks."

"We're done here," Hunter said and moved straight back to the front entrance.

He couldn't trust anyone.

The crescent moon hung in a bed of stars outside the giant windows surrounding Zyne's dim office. Hunter sat across from him and Clara, who kept her hand intertwined with his. The cardboard cylinder Hunter was sent to get stood upright on the coffee table between them.

Hunter still fumed from his meeting with Sams earlier. Neither he nor his father had any allies left. Maybe Daniel was right and Zyne was the only way to keep the city running. He certainly did a good job of keeping Clara running for him. If he could reign in her power, the city should be no problem.

Zyne popped off the top of the cardboard cylinder, letting it fall to the floor and roll around on the carpet. Reaching inside, he pulled out a clump of brown paper twisted around the sculpture within. Zyne set it back down on the table with a clank.

He peeled back the paper, stuffing it back into the empty cylinder. Hunter scoffed at the small statue. It was a bodybuilder hunched over, balancing a globe on his shoulders. Zyne swept all the remaining paper off the table and stared at it.

Touching the top of the globe, Zyne closed his eyes and whispered to himself. A tiny white light spun around the inside. The rest of the sculpture glowed blue as the light intensified. Zyne gripped the globe as wisps of darkness bled off his arm to cover up the light.

Hunter cringed with anticipation as his stomach

churned. Zyne pushed further into his trance, leaving Hunter and Clara to exchange looks as they waited. Neither was brave enough to interrupt.

Zyne pulled his hand away. The glow on the sculpture died away, leaving only the lifeless brass behind.

"Sams is ready to move with us," Zyne said, looking to Clara. "We have to find Matt before Astrous does."

"Thomas and Emily are following me," she replied, resting her head against her fist. "Seems like I'm the only one who can track him down."

"What does Matt have to do with this?" Hunter asked.

"His power is fresh and raw," Zyne began. "And I will use it to shut down the portal in the Shifting Plains that connects our two realms. This will keep out any new Shades from being pulled back here."

"I didn't know that was possible."

"That's why I need your uncle, Hunter. I've figured out a way to do it, but he is the only one who can complete the seal."

"What seal?"

Clara stared him down. "Raven blood will close out the portal. We can draw out the Shade from Matt and use Matt's blood to close it down."

"The Shade within him will act as a binder for his blood," Zyne explained. "Blood sacrifices created the portal, and a final sacrifice will complete the cycle and shut it down." He stood up. "Now, if the two of you will excuse me, I have to go downstairs to check on some other business."

Clara followed Zyne out of the room, leaving Hunter to try and figure out the statue's meaning.

People filled the smoky room with excited chatter as they squeezed past each other on their way to and from the bar. Multicolored lights bathed their skin in hues of greens and blues. Clara watched them refill their drinks and take turns puffing on the nearby hookahs. The local media jumped all over the story of how she planned to reopen her deceased parents' club, drawing in most of this crowd by appealing to their morbid curiosity. However it happened, Clara was glad to serve the largest crowd in its history; a great start to her new side venture.

Two familiar smiles broke through the monotony of the crowd. She waved at her friends to get their attention. A boisterous woman wrapped in a blue party dress that was obviously designed for someone smaller charged straight for her, dragging along a helpless man who did his best to dodge the movement around them.

"Hey girl!" Olivia said, wrapping Clara up in a hug while trying not to spill her drink. "It's so good to see you again. You're looking well, and cute as a button in that orange dress. Your mother would be proud to see you in such radiance!"

Clara put her hands on her hips and turned to the side. "It's a bit tighter than she would have been comfortable with though."

"You look great anyway. You do remember Raoul, right?" Olivia asked, pointing to the dark-haired man next to her.

"Ha! I'll never forget the two of you. How else was I supposed to get through college?"

"You seem to be doing as well as you look, Clara," Raoul said with his exceptional smile.

"Yeah, no kidding," Olivia added. "All compliments of your new boyfriend?" She nudged Clara in the rib.

"Well, he did have a small part in the re-opening."

Olivia raised her eyebrows. "Oh really? Are we going to get to meet him tonight? I need a picture, because no one believes that I know the girlfriend of Arthur Zyne."

Clara shook her head. "No, actually. He has other business to get to tonight. So, what are the two of you up to these days?"

"Ah, you know," Olivia answered. "Just working at that piddling little software company you passed on your way to the top. Raoul here is doing IT work for the med center. But anyway, what's it like to walk in Mandrake Tower knowing you practically own the place?"

"I assure you, I don't own the place."

Olivia cocked her head back. "Hey, as long as you own his heart you do. Remember that." She held up a finger with the hand clasping her drink and took another sip.

"So, you really holding up okay?" Raoul asked while he still had the chance.

"Yeah, I miss them, but I can keep them alive with this place."

"And apart from that, you should get out more," Olivia added.

"I know," Clara said, feeling just how much she missed

seeing her friends. "Hey, there is a new place we could try. It's called Stonegate up by the Arch. Actually, I think it's attached."

"Sounds like fun. Maybe we should make it out there tonight?"

Raoul shook his head. "Not unless you want to volunteer to be the DD for tonight, because I'm not buying a taxi to go all the way out there when I can drink here."

"Fine, whatever," Olivia said with her palm held up to his face. "But I do know of another place within walking distance that is going to be awesome tonight."

A group of girls walked in front of them, drawing Olivia's critical eye. She snapped her head back to Clara.

"Clara, did you see that? Looks like they have fang bites on their neck!"

"What?" Clara asked, looking to see what she was talking about.

Sure enough, the trio of girls now lounging on some furniture had twin black dots with trailing crimson lines near their throats.

"You guys haven't heard about that yet?" Raoul asked.

"No, I can't keep up with what all the kids are doing these days," Clara said.

"They've 'taken the vampire's mark'. They get out an eye dropper and make fake bloodstains on themselves. Sometimes they'll use a straight razor to make small incisions for a heightened experience," he explained.

"Why?"

"I don't know. Because they're too old to be cutting their wrists for attention and would rather fantasize about

Louisiana vampires   sweeping them off their feet?" He shook his head.

Olivia lightly slapped his shoulder. "That's terrible."

"I've got to get a closer look," Clara said, walking toward the group of girls hanging all over their couch.

She didn't look directly at them but made a pass close enough to sneak a better glance. Twin lines of crimson streaks ran up from their necklines a finger-length's distance. Heightening her senses, she felt something more from it, like a radiating energy. That wasn't food coloring on their necks, and only one family's blood in this area would call out to her like that.

Clara went back to her friends to get any other information they had about it, but Olivia had convinced Raoul to follow her to the other club she had been talking about. Clara didn't really want to leave the Hooka on re-opening night, but running it wasn't as fulfilling as she had hoped. If she had to work the crowd without Olivia, she would be lost. She gave up and followed Olivia outside.

Clara and Raoul soon found Olivia's term for a "couple of blocks" meant at least six blocks from the Hooka. They entered the dingy place that Clara didn't pay attention to the name of. Olivia dragged them through the bar area to a room in the back blaring with live music. They posted up against the wall and watched the band for several minutes.

The guitarist jumped around on the tiny stage, fingers crawling all over his strings. Shrill notes of his solo blasted right into Clara's ears. The solo ended, and the local band went back into its chorus with their singer trying to garner support from the crowd. There were a few people bobbing their heads, but most of the room seemed unimpressed.

"I love these guys," Olivia yelled to Clara over the loudspeakers.

"I think you've had too much to drink," Clara yelled back.

Olivia smiled and tipped her glass back to her lips to finish it.

"Not yet!" She grabbed Clara's arm and dragged her back to the bar in the adjoining room. Clara looked at Raoul to save her, but he just gave a salute and went back to talking to the girls beside him.

A handful of people shot pool while another group sat around the bar drinking and listening to the band at a more tolerable level. Olivia slammed her tumbler in front of the bartender.

"One more round, please," she requested and turned to Clara. "You going to continue to force me to drink alone? I'll even buy!"

"Get me a root beer then," Clara said.

"Seriously?" Olivia turned back to the bartender. "And a root beer for my all-too-sober friend."

The bartender filled up Olivia's tumbler and slid down a bottle of Abita root beer to Clara. Ever since coming into her immortal side, alcohol didn't have the same effect it used to. Now it was just a bitter drink without any benefits. Thankfully, root beer still tasted just as delicious as before.

"You should listen to your friend here and loosen up," a guy said from across the bar. He looked a bit familiar.

Olivia sauntered over beside him. "I keep trying to tell her that we're still young enough to party like college kids.

Guess it's the job pressure that keeps her from drinking; weird, right?"

"Completely weird," he replied, extending his hand to her. "Thomas."

"Olivia."

She grabbed his hand, but instead of a shake, he brought her hand to his lips. She giggled.

Clara sat on the other side of Thomas, who brought his smiling face around to her.

"I don't think we've met," Thomas said. "Not officially anyway. I'm sure we've heard plenty through our respective bosses."

Olivia peeked out from around Thomas's back. "You know this guy? Since when do you keep a secret list of cute guys from me?"

"Since they work for a competing company."

"Yeah, since our companies battle against each other, why shouldn't we?" Thomas raised his glass to her. "By the way, that seat is taken."

"By whom? You didn't drag Astrous out with you?"

"Nah," Tomas replied, motioning behind Clara.

Clara turned around to meet another fake smile from a female Shade.

"Glad to meet another supporter of the local music scene," the Shade said, extending her hand. "I'm Emily, glad to meet the legend in person. Though, don't you have your own club to run right now?"

"I've got really good managers to cover for me," Clara explained, shaking her hand.

"Can't get your hands too dirty can you?" Thomas

asked. "Zyne really has you sold on his way of handling things from the top."

Clara moved out of her chair. "If he doesn't control this city, then all that's left is for the rats to take over the streets."

"Man, you guys are too serious about this stuff," Olivia interjected. "It's just software. Just let the computers talk." She hopped down and headed back to the stage room.

"You guys watching me?" Clara asked.

Thomas leaned into her. "Every move you make, we'll be there waiting on the perfect moment to strike." He scowled at her for a moment and broke into laughter.

Emily laughed. "We're just here to have a good time. Zyne doesn't let you out to play?"

"Why else would I be here?"

"So, you're not hunting down Matt?" Emily asked with a straight face.

"Tricky question, I know," Thomas offered. "I mean, you don't know how much we know, and it is strange you would happen to run into us while you are out with friends in a safe place."

Clara reached out and clamped down on his forearm, garnering a few looks from the other patrons around the bar. She smiled and let him go. He smirked at her.

"Perfect," Thomas replied. "Now we have you hooked. Perhaps you should stop looking right now and we'll have an agreement."

"You've been a good bloodhound so far," Emily added. "But now the real Shades have to finish this."

Clara found her hand in her pocket squeezing her coin. Emily looked down at her, taking another gulp from her bottle.

"I haven't been in a good bar fight in a while," Emily challenged. "Can you really handle the both of us without your master here to protect you?"

Clara placed her coin on the bar and spun it like a top. Sparks of blue fluttered around it. Now everyone at the bar was looking at the three of them.

"Oh, I'm ready," Clara said.

Thomas snatched the spinning coin and dropped it on the ground in front of Clara. He wiped his blackened fingers against his pant leg. With his other hand, he finished his beer and slapped it back down. He gave Clara a nod and dragged Emily outside.

Clara picked up her coin and went back to finish listening to the local band. She hoped there would be a mosh pit to calm down in.

The night grew late as Clara helped Olivia and Raoul into a cab.

"Aren' you comin'?" Olivia managed.

Clara smiled, "No, you need to go home and make sure Raoul gets home too."

She double checked with the cab driver that he had both addresses and sent them on their way. The streets were quiet and empty as usual at this hour. Heading back toward Mandrake Tower a few blocks away, she heard a flutter of wings behind her. A brilliant blue Illumin glided down at her from the roof of the building across the street. Clara reached out to slip into her Shade form. Black wings stretched out from her back as she crouched down, preparing to launch an attack.

The Illumin landed on the sidewalk in a guarded stance and yelled, "Stop!"

It was Gabriella. Clara pulled her power back inside, feeling her wings disappear.

"Get out of here," Clara said.

Gabriella's light died off as she returned to her mortal state. "I need you to confirm if Astrous is involved with a homicide."

"What do I care about police business?"

Gabriella walked straight up to her. "Thomas left a corpse in an alley."

Now she was interested. "Let's go then."

They ended up in an alley several blocks away standing over the twisted corpse of a young club patron still wearing her party dress. Vampire lines ran down her neck but ended in a gash that spilled out a pool of blood around her.

"She's missing more than the blood she's lying in," Gabriella informed. "I can't trace anything on it, but thought you might. And given we both hate Astrous, can you at least confirm this is him?"

Clara's phone sounded off with both Olivia and Raoul texting her as to why she hadn't joined them this evening. She was glad to know they were both all right. Looking back at the corpse, she bent down and closed her eyes to heighten her senses.

As in the Hooka Palooka, the blood streaks on the

victim's neck called out to her. She reached down and traced along the dark lines. A warm pulse beat against her fingers, not from the woman, but from Clara's reaction to the blood. There was no question that this was Raven blood, and it was laced with the same power she had tracked down before.

She looked up at Gabriella, "This is Matt's blood on her neck. I've seen several people around town with this same fashion trend. A few of whom I ran into at the Hooka Palooka."

"Can you track it down from here?"

Clara looked at the woman killed in the prime of her life. Energy passed through her lifeless corpse like a trail of dim red light off into the darkness of the alley. The power she felt reminded her of when Arthur first sent her out in search of the relic. However, this time it felt much more potent and real.

"No doubt this is Matt's blood on her neck, but Thomas must have cleaned up this kill," Clara said, dipping back to reality. "I can't trace it anywhere. Actually…" Clara paused, a sinking feeling weighing her down. "This was a message for me. I ran into him tonight while out with some friends, and he pretty much threatened their safety if I kept hunting for Matt."

"That's enough to act on. Want to come with me to pay him a visit?" Gabriella asked.

Clara smiled. "Definitely."

"Did you really think he was just going to let us in?" Clara asked, looking over Astrous's mansion from the passenger seat of Gabriella's police cruiser.

"He should have come out to meet us at least," Gabriella said. The speaker grew silent again as the attendant on the other end ignored them.

Clara opened the door and stepped outside. "Let's go."

"Don't cross that gate!" Gabriella shouted after her.

Clara jumped up, letting her power break through. Her wings stretched out of her back and carried her the rest of the way to the top of the gate. Grabbing onto the tiny spires of iron, she looked down at Gabriella.

"I've got to protect my friends."

She launched off the gate and glided down into the yard to wait. Two loud howls pierced the muggy night air just before Astrous's dogs rounded the other side of his mansion and headed straight for Clara. They pounded the ground in a flurry of claws and teeth.

Clara sprang over them at the last minute. Her wings twisted her around in the air, and she fell upon the creatures, knocking them away in opposite directions.

They growled and darted back at her. She crouched, facing one of them. As it lunged at her, she gave it her forearm to chew on and slammed her fist into its belly. Hurling it overhead, she dropped it down upon the other one that had tried to bite her leg. They stumbled over each other to try to get back up.

Clara put her fingers on the ground in front of their writhing bodies and pushed down. She felt the presence of the Shifting Plains and the spires on Mandrake Tower. Just like Zyne taught her, into the mortal plane she pulled out a set of tendrils that wrapped around Astrous's two beasts.

She could see down into the Shifting Plains at the strong roots that anchored these small tendrils. Touched them with her senses, she willed pain through them. The beasts writhed and howled.

Kneeling down, Clara pushed into the ground to try to drop the beasts back into the Shifting Plains. Her muscles protested, but she pressed even harder. The beasts fought to stay above ground.

Clara saw a blue light charge overhead as Gabriella joined the fight. While Calra was distracted, a fist rammed into her face. Her connection with the Shifting Plains loosened enough for the beasts to wriggle out of the tendrils and run away. The fist came back for her, but she caught it and threw the guy onto his back.

Thomas looked up at her with a darkened face. She stomped down at his chest, but he rolled out of the way. Snatching her coin out of her pocket, she moved to throw it in the air. Another hand caught her wrist and her coin tumbled to the ground. A silver knife slashed out at her and caught her side, leaving a trail of black blood.

Clara leapt into the air, dragging Emily up with her. Emily's wings spread out from behind her and pulled away, but Clara held on. She whipped around her free hand and knocked Emily's jaw to the side. Using her wings, Clara pulled them back toward the ground and summoned another set of tendrils that crawled up through the ground and snaked around Emily's ankles.

"Not powerful enough," Thomas shouted from behind her, wrapping his arms around her neck.

He dragged her backward, but she maintained her connection to the tendrils. She felt the cold barrel of a gun pointing at her lower spine.

"You don't want to find out what I've loaded this with," Thomas threatened. "Look!"

He turned her to face the porch where Astrous stood with his arms crossed. A few paces out from him, Gabriella stood triumphant against three Shades that lay at her feet.

"Three of you couldn't even take out Gabriella?" Clara taunted. "I took her down myself."

Thomas said nothing but pushed her toward Astrous. She released her grip on the tendrils, freeing Emily. Clara looked around for the beasts that first attacked her but couldn't find them. She smiled, imagining them cowering behind the house.

Thomas stopped the two of them at the base of the stairs. Astrous bounded down the steps, wearing a pinstripe suit that had probably survived the Great Depression.

"Clara Raimes , it is good to finally meet you," Astrous said with antiquated charm, sticking his hand out for her.

She grabbed it and shook. "Astrous, is there anything else I can do besides stand here with a gun in my back?"

Astrous nodded to Thomas who backed away from her. "There, now we can talk. Why are you here, and why are you with her?" He pointed to Gabriella who hadn't moved an inch.

"We girls have to stick together. Can't let you boys have all the fun," Clara replied.

He clasped his hands across his stomach. "Ah well, I'm sorry to inform you that your fun ends here. I don't have Matt, but I do find it just as curious as you that his blood is being distributed around town."

Gabriella took a couple of steps toward him. "Why couldn't you just have told us that before we jumped the gate?"

"I had to know how desperate you were to know. Seems Matt is wanted by all. Please, see for yourself." He gestured to Clara.

She closed her eyes and pushed out with her senses, finding no traces of his blood nearby. Even Astrous couldn't have cleaned up Matt's scent that well. Still, she felt all around the property, watching it cycle around her as she searched in vain. Satisfied, she dropped back to reality.

"He's not here, Gabriella," Clara said in defeat.

"See, now why couldn't you have done that before you jumped my gate?" Astrous asked, pointing a finger at Clara. "Perhaps you came to learn more of your father and the present tortures he endures."

Gabriella walked up to her side and pulled her away. "Let's go."

"No," Clara said, moving toward Astrous. "When I get my father back, all of you will pay."

Astrous took a few steps toward her. "Even if Zyne is able to bring him out of his own apathy, he won't be who you remember. He was one of the most powerful and vicious

Shades this world has seen. Do you really want to meet the true Nathan?"

"I've already seen how he was, and I will see him rise again in his power."

"No," Astrous shook his head. "You've only seen what Zyne has shown you. Even now, I can feel him shielding you from the truth."

Clara tightened her fists at her side.

"You are not yet attuned to your power, Clara, so you won't feel what I do, but Gabriella can tell you." He motioned to her.

Clara looked at her for support. She nodded slightly. Confusion raged inside Clara.

She tried to think of something. "I can feel-"

"You are nothing to Zyne! He used you to break your mother's grip around Nathan's throat. By sneaking into your mind," Astrous continued, stroking her face with the back of his hand. "He found the way underneath Jailyn's protection. He could feel, just as I do now, your unbridled potential. The union of your parents left you with such raw power that, should you desire, could smite us all. Pity you can't see the chains with which he has you bound."

Thomas and Emily stood beside Astrous. Clara shook her head and turned away, walking straight back to the gate. Gabriella joined her.

"Go back to your master and see if he'll give you the truth, Clara!" Astrous yelled out after them.

When they returned to Gabriella's police cruiser, Clara's fury burned hotter than before. A couple of times on the trip back to Mandrake Tower, Gabriella almost broke the silence but wisely stopped herself at the last minute. Clara stared at the dark streets for the entire ride, wanting answers, but too afraid of discovering the truth. When she saw Arthur again, she would make him take her down to the Shifting Plains so she could put to rest Astrous's crazy accusations. She hoped they were just that, but an itch at the back of her mind gave her doubt.

Unhappy with Zyne's late night summons, Hunter stumbled to the elevator through the dark hallway. He rode it upward, wiping the sleep from his eyes. Zyne waited for him in his lobby.

"Have a seat, Hunter." Zyne motioned to the couch in front of him.

Hunter sat down and listened.

"Time to sow discord among the family ranks," Zyne began. "Sams has been getting reacquainted with your father, and I trust you more than I trust him."

"How is that?" Hunter asked.

"You have simple tastes. Power is easy for me to come by, so I can extend it to you without worry of you betraying me. You understand that to wield more power, you must surround yourself with those more powerful than you."

Hunter hated being reduced so simplistically. "What do you want me to do now?"

"Go tonight and visit your sister, secretly of course, and deliver to her a warning about Sams' ties to myself. That should get your father to keep him at arm's length."

He remembered how Katy fled when he lay bleeding on the ground. "She left me for dead back at the cabin. At best she won't speak to me."

"You are twins recently separated by Shade and Illumin. Why wouldn't she want to speak with you? She wants to save you from yourself. Use that against her."

Hunter crossed his arms and sat back. "And what if some Illumin captures me trying to sneak around? Put me to work doing what I know, not running these dangerous errands."

A trickle of fear dropped into Hunter's heart as Zyne's eyes grew ever blacker.

"Quit testing me, Hunter. I have lived through every era of your school history books. I see the patterns of humanity, and I know what I'm doing. Go warn your sister of the dangers she faces."

Fear overtook Hunter. He nodded and dashed for the elevator. He pressed the button, using the frame to hold his shaking legs upright.

Zyne grabbed him by the neck and pulled him back so Hunter's ear was next to Zyne's mouth. Hunter shut his eyes.

"Astrous lets traitors live. I'm not so foolish."

The elevator doors opened, and Hunter stumbled inside. He scrambled to press the lobby button. A dark set of eyes smiled at him until the doors shut. Katy had to know what the family was up against.

Hunter ran to his car and raced down the highway,

finally out from underneath Zyne's power. He was done being treated like a caged animal. He had only one person he could really turn to–Daniel.

Pulling up to Daniel's shop, he was relieved to see the lights still on in the back. He nearly tripped over himself getting out of the compact car Zyne had forced him to drive. If Daniel couldn't get him out of Zyne's prison, no one else could.

He threw open the doors and went straight up to Daniel. "Can I please talk?"

Daniel nodded. "You talked to your father since you've been back? Because I have."

"Uncle Daniel, I need your help," Hunter begged. It felt so demeaning to ask his uncle to bail him out of another problem.

"Maybe you should have gone to him anyway, like I did. He let me in on what you did to Matt right after I helped you save him. Care to explain why you kept him locked up in a cabin instead of coming back to me?"

Hunter tried to think of something. "It was Astrous, he had me–"

"That's your problem right there!" Daniel yelled. "You went to Astrous instead of me. You took that dishonorable, slimy demon to my son and let him torture to his heart's content. I know what Astrous is made of, and you are lucky Zyne pulled you away from him."

"I actually protected Matt from Astrous until he forced his way through me to your son," Hunter protested, trying to get back to the subject at hand. "Whatever you think I should do to make up for that I will. Just please, help me get away from Zyne. Every time he gets near me I feel like I'm changing into something else. He's got me doing all this stuff for him that will come back on all of us, I'm sure of it. He's even got–"

Daniel grabbed his shirt and breathed out through his teeth. "Our punishment for being family outcasts is we're forced to work with Zyne because he is the only Shade that works for us. I know the pain you're feeling. I live with it every day. This shop is my answer to it. Your dad cares more about our name than who we are. The only way you're going to learn this is to get in deep with the wrong kind of people. Since Astrous didn't teach you, you're now in the hands of a master manipulator."

Hunter stood there in silence until Daniel pushed him away.

"I don't care anymore," Daniel said. "Not that I ever did. Now get out of my shop. I have my own demons to dance with."

Angry, Hunter spun around and stormed back into the heat of the parking lot. A faint thumping grew louder and rumbled toward him. Hunter jumped into his car and watched a huge white SUV pull in. The rumbling bass stopped when the SUV parked. What was his uncle up to tonight?

He drove to a gas station a couple miles down the road. Fairly sure Daniel hadn't noticed his car, he went inside and bought a Coke, keeping careful watch of the road. As he was paying, he saw the SUV zip past the station outside.

He finished at the counter and ran back to his car. Following the SUV from a safe distance, they traveled to downtown Shreveport and got on the parkway by the river.

Hunter followed them a few miles down until they exited into Veterans' Park, which divided the parkway to either side of it. Typical for this time of night, rows of bikes filled the concrete parking lot while their owners lounged around wooden picnic tables.

Taking the next exit, he doubled back and parked in the lot for the large, open field that lay before the disc golf course in the park. Cutting off all his lights, he watched the SUV to see what it would do. Several trees broke up the gently rolling hills of the disc golf course, but Hunter could still make out what was going on in the parking lot at the other end.

Flanked by his gangsters, Daniel started talking with one of the bikers. A fight erupted after Daniel dropped one of the bikers to the ground. The gangsters kept the bikers at bay until they were able to make it back to the SUV and escape.

Hunter tried to make sense of what he had seen. After the big speech he had just given Hunter, why wouldn't Daniel take his own advice? Hunter literally just saw him in league with Shades that had no commitment to anything that Daniel could control. Not to mention that they were small-time compared to Zyne.

With the SUV driving off, Hunter wanted a closer look. Getting back on the parkway, he drove down and entered Veterans' Park. The long rows of sports bikes now lay on the ground with an angry mob working to pick them up.

Hunter smiled at the opportunity. Zyne had told him to sow discord, so here he would. He psyched himself up for the challenge. Stepping out with a purpose, he strutted over to the group.

"Having trouble with your bikes, gentlemen?" he called out to no one in particular.

An Asian guy dressed in a red jumpsuit drew out a sword and jumped over at him. Red orbs peered out from his eye sockets.

Hunter threw his hands in the air. "I know what it's like to have everything stripped away before your eyes."

The guy walked toward him with his sword pointed at Hunter's throat.

"It's just a sword, man," Hunter said. "But I can make it into a tool to reclaim your destiny."

The guy jumped at him and grabbed the hair on the back of his head. He held him close enough for Hunter's senses to go numb in the Shade's presence. "Another Raven?" he asked, releasing Hunter.

"A savant," Hunter said, dusting himself off. "No one will ever be able to overpower you like that again, should you employ my services."

"Bring the Raven," a voice called out.

The Shade pushed him past the lines of bikes and slung him into the ground next to another Shade hunched over the lifeless body of an Asian woman dressed in tight leather. He noticed the charred symbol of a raven on her sternum through a burnt hole in her leather jacket.

Glowing red eyes surrounded Hunter again. The guy stood over him and pointed to the body. Hunter understood. He looked her over again, checking for a pulse. Whatever Shade had inhabited this body had been pulled out by Daniel through some means Hunter didn't even know was possible.

"Looks like my uncle caught you by surprise," Hunter

said, thinking ahead. "I can bring him down and restore this broken Shade. Throw her body on ice, and I'll tell you how we can get her back."

"Soren." The guy introduced himself with a bow.

"Hunter," he replied, bowing in respect, or attempting to anyway.

"The Dynasty only deals with its own, and we are more than familiar with the Raven weapons."

"Then I'm sure you know how well mine work."

"We also know how you dealt with Astrous."

"I've fired him as a client and am shopping for new business."

"The Dynasty requires loyalty and honor. If you can demonstrate your commitment to these, you will have a place among us."

Now they were getting somewhere. It was just another game to play, another group to manipulate.

"Tell me what I must do," Hunter said, trying not to smirk.

Soren smiled down at him with all the hubris of an over-confident emperor of old. "We shall prepare to host an invitation. Meet us at the old graveyard behind the city after dawn. There, we will determine your worth."

Hunter nodded and walked back to his car. He still had plenty of time to make it out to Katy and get back. Taking off down the road, the rest of the Dynasty gathered themselves together and drove the opposite direction toward Downtown.

Morning came into full bloom as Hunter sped away from his dad's mansion to the meeting place he had set up with Soren. The warning given to his sister was such a mixture of truths and lies that Hunter didn't know if it made sense anymore. No matter now. It felt good to be officially back in the game.

He drove past Downtown to an old graveyard. Parking on the side of the road, he looked around to see if anyone had followed him. The gate was closed, but he didn't have much trouble jumping the fence. He made his way to the top of the central hill where a cluster of silhouettes waited on him.

"Hunter Raven at your service," he said bowing low.

"The Raven steps out on his own, as he has before," Soren said, moving out from his group. "Only in this part of the world have I seen one sharing the blood mark to align with the Shade."

"Because you haven't seen me," Hunter replied, following Soren as he began circling around him.

"We are the Dynasty and have crossed the world to settle here."

"You'll never get more than a foothold here without my help. Unless you want to take on Astrous and Zyne yourselves."

Soren stopped walking and just looked at him. "If you help us regain our deity, we will hear you further."

"I can work with that, but I need more than just your

word; I need your help."

Soren approached him, staring into him with his red eyes. "Careful what you request, Hunter, or you may create a debt too great even for all of your wealth."

"My wealth is right here," Hunter said pointing to his head. "Give me a sword and a strand of hair. I'll give you a taste of what I can do."

Soren pulled out the thick sword from his back and plucked out a strand of hair. He handed both to Hunter. Kneeling down, Hunter placed the sword on the ground and stretched out the short strand of hair before him.

He broke the hair into two strands and put the hilt of the sword between his knees with the blade facing upward. Starting with the point, he placed the two strands of hair on either side of the blade's cutting edge. As he moved his fingers across the hair, careful to not cut himself, small black puffs of smoke eased out of the hair.

Hunter knelt there rubbing the hair into the blade until the tip of the sword look like it had been dipped in tar. He blew on it and trails of black smoke fled. With a smile he stood to his feet and handed Soren back his sword.

"If this doesn't slice through the next Illumin to cross your path, you'll know I lied to you."

Soren nodded and sheathed his sword. He gave Hunter one last bow before turning around and disappearing into the night with the rest of the group. Hunter looked around but saw nothing except the creepy scene of crumbling headstones. He walked back to the car, eager to see what tomorrow would bring him.

"Babe, you sure you still want to do this?" Arthur asked from behind Clara. He moved closer, wrapping her up with his arms.

She stared at the lone painting in the otherwise stark room. A simple landscape of green hills contrasted with tufts of wispy clouds in a pure blue sky lay in a golden frame. The hills drew her deeper into the painting, like she could actually be standing in the fictional scene.

"I have to see them," she finally answered.

"Alright." He kissed her neck and let her go, moving around to face her. "The Shifting Plains is a strange place, and you'll have trouble adjusting to it the first time. Don't push yourself. The Illumin that go down there don't make it very long before they start losing themselves to its power. As you've felt, Shades grow stronger and can manipulate the world however they wish."

"So, you have no idea how I'm going to react?"

He shook his head. "Not when you're actually down there, but we'll find out, just hold on."

He moved up to the painting and stared at it for a moment. Then, he swept his fingers out from the center. Blue and green streaks followed Arthur's motion off the painting and into in the air. He kept going back to the center of the painting to pull out more colorful streaks until they began curving toward Clara.

She moved back, unsure of what she should do.

"Reach out and touch faith!" Arthur said.

The streaks tapped against her arms with a tingling that left goose bumps. As she tried to sweep them away, they only tangled around her even more. The moment they wrapped around her, their colors died away to differing shades of grey. The tingling grew into a worsening itch over her skin.

Arthur turned around with a smile across his face. He moved in close and held her in just the right way to make her feel safe. Leaning down, he kissed her. She held on to him, afraid to let go.

The itching started to burn, but she held her eyes shut and focused on kissing Arthur. He pulled away, taking all the burning with him. Clara opened her eyes to a world set upon by darkness. A deep crimson sky overshadowed the craggy ground that spread out all around her. The stench of smoke permeated everything.

"Welcome to the world below," Arthur said, spreading his arms outward.

It was unlike anything she expected, completely foreign. "It's nice," she lied.

"And my greatest creation." He gestured behind her.

She looked up at a massive tower that broke through the terrain and stuck its four corner spires high into the sky. "Mandrake Tower," she said in amazement.

"You always wanted to see exactly where we pull the tendrils from, so there you go. Those are the roots that allow us to feed them into the Earth."

"So, my father is in there right now?"

Arthur stepped beside her and grabbed her hand. "Yes he is. And like you he needs to see your mother. Let me show you where she is, and you can lead her to him. However, you can't go to her like this. You'll need to create a disguise."

Clara hesitated at the thought of seeing her mother again, even in this place. Remembering just how her mother had dominated her life brought back all the anger she had forgotten. Their last argument over where she should interview buzzed through her head again.

"That's the one," Arthur said, breaking her train of thought.

"What?"

"Your feelings of vulnerability right now–follow them."

"How did you even–" She stopped and felt a deeper connection to the world around her.

It was like everything worked to show its purpose instead of its physical direction. When she looked at Arthur, she could tell his feelings for her were strong bonds that would never break. The tower behind her stood like a beacon of security, imbuing her with the power to accomplish the task at hand.

"Weird," she said. It was the only way she could describe the feelings.

"Yeah, this place will do that. Now just–"

"Shh," she cut him off and concentrated on her childhood.

All the feelings of security from her parents flooded into her and altered her perception of the Shifting Plains. Imagining herself playing as a little girl again, she sat down on the ground to wait. Hot air kicked up flecks of ash that swirled around her and blocked her sight.

After the wind died down, she stood up and noticed that

Arthur had grown a bit taller.

"Weird," she squeaked.

Covering her mouth, she felt a tiny set of hands against her premature lips. Holding her hands outward, they were just as she remembered from her childhood. Looking down, she was wearing a blue sundress from the memory she had just relived inside the ash cloud.

"Looks like you figured it out," Arthur said, offering his hand.

She took it as any child would with a trusted adult, and he led them toward the horizon in search of her mother.

The angry banging at his door disrupted Hunter's sleep. He threw his covers off and stumbled to the door, snatching it open. Zyne pushed his way inside.

"It's your place anyway, I guess," Hunter mumbled.

"Sleep is one thing I'll never emulate," Zyne replied. "It's such a waste of time, and I hate when my time gets wasted."

"I know what you mean."

Zync ignored the comment and moved on. "Clara has an amazing ability to follow a Shade's power residue. It's how she was able to find Matt originally, before he broke out of the Relic. Astrous has discovered some way to interfere with that now. Have you heard of this thing called 'taking the vampire's mark'?"

"Yeah. Everyone on this floor won't stop talking about it. Don't they like drip iodine on themselves?"

"Only the ones who can't afford the real thing."

"Which is?" Now Hunter was actually interested.

"It's Matt's blood, or that's what Clara thinks. To her, it feels a bit like Raven blood with a dark undertone."

"Apt description. Now what do you want me for?"

"This is where I give you what you want. Clara needs to find where Matt is hiding, but can't because of whatever Astrous is doing to the bodies. Figure out a way to break through Astrous's tricks so Clara can track down the source of power."

Hunter considered it for a moment. "Okay, do you have one of these people I can work with?"

Zyne scoffed at him. "What? You think I keep a stash of people locked away here? Go out and find someone. I'm sure if you throw around enough money at a club, one of them is bound to turn up."

"Except I have no money right now."

"Take Clara with you; she'll cover your expenses. Right now, though, she is doing some soul-searching down in the Shifting Plains, so you'll have to wait a while. Use the downtime to rack your brain as to how you intend to pull this off."

Zyne left the room with the door open. Hunter shut it and fell back down on his bed.

His eyes shot open with realization.

Daniel had taken Tai Mei away to weaken the Dynasty while he went straight for Matt. Or perhaps it was just a test for whatever device he planned to use on Matt. Either way, his next stop would be for Matt, and he would do exactly to Matt what he had done to Tai Mei.

A half-eaten burger lay on the plate in front of Hunter as he stared out of the large windows in the U-club. What little nightlife Shreveport had was now in full force. People in various stages of their twenties and thirties traveled from one club to the next in search of a little fun. If Clara didn't show back up soon, they would have it uninterrupted.

Right on cue, Clara waltzed through the dining room right up to his table. She peered down at him with her arms crossed.

"Well," he said, getting up. "Let's go."

"Go where?" she asked. "I just got back."

"To the club!"

"I'm not even dressed for that!" She protested.

It was true. She wore a pair of old jeans and a t-shirt for some video game.

"Do you have clothes here?"

"Yes, I'll meet you down in the lobby in 20 minutes."

With that, she went back to the elevators and disappeared again. Rolling his eyes, he headed down in the lobby to wait. He made casual conversation with the guy behind the reception desk to try to pass the time.

After at least 40 minutes, Clara stepped off the elevator. Her hair was bundled up in rich waves that tumbled down her right shoulder. She wore an emerald green dress that fit her just right and completely removed all Hunter's thoughts of her ugly t-shirt.

"You clean up good," he said.

She smiled. "You had all four years of high school to notice me. Why are you just seeing me now?"

Speechless, he held the door open for her and watched her walk outside ahead of him. It was crazy how her immortality had transformed her from some backroom nerd to a nice piece of arm candy. It was just too bad she was Zyne's girl. Even Hunter wasn't stupid enough to try to cut in on that. This was a onetime thing, but he was going to make it the most convincing onetime thing of his life.

Clara held on to Hunter's arm as they entered the grimy club. In the back of the dark room, the DJ blasted monotonous techno mixes for the patrons attempting to dance out on the floor. They all writhed around in a drunken stupor, laughing as they fell further behind the beat with their feet. This is why she quit going out with Olivia, because there was no fun for her to have.

"I still can't believe the EDM craze took this long to hit Shreveport," Hunter shouted in her ear over the booming speakers.

"Whatever happened to calling it techno?"

"Calling it 'electronic dance music' sounds less nerdy. When things go mainstream, they need to be re-branded."

"So stupid."

She looked over the crowd, trying to pinpoint a few targets. She could almost close her eyes and randomly pick one with how many worked the dance floor. The potency of the blood emanating off them intoxicated her.

"Go buy me a drink," she said to Hunter. "And I'll grab us a table."

"What do you want?"

"It doesn't really matter."

He headed for the bar, and she moved to the side of the room to place her black handbag on one of the empty round tables. A couple of guys watched her as she took her seat at the table, carefully crossing her legs. These things came so easy for her now that she had stopped caring about climbing up the social strata. One table of three guys kept sending curious glances her way. She pretended not to notice.

Hunter returned and handed her a martini glass with some multicolored liquid in it.

"Hope you aren't planning on roofie-ing me," she said.

"If only," he said, lifting a clear tumbler to his mouth. "So, which one should I talk to?"

"Hmm.." She thought about it while sipping on the mystery concoction. It was so fruity she doubted it even contained alcohol. Looking back over the dance floor, she pointed out the strongest impression. "Talk to that redhead there."

Hunter looked at the woman who was throwing her long, thin hair from side to side with the twisting of her head. Blue laser lights traced over her pale skin. Her swaying dance made her look drunk, but Clara saw the power that confused her mind.

Concentrating on what her supernatural vison could see, Clara watched crimson trails bleed off the girl's neck out into the room. It swirled around to connect with a few other clouds of energy rising off the marked dancers bouncing around the club. Like trying to figure out the shapes of clouds on a normal summer day, she tried to see where they led.

Outside the room, past Clara's ethereal senses, a darker cloud pressed down against her and everyone on the dance floor. At its center, a human form screamed down at her. Taking another sip from her drink to remind her just where she was, the vision from her visit to the Shifting Plains continued.

The human form was tethered to a jagged spire curving over his head. His face looked at her through agony, but reflected a pity that cut into her.

"Daddy," she whispered.

Hearing her voice, the vision changed. She watched her father push a younger version of herself in a swing. She watched one of her own memories play out before her. In that moment, she recognized her father trying to give her the most important lesson of her life.

She watched her child self transform into adulthood and ride the swing back down to demand her father return to her and Arthur. With honesty in his eyes, he warned her that Arthur controlled her life, but she refused to see it.

Now, as she peered back at this reflection of the past, she saw Arthur's power overshadowing her, forcing her to manipulate her own father. None of it was her choice or desire, it was all what Arthur wanted of her. Astrous had been right!

"No!" she shouted, bringing her glass down into the table.

Tiny glass shards spilled out with the remains of her drink onto the floor. Several others around the club looked at her as Hunter rushed up to her side. The redhead trailed behind him.

"You okay?" Hunter asked.

She put a hand to her forehead. "Yes. I just forgot where I was for a second."

Waving him away, she reminded herself that she had already confronted her father in the Shifting Plains. What she had just seen had already happened. How could it have come back to her like this?

She left a good tip next to the pool of alcohol on the table and left before Hunter could stop her. Only Arthur could answer these questions for her, but there was someone else who might could help her.

"What's wrong with your girlfriend?" Justine asked Hunter.

He turned back to her and mimicked her drunken dancing. "Nothing. And she's not my girlfriend. In fact, her boyfriend would grind me into pulp if I ever hit on her."

"Haha!" Justine cocked her head back as the music boomed around them. "Not mine! We sort of have an open relationship."

"Open enough for me to steal you away?" Hunter asked with a smirk.

A hand slapped against his shoulder and Thomas walked from behind him to join Justine's side. "Steal away, Hunter. Justine would be one lucky girl to wind up with you. Though, she might like the both of us."

"There you are!" she exclaimed, pulling down on his shirt collar to get him to kiss her.

"So, Hunter," he continued. "You cool with open relationships?"

Hunter took a couple of steps back.

Thomas draped his hand across Justine's shoulders and said to her, "I think he wants to but just can't let himself, babe."

"Awww, come on Hunter, it will be fun!" She threw her hands up into the air and dashed for him.

Hunter caught her just before she lost balance. "Sorry, Justine. Wouldn't want you to come between friends."

Justine laughed with a drunken howl.

"I get it." Thomas smiled at him. "You don't like to share." He leaned in face to face. "Sometimes, neither do I. Which is why I'm working to hide all these 'bitten' people from your girlfriend."

Justine punched Hunter in the shoulder. "I thought you said she wasn't your girlfriend."

"She's not!" Hunter said, pushing through Thomas on the way to the door.

"Wait!" Thomas yelled.

Hunter turned back around.

"Don't you even want to know where I pick these lovely

girls up?" Thomas asked. Justine smiled at him and kissed his cheek.

"Tell me," Hunter demanded.

"Just for old times' sake. Head up to the new Stonegate club next to the Arch and you'll find all the easy love you can stomach."

Justine went back to writhing around among the other dancers. Hunter shook his head and left. At least this time he would have valuable information for Zyne.

Thirty minutes passed of Hunter sitting alone in the car with the summer night's heat beating against him. Sweat trickled down his face, but he remained intent on the Arch, watching all who went in and left at this late hour. Just as Thomas had said, groups of attractive women periodically left together in a collective stupor. Even to Hunter, it felt strange that such a prestigious restaurant would actively cultivate a party crowd.

He still felt nervous parking at the opposite end of the lot. The Arch was a staple of the Raven family. In fact, he wouldn't be surprised if there was one in there now. At any rate, the wait staff would probably still know him by name, so there was no way he could get a closer look.

The roar of a motorcycle rumbled beside his car. Turning his head, he saw a biker wearing a red jumpsuit get off right next to him. The biker pulled off his helmet, revealing himself to be Soren.

Hunter rolled down his window. "Can I help you?"

"The Dynasty accepts your weapon and extends an opportunity to join us."

"I wish I would have known you were following me. Do you know what is in there?" Hunter nodded toward the Arch.

Soren tilted his head to the side and stared into space for a second. "Yes, he's the reason we have traveled here," he said, throwing his helmet back on.

With that, Soren fell across the hood of Hunter's car. Hunter turned to see what had happened when his door flew out into the parking lot. A hand reached in and grabbed his throat. Struggling the entire way, he found himself looking into Jarvis's eyes.

"You come to meet your lost cousin?" Jarvis asked.

"Cousin?" Hunter tried to think with Jarvis pressing him against the side of his car.

Soren made it back to his feet and ran back at Jarvis. Letting Hunter go, Jarvis reached up to intercept Soren and slammed him onto the concrete.

"I already beat your leader; don't make me grind you up!" Jarvis yelled. Jarvis kicked Soren into his bike, knocking it over.

Soren grabbed the hilt of his sword planted at the back of his seat and pulled it out. "The Dynasty has come for all of you!" He thrust the blade into Jarvis.

Hunter watched as his modified weapon burned through the massive Shade's chest. Jarvis cried out and dropped to his knees. Soren pulled his sword out and kicked Jarvis on his back. He shook on the concrete with black liquid pouring out of the wound.

Hunter rushed back in his car and started it up. Soren followed suit and jumped back on his bike. They both had to get out of there before Jarvis recovered. Hunter wasn't sure how drastic of an effect the blade had.

Soren pulled out in front of him and led the both of them back to Veterans' park where the rest of the Dynasty gathered. Hunter wasn't sure if they were looking at him because he was an outsider or his car now lacked a door.

After parking, he realized he was shaking from the adrenaline flowing through him. Soren didn't let him rest a bit before he was standing outside his car again.

"When will you get our deity back?" Soren demanded as if nothing had gone wrong tonight.

"I think we just stumbled onto bigger concerns, Soren," Hunter began. "I'm sure whatever you felt back there at the Arch was from my cousin. The Shade has taken root inside him and will manifest soon enough. I think my uncle, who took your deity from you plans to do the same with him. Keep a watch on the Arch and we can move in just as soon as I tell Zyne."

"No, we will handle this."

"You barely handled Jarvis back there. Zyne will be enough to distract Matt while I get the ring from my uncle. Then we can take what belongs to us."

Soren nodded. "We will be behind you. Free Tai Mei and she can handle this new Shade."

Hunter didn't have time to point out how easily she had fallen. He just agreed and went back to Mandrake tower to talk reason into an unreasonable being.

Still wearing her party dress, Clara hung her feet over the side of the building and stared down into the empty streets below. Her phone sang a tune, and she snatched it out of her handbag to read a text from Olivia inviting her to check out the new Stonegate club tonight. Clara replied that she wasn't feeling well and hoped that would be the end of it.

"I can't even talk to my real friends about this, so thanks," Clara said to the Illumin standing behind her.

"Not sure what good I am since I don't have any answers for you, Clara," Gabriella replied.

With a sigh, she faced Gabriella, "Nothing? Even after I saved you from Astrous?"

Clara's phone sang again, but Clara ignored it.

"And not long before that, you beat me into the ground for protecting Matt. I still don't trust you, so don't get confused. Right now, our mutual interest in finding Matt is the only thing keeping us from charging at each other's throats." Gabriella's blue eyes looked ice cold.

"A couple of months ago, I was a typical college grad excited about finding the perfect job. Now I'm trying to understand how this world that I've been blind to for so long works. I can't make sense out of any of it. This is your chance to convert me to your side, and you are blowing it."

Blue sparks flickered out of Gabriella's eyes. "Here is how your world works. You are immortal, but act like a high school girl unsure about her crush. All of my kind has told you of Zyne's true nature, but you've ignored us. You've chosen him and now ask me again whether or not he pulls your strings?"

Gabriella stepped forward, walking along the building's edge. Clara felt the darkness inside her rise up and leak out through her skin. She fought her impulses and let Gabriella come within arm's length.

"Yes, Zyne has controlled you. Think back to your 'spiritual awakening' as you put it. The only thing I can think of is that he broke through whatever your parents held over you and took control from them. You are still a puppet; you've just changed handlers." Gabriella paused for a second. "Now there is something you need to decide. Who is worse? Zyne or your mother? I'm not that fond of her either. She started you down this crazy road."

Clara stepped down from the ledge, looking up at Gabriella. "Is that my fate? To always be controlled by someone else?"

"As powerful as we are, Clara, we are all controlled by something. At times, even the Illumin bend to the will of the Ravens. Then again, perhaps Shades do as well." Gabriella nodded to Mandrake Tower.

Snapping around, Clara watched Hunter jump out of his car and bolt inside. Her present conversation would have to wait. She moved to jump down the side of the building.

"Don't go far, just let me see what he wants."

Hunter dashed into an empty lobby at the top of Mandrake Tower. He ran around to get to Zyne's office, only to find it equally as empty.

"Zyne! Get here now!" he yelled to the darkness.

Moving to the light switch, he lit up the lonely office. Zyne wasn't there. Scouring the rest of the floor, he gave up his search and went back to the elevator.

A silhouette peered at him from the darkness. He jumped back against the wall, clambering for the light. Light flickered on all around him, turning the silhouette into the angry form of Clara standing over him.

"Get up you jittery idiot," she breathed down at him.

He sucked in a few breaths. "Sorry, you scared me. When did you get here?"

The sound of elevator doors closing answered his question. Embarrassed, he pulled himself to his feet.

"Just now. What are you doing here?"

"Trying to sound the alarm. Matt's running the Arch as his hidden base. And he already has Shades protecting the place."

Her eyes widened. "Where is Arthur?"

"I don't know. Not here. Shouldn't you know?"

"Let's go." She grabbed his arm and pulled him toward the elevator while checking her phone.

"What's your plan?"

As the doors shut them inside, she turned to him. "Right

now, I only trust one person, and you are not her. Shut your mouth and do what I say without question."

He cocked his head, deciding he should keep his snide comment to himself.

With Hunter in tow, Clara burst outside Mandrake tower, ending her unanswered call to Olivia. She had to get her away from Matt before she ended up like the rest of the girls. Desperate, she sent a text asking Olivia to come and pick her up before heading up to Stonegate. After the text sent, Clara waved up at Gabriella for her to join them.

Gabriella glided down on light blue wings that disappeared as soon as she hit the ground. Hunter shrank back from her.

"What are you scared of, Hunter?" Gabriella asked with narrowed eyes.

Clara looked up from her phone. "It doesn't matter whose side we are on. Hunter has found Matt down at the Arch's new Stonegate club, and my friend has been lured into the trap. I need your help, Gabriella."

"He's there right now?" she asked.

Clara's phone interrupted them. She saw it was Oliva and answered.

"Hello?" Clara practically shouted.

"Hey girl!" Oliva shouted over the phone in a drunken slur. "Where are you? I texted you like forever ago. You've got to join the party!"

"Olivia, listen, you need to get out of there!" Clara said in a frantic tone.

"You must be crazy," Olivia replied. "I just met the owner, and he says the two of you have met before. Here, see if you can remember him..."

Olivia's voice cut off as she shuffled her phone to someone else.

"Hello Clara," a cool male voice replied. "I hear you've been looking for me. Though, I'm glad your friend found me first. She's pretty fun to hang out with, plus I do love older women."

"Put her in a cab and send her home, Matt," Clara uttered. Both Hunter and Gabriella perked up at Matt's name.

"I don't think she really wants to go home, though. She keeps begging me to take the Vampire's Mark. I'm not sure she's really ready for that, but I may give in if she keeps begging. I just can't resist those sapphire eyes."

Clara heard Olivia giggle in the background. She ended the call.

"Matt's at Stonegate right now holding my friend hostage."

Clara turned to reenter Mandrake tower and summon a Shade taskforce when Gabriella stopped her with a gentle hand on her shoulder.

"Not them, Clara," Gabriella said. "The Illumin will help you. Let's go."

Gabriella probably thought forcing Hunter to ride along with them would be a way to keep him from interfering with their rescue attempt. Once they made it to the Arch and she saw the Dynasty waiting to take his commands, she would see differently. While she drove the three of them in her police cruiser, he texted Soren to keep him updated.

Both the police radio and Gabriella's phone sounded off with communication from various Illumin around the city. Mostly, they directed her to talk to Sams, which made him feel a bit uncomfortable, seeing as how Sams was working with Zyne. When she finally got him on the phone, it wasn't pretty.

"Matt's holding human lives, Sams; how can you say it's no credible threat?"

Hunter met Clara's knowing look and they sat in uncomfortable silence while Gabriella continued arguing.

"No, we have to deal with this now. If we wait, he'll have grown too strong. You already know about the marks he's putting on club-goers. Now that I've found the source, we have to take it down."

She paused. Hunter could feel her frustration. He wondered if Clara would tell her why Sams was really stalling.

"I don't care what you say! I'm going to tear this place apart with or without support. You sound just like Jailyn right after she washed out."

Gabriella cut off the call and ignored the immediate return call.

She looked at Clara. "Sorry, I didn't mean to bring your mother into that."

"It's alright," Clara said with indifference. "I'm not her biggest fan either. So, it's just the three of us?"

"Yep," she replied.

They pulled into the shopping center sitting across from the Arch, Stonegate, and the surrounding boutique shops. Hunter scanned to find several bikes parked over there, confirming that the Dynasty was waiting on him. They weren't going to be alone.

"Let's figure this out," Clara said.

Hunter was studying the Arch when a familiar white SUV pulled into its parking lot, trailed by Daniel's car. Martellus and the rest of his thugs got out to wait for Daniel.

"The trap is for Daniel!" Hunter exclaimed and jumped out of the car.

He bolted across the empty street, catching Daniel just in time. He managed a few words of warning before Jarvis wrapped him up and pulled him away. He struggled, but was no match for the Shade's strength. Daniel watched him struggle with mere pity in his eyes.

Hunter kicked his heels into the pavement, trying to get some leverage, but they only scraped along the surface as Jarvis pulled him around the corner. Daniel kept walking toward Stonegate, ignoring him.

"Better get out of here, Hunter, if you know what's good for you," Jarvis said, pinning him against the brick wall.

Hunter threw up his hands. "Point made, just let me go."

Jarvis looked around the corner and nodded at some unseen person. He looked back at Hunter. "You've lost, now get out of here. Your uncle is with us, and we will protect him."

Jarvis released his grip and walked back around the corner. Hunter watched him enter Stonegate, waving to the full set of guards standing watch. The guards wouldn't let anyone inside from the growing line of hopeful partygoers. If they only knew what they would be walking into, they wouldn't be so anxious.

Clara and Gabriella waited for him in the middle of the parking lot. The guards at the door watched the three of them, but at this point, it didn't really matter.

A shadow moved out between two trucks right for him. His stomach tightened with fear until he saw it was only Soren. Several more of the Dynasty appeared beside him.

"New friends, Hunter?" Gabriella asked.

He jerked around in surprise. Neither she nor Clara looked too happy.

Soren answered. "The Dynasty fiercely protects its own. The Raven will join in our crusade."

Clara narrowed her eyes at Hunter. He straightened himself up, deciding the time had come to make his move.

Hunter spoke next. "The Dynasty is here to fight on our side, Gabriella. None of us want to see Matt get a hold on this area. Now, here is how this will go down. You and Clara will rush in to disrupt whatever Daniel thinks he is doing, and then the Dynasty and I will come in next to take Matt and his new thugs down."

Clara shook her head. "No, we need to attack in force, together before..." She snapped her head toward the club. "Olivia," she whispered and ran to the entrance, her immaterial wings unfurling behind her.

Gabriella pushed Hunter out of the way and chased Clara.

"Glad that worked out," Hunter remarked to Soren. "Let's get ready."

The Dynasty watched Clara smash through the front of the club and toss her coin ahead of her. After she and Gabriella disappeared inside, they advanced. The entire line of clubanites who had waited for hours to get into Stonegate suddenly lost their desire to party and fled to their cars. Screams erupted from within the club, and more fleeing patrons rushed out into the parking lot to join the others.

Hunter dodged the panicking cowards and kept running toward the door. He heard crashing and saw brief flashes of light from within the dark room. After a few more moments, Daniel burst outside and bolted for his car.

"That's it! Matt should be down!" Hunter exclaimed.

They poured inside through the doors that Clara and Gabriella had broken through. Matt stood on a table, holding a terrified blonde woman in his arms. Martellus and Jarvis stood to either side of him while Gabriella lay on the ground. Clara lay against the right wall.

"My long lost cousin, come to join me?" Matt asked, looking directly at him. The woman tried to cry out, but Matt whispered something in her ear, and she quieted down.

Hunter saw him clutching Daniel's ring in his hand and froze for a second. "You know what you're holding right there?" he said, coming to his senses again.

"I'd say an armful of fun," Matt replied, placing his forehead against the woman's. Her eyes cried out for Hunter to save her. "Oh, you mean the ring," Matt said with fake surprise. He slipped it on and spun it around. "Nope, not a clue, but I'll bet you can show me how to use it."

Gabriella and Clara made it to their feet and edged toward Matt. Matt held his hand out to them and signaled Martellus and Jarvis to get between them.

"I believe we are having the famous Mexican standoff," Matt declared to the room. "However, how many sides do we really have?"

"There are no sides," Soren answered. "Only the Dynasty."

"Oh, the Dynasty?" Matt replied. "And how can you get your leader back when she is literally wrapped around my finger?" He pointed to the ring.

Soren jumped at him, rolling through the air and bringing his sword down at Matt. Matt let go of the woman to reach up and grab the blade, twisting it out of Soren's grip. He turned and jabbed his elbow up into Soren's jaw. An unearthly crack made Hunter cringe as Soren fell onto his back. Before the woman could scramble toward Clara, Matt wrapped her up again, pulling her back to his chest.

"I am the power here!" Matt screamed, tossing the sword aside. "Your Dynasty begins anew with me! First, however, I'll subjugate your former leader." He looked at Clara. "This is why I invited your precious friend here today.

She needs to understand why you are so weird."

Matt spun the ring and pressed it into the woman's throat. Her face darkened with agony and a silent scream.

Stumbling to his feet, Soren charged Matt again, this time launching out with a kick that sent Matt flying backward against the far wall and the woman falling to the side. Like a blur, Soren pressed ahead, attacking so fast, Hunter had no idea what was going on. It was like watching a karate movie in fast forward.

"Olivia," Clara cried, dashing for the woman, but Jarvis stopped her while Martellus grabbed Olivia.

Hunter backed up to watch two fights play out at the same time.

Clara spun into the air, twisting out of Jarvis's grip and kicking him backward. She flew down at a shocked Martellus while the dagger in her hand grew into a full sword. Martellus twisted Olivia to face the blade, but Clara quickly pulled the sword back and swooped over him. When she was directly above him, she stabbed into his back. He released his grip and Olivia ran free. Clara pushed the sword until it pierced him through his chest.

Clara pulled her sword free and kicked Martellus away. He clutched his burning chest, hunched over on the ground. Olivia stumbled toward the exit. Clara moved to her side and led her out of the club. The rest of the Shades were too focused on the other fight to pay them much mind.

Matt laughed while Soren pummeled him with attacks. Another loud crack sent Hunter cringing. Matt stood upright like a dirty stone statue. Soren stumbled away from him, clutching his hand. With a smile, Matt moved again, grabbing

Soren by the throat and slamming him into the ground. His skin remained grey with black streaks that moved wildly about. Everyone else in the room just watched Matt sit atop his enemy.

"You don't have enough finesse to match my power!" Matt spun up the ring and let it hover above Soren's throat.

"No!" Hunter shouted, moving to intervene. Gabriella grabbed him and held him back.

"It's over," she whispered. "Now watch your failure."

"Didn't you want your deity back?" Matt asked Soren.

"Not in an unworthy vessel," Soren answered.

"Accept me as your new deity, and I'll return her to a worthy vessel– bound to me of course–but at least she'll be free. We'll forge this world into what we need it to be. From now on, I'm the only Raven you need to deal with, and the only one who can give you what you need."

"No loyalty among Shades!" Hunter yelled, breaking out of Gabriella's hold. Martellus walked up to him.

"Loyalty?" Matt said, dragging Soren over to them. "You've only ever known self-preservation. Now leave me to my spoils before I remember what you did to me. Don't think I've forgotten, or that you won't suffer because of it."

Matt started laughing. Hunter's rage held him in place until Gabriella pulled him through the crowd of Shades lining up to form a new Dynasty.

Clara helped Olivia crawl into her bed. Even in her

drunken stupor, she was bound to remember something about what had happened. Hunter assured her otherwise, saying that the Ravens' thoroughness covered close encounters like these. The morning would tell the truth.

Olivia rolled onto her stomach, fast asleep. Clara was glad she was safe, but anger at the Shade's touch quickly returned. Everything Shades touched decayed. And if Gabriella was right about Zyne touching her mind, that meant...

She stood up, refusing to follow the thought and left Olivia's apartment. She rejoined Gabriella and Hunter, ready to be dropped back off at Mandrake Tower. They rode in silence.

Gabriella pulled to a stop outside Mandrake Tower and waited for them to get out.

"Thanks for everything, Gabriella," Clara said before getting out.

Gabriella's tired eyes looked to see that Hunter was out of earshot. "Just call me again when you see Zyne for what he is."

"I know what he is," Clara replied. "And don't worry, I'll take good care of him."

She joined Hunter, who remained silent, hopefully thinking over his error. In a few minutes he would get what was coming. Arthur's comforting presence radiated all the way down and grew stronger as they made their way to the top. When they arrived at the top, his presence crawled inside her mind. She had never paid much attention to this before, but now it felt more of a violation than comfort.

Moving into the back office, they found Arthur and

Daniel sitting around the statue given to him by Sams. Clara felt new tremors in the air she hadn't ever felt before. The sickening look the both of them gave her ramped up her fears.

"Babe," Arthur said, rushing to take her in his arms. He kissed her with all the intensity she missed. Still, his unconscious power tried to invade her mind, numbing her.

"What's wrong?"

"Hunter," Daniel spoke in a low voice. "Let's go discuss other important matters."

"Sure," Hunter replied, letting Daniel take him out of there. From his smirk, Clara saw he thought he had gotten away with his attempted mutiny. She would see to that later.

"I don't care what it is, just hold me for a moment," Clara said, pulling Arthur closer to her, trying to remember why she loved him.

"I should be devastated but have no true concept of sorrow," he whispered.

"Just tell me," she answered, closing her eyes to brace herself.

Before he continued, she felt his raw emotion sweep through her. The portal to the Shade realm flashed before her eyes. She watched her father wade out in the dark sea to reach the impossible point where the sky bent down to kiss the ground. Guardians of stone crumbled against him, ripping apart the fabric of his being with each step he took.

Nathan's last thoughts of Clara streamed into her mind. Her world shattered around her until she was in her father's arms one last time. Looking into his eyes, he said goodbye in the only way he could.

"Be free," Nathan bid her as he faded away.

Clara's heart burned with loss greater than the day she sat before the white caskets of her parents. This time, she knew her father was permanently removed from her life. The walls of Mandrake rose up around her like the prison it was. Tears rolled down her cheeks.

The man holding her let her father destroy himself! She pushed against him with all her might. Arthur, no, Zyne, flew across the room and crashed into his wall of books. A few of them rained down on his head. The curtain he had drawn over her eyes lifted, ripped away by the remnant of her father she now carried inside her.

"This isn't how I saw our future, Zyne! My father lived to rejoin my mother and fight against the two of us!"

"If any of us could accurately see the future, then why would we make such rash decisions?" he countered, getting back on his feet. "Your father made a choice neither of us could see. What you took to be the definite future were only dim reflections."

Another wave of burning pain shook across her chest, sending her onto the floor in pain. Zyne moved to help her, but she thrust him back as best she could. She disconnected from reality again and fell into her past.

She again saw the scene at her house where she came into her supernatural form. Only this time, she saw the strings wielded by Zyne that pulled her into his plan. He hid her true consciousness and used her Shade to enact his revenge against her parents. It was never her choice to do that, but rather his manipulation of her.

All through the moments that followed, she watched

herself being led along with Zyne at her side, happy to guide her through the difficult time of losing her parents and having a spiritual awakening. Throughout all of it, a cloud surrounded her, dampening her senses to the truth.

"You chose my parents' fate on my behalf," she cried, arriving back in the present moment. She sobbed on her knees, scraping her forehead against the carpet to ease the pain inside her.

"The truth isn't what you always want to hear. I'm sorry," he said, slumping into a couch against the wall. "I did it for us."

Pounding the carpet with her fists, she launched back up on her feet. A renewed vigor charged through her. As she watched her reflection against the wall of glass, her wings snapped out from behind her, and her skin decayed into patches of black and grey.

"This is what you did for 'us'. You chose who I would be." Turning back to face him, she just shook her head. "I'm taking my choices back!"

She took off straight into the glass, blasting through it, leaving it to rain down onto the street in tiny shards. Flying high over the sleeping city, she wept the tears of mourning she should have wept at her father's funeral.

"Now you are the one offering him power," Zyne told Hunter while knocking on the door. "So, relax and gloat with me."

The door swung back, and Thomas greeted them both with a smile. "Hunter and Zyne. Always a pleasure, come in."

Hunter nodded to him as they passed into the familiar house of Astrous. Thomas led them to the very room where Hunter had originally negotiated his plan with Astrous. Everything looked the same with its stuffy antique furniture that displayed tastes too old to cope with the changing times.

Astrous waited for them in a blue high-backed chair and bid them to sit with him by a simple wave of his hand. Hunter sat on a creaking wooden bench, watching the two rivals look each other over with judgment in their eyes. Each wanted power in his own way.

Emily joined them for a nice and awkward silence.

"I don't often come down from my tower to interact with the rest of my brethren," Zyne began. "So know I have come here out of the largest necessity."

"Oh, I know," Astrous cut him off, clasping his hands in his lap. "When trouble strikes at home, where else can you turn but your enemy?"

Zyne ignored the cheap shot. "The enemy of my enemy is my friend. Even for human wisdom, I agree with it. I've tracked Matt down while Thomas and Emily here have been hanging out at nightclubs." Emily bristled at the mention of her but kept silent. "He has rallied most of the Shades that are not pledged to either you or me. That wouldn't concern me, but I've also felt his power, and if the two of us don't put him in his place, we won't have any city left to create banter over."

Astrous nodded his head thoughtfully and pointed both index fingers at Zyne. "Yes, you are correct. I have sent Thomas and Emily out on nightclub runs to make sure that your girlfriend, oh, excuse me, your ex-girlfriend, kept looking their way instead of mine. And while you were wasting time trying to break through Nathan's ennui, I mingled within Shreveport's high society."

A pair of dress shoes clicked against the hardwood floor in the hallway. Hunter turned and watched Matt enter the room, dressed in all the retro finery Astrous usually wore. His eyes were ablaze with just as much power as when Hunter last saw him.

Smiling, Astrous stared right into Hunter. "Thank you, son, for introducing me to your cousin; I can never repay you for that encounter. So, to make it up to you, I'll let you walk out of here alive."

Zyne stood to face Matt. His fingers twitched at his side. Matt looked him up and down.

Matt said coolly, "If you're on your way out, best get to it."

Astrous's smile widened even more. "This is how the

giants fall, Zyne–by ignoring the subtle cracks running through them as they struggle to balance the world on their shoulders. You've lost both your greatest love and greatest ally. When you try to scrape together the ashes of your empire, they will scatter underneath my winds of change."

Clouds of darkness poured out of Zyne as he twisted back around to Astrous, who remained seated with a sadistic grin. Tendrils slithered down Zyne's arms, stopping at the floor. But as if sensing the lost cause, Zyne retracted his tendrils and stormed out of the house, leaving Hunter.

Hunter went to follow him, but Matt moved in his way.

"I wish we could have known each other before all of this, cousin," Matt said. "Would have been cool to see how the other half lives."

"I think you are seeing it now," Hunter replied. "If there is even any part of you left."

Matt reached over to pat him on the back. "Oh, I'm all here. So are my feelings of pain and rejection. Don't worry, we'll deal with those very soon."

Matt stepped out of the way, allowing Hunter to catch up with Zyne under the heat of the summer sun. For a moment he thought he saw a tear in the Shade's eye. Wiping his own blanket of sweat away, Hunter dismissed the thought. Nothing could break Zyne's power or Hunter's newfound devotion to it.

Only one certainty remained: Astrous meant to bring war to Shreveport.

About the Authors

Jason Craft

Born and raised in northwest Louisiana, Jason did very little to escape the area outside of writing about fantastical worlds. He is a legitimate nerd who enjoys PC gaming, arguing about time paradoxes, and the indomitable table-top game, Warhammer 40K. One day he plans to have his entire Tau Empire army fully painted. He currently resides in Shreveport, Louisiana and is employed as a full-time computer programmer to support his writing and nerd habits. You can catch him on the interwebs by his handle, VigRoco. Challenge him to a Planetary Annihilation match, and he will gracefully lose to you.

Blog: http://VigRoco.com
Facebook: http://facebook.com/VigRoco
Twitter: http://twitter.com/VigRoco

Amanda White

Amanda has lived in various Louisiana cities and has grown to know and love the state's rich culture. She works in the field of Psychology and enjoys using her knowledge to enrich her characters. When not working or writing, she enjoys biking, running, reading, and spending time with her friends and family.

Facebook: http://facebook.com/amanda.white.54772

www.ingramcontent.com/pod-product-compliance
Lightning Source LLC
Chambersburg PA
CBHW021454240626
47154CB00002B/369